Someone was unlocking her door

Panic held Bri frozen for a moment, but then she reclaimed her wits and reached for the phone.

As soon as she lifted the receiver, she realized the phone was dead. Paralyzed with fear, she watched the door open.

Scream, Bri told herself. But even as she opened her mouth, no sound came out. She was too terrified.

She lay in bed hearing the sound of footsteps crossing her room. She clutched the receiver of the phone like a weapon. Who was it? Who was inexorably drawing nearer and nearer to her?

And then she picked up the familiar scent. A distinctive perfume. She huddled under the covers, the receiver hidden from view. This time she wouldn't be caught sleeping. This time she would strike back.

ABOUT THE AUTHOR

Elise Title and her family live in a small New England college town. Elise says she enjoys combining the unending variety inherent in small-town life with the scandals and excitement she can invent for her totally fictional town of Thornhill. Her first two Thornhill novels were Harlequin Intrigue #160 *Shadow of the Moon* and #180 *Stage Whispers*.

Books by Elise Title

HARLEQUIN INTRIGUE
149–THE FACE IN THE MIRROR
160–SHADOW OF THE MOON*
180–STAGE WHISPERS*
*Thornhill Mysteries

HARLEQUIN AMERICAN ROMANCE
377–TILL THE END OF TIME
397–NEARLY PARADISE

HARLEQUIN TEMPTATION
412–ADAM & EVE
416–FOR THE LOVE OF PETE

HARLEQUIN SUPERROMANCE
478–TROUBLE IN EDEN

Don't miss any of our special offers. Write to us at the following address for information on our newest releases.

Harlequin Reader Service
P.O. Box 1397, Buffalo, NY 14240
Canadian address: P.O. Box 603,
Fort Erie, Ont. L2A 5X3

No Right Turn

Turn

Elise Title

Harlequin Books

TORONTO • NEW YORK • LONDON
AMSTERDAM • PARIS • SYDNEY • HAMBURG
STOCKHOLM • ATHENS • TOKYO • MILAN
MADRID • WARSAW • BUDAPEST • AUCKLAND

To David and Rebecca, with special love

Harlequin Intrigue edition published January 1993

ISBN 0-373-22209-2

NO RIGHT TURN

Printed in U.S.A.

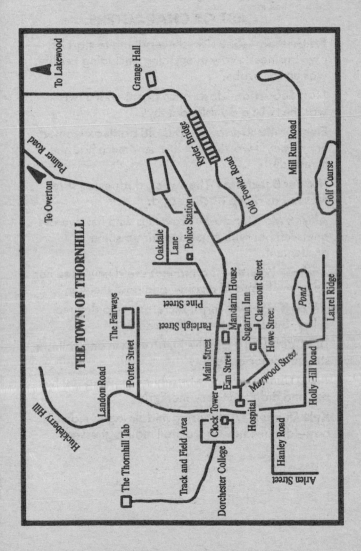

THE TOWN OF THORNHILL

CAST OF CHARACTERS

Bri Graham—She risked everything to start her own business. Now everything, including her life, was up for grabs.

Matt Sebastian—Insurance agent with a twist—was the twist a double identity?

Eleanor MacDermott—This old battleax wanted her money's worth—but just how much had she invested?

Harriet Beecham—The sweet, doddering sister was not as dumb as she acted.

Allison MacDermott—Traveling with her two old aunts left her with a need to stir up some excitement.

Andrew Weston—Bri thought she'd never see her absentee husband again—and now she won't.

Jillian Knight—A legal secretary who defined sultry, but could she spell murder?

Tim Campbell—Did the handsome young college student major in deceit?

Anna Campbell—She barely acknowledged her son and didn't act very motherly.

Kyle Dunner—A dithering middle-aged mama's boy—did he know more than mama guessed?

Prologue

Egyptian Curator Commits Suicide

Cairo, Egypt.

Selim Khaffir, distinguished curator of the Cairo Antiquities Museum, committed suicide yesterday. His wife discovered him hanging from a noose in the den of his Cairo apartment, when she returned home from work early last evening. According to the coroner, Mr. Khaffir had been dead for several hours. A very distraught Mrs. Khaffir reported that her husband had been despondent over a valuable antique papyrus scroll which was stolen one week ago from his museum. At the time of his death, Mr. Khaffir was himself under investigation for the robbery. The noted curator left a brief note, begging his wife's forgiveness for the shame and disgrace he brought on the family name, declaring himself innocent of all charges and naming an American acquaintance as the guilty party. The name is being withheld by the police pending further investigation.

Chapter One

"And another thing, Miss Graham. Air flow is quite important. My sister and I were on a bus tour to Quebec last winter and the air flow was abysmal, wasn't it, Harriet? Impossibly stuffy. I was dangerously close to a fainting spell on several occasions. Not, mind you, that I'm giving to having the vapors by any means. I'm in perfect health."

Eleanor McDermott, a large, cantankerous woman in her late sixties with curly, close-cropped, blue-white hair, sat on the divan holding court, while her slightly younger gray-haired sister sat meekly to her right, primly sipping tea. On Mrs. McDermott's left, sat her teenaged granddaughter, Allison, who munched distractedly on a ragged cuticle and made no effort to hide her boredom.

Harriet Beecham smiled sweetly. "And the seats were quite narrow as I recall. Don't forget how upsetting that was, Sister."

Brianna Graham, the owner and tour guide of the Boston-based Valentine Tours, forced back a smile as she observed the tiny woman. It was difficult to imagine a seat that would not accommodate the scrawny Miss Beecham.

"As I've explained," Bri said, surreptitiously checking her watch, then tucking her shoulder-length auburn hair behind her ears, "we won't be traveling by bus but by a customized van. There'll be ten of us altogether and the seats are *quite* large and comfortable. Unfortunately the garage is doing some last-minute finishing work on the van, but if you'd like to come back in a couple of days..."

"The tour leaves in precisely four days," Eleanor McDermott reminded Bri. "If we're delayed because of this customized van of yours not being ready we will most certainly miss the peak of fall foliage." Turning to her granddaughter, she swiped at the girl's hand to stop her from her nibbling on her fingernails. "Allison is visiting from California and she's never seen fall foliage in New England. If I'm going to all this expense, I expect her to see the leaves at their very best."

Bri forced a cheery smile on her face, but it was hard to keep from looking slightly withered. Her interview with the two elderly women—she didn't include Allison since the teenager had barely said two words—had been dragging on for close to an hour, a half hour more than she'd allotted. She still had one more interview to go and was worried that the young man in the waiting room might be growing impatient and irritable. Then again, so was she. The only difference was, she couldn't show it.

"I assure you, Mrs. McDermott, we'll leave right on schedule." Bri glanced down at the paper on her desk. "And I've made note of all your special needs and requirements—adjoining suites with private baths at each of the inns we'll be stopping at during the eight-day trip, a careful listing of each of your dietary requirements, a request for down pillows and thermostats in your rooms. As for the van, I can guarantee it will have very comfortable seats, excellent air flow and terrific springs. And I'm certain you'll like all of the other tour members."

Eleanor McDermott frowned. "Ten of us, you said?" She glanced at her granddaughter who'd gone back to her cuticle attack. This time the older woman didn't interfere. Instead she turned back to Bri. "I do hope it's going to be a *respectable* group. And not a bunch of old biddies. I absolutely detest those senior citizen tours, everyone talking about their rheumatism or lumbago all day long..."

"Oh yes," Harriet Beecham piped in, "and discussing their medicines every chance they get. Red pills for the morning, yellow ones at lunch, blue ones after dinner. I only take one little green pill before I go to bed and then, of course, two white tablets for indigestion."

"Enough, Harriet. What I'm saying, Miss Graham, is that we prefer tours that have a good mix when it comes to age."

"Actually, you and your sister are the only—" Allison almost said *old biddies*, but caught herself in time "—senior citizens on the tour. Besides yourselves, there's a middle-aged investor, a businessman in his thirties, an insurance agent in his late twenties, a young, attractive legal secretary and a bright, handsome, young Harvard college student and his mother."

Bri was not surprised to see Allison perk up a bit at the mention of the college student. "I've already interviewed all but two of them and they're a very nice, quiet group," she hurried on. "And I've got Mr. Sebastian, the insurance agent, waiting just outside for his interview." Bri hoped Mrs. McDermott would get the hint that it was time for her to gather up her sister and granddaughter and exit.

Mrs. McDermott, however, appeared impervious to such subtleties. "And the other one?"

"The other one?" Bri asked.

"Number ten. The one you haven't interviewed."

"Oh, that's Mr. Weston. He's a businessman and he may be out of town until the day of our trip. But I had a nice long chat on the phone with his secretary when she booked the trip. And I'm sure he's very respectable." Bri pushed herself away from her desk and started to rise.

Mrs. McDermott eyed her sharply. "I don't recall seeing any advertisements for Valentine Tours before this one for the fall foliage."

The last thing Bri wanted was for her tour members to worry about her being a novice in the business. But she decided the best way to deal with Mrs. McDermott was straight from the shoulder. "This fall foliage tour is actually my maiden voyage. But I've traveled up to New England many times, and I want to assure you, Mrs. McDermott, that I've done meticulous preparation for this trip. My primary goal is to see to it that everyone has a wonderful time on the tour. And I've done everything possible to make sure things run smoothly and comfortably. The van is as luxurious as any touring vehicle on the road. The New England towns I've chosen as stopovers are incredibly picturesque and charming, especially Thornhill."

At the mention of Thornhill, Bri faltered. Six months ago she had spent her honeymoon in the picturesque little college town of Thornhill. Four blissful days and four glorious nights with her husband John Fossier, in a storybook historic inn close to the elite Dorchester College where John had been an undergraduate. Bri had fallen in love with the town, she and John vowing to come back each year for their anniversary.

Little did she know at the time that they weren't even going to make it back for their first anniversary. Two months after they'd settled happily into married life in Weymouth, just south of Boston, John had walked out on her. No explanation, no fight, not even an argument. A couple of weeks later, she'd received one bland postcard from him postmarked the Canary Islands that said, "Sorry things didn't work out," and then not another word. Just a week ago Bri was finally able to file for a divorce on the grounds of desertion.

"We're so looking forward to the trip," a meek voice said softly, shaking Bri from her ruminations. "My sister disagrees, but I always feel that autumn is the perfect season. Is it your favorite, Miss Graham?"

Before Bri could respond, Eleanor McDermott rose. "That's neither here nor there, Harriet," she said sharply, removing the teacup from her sister's hand and depositing it on the desk. "Miss Graham has more to occupy her mind than the seasons. She needs to get on with her work. And we need to get on with ours. We have four days to show Allison the important historical sights of Boston."

Allison's bored expression took on a pained look. Bri felt sorry for her.

"Come, Allison. Don't forget your handbag, Harriet. You're always leaving something behind." That said, Eleanor McDermott started for the door, Allison in tow, Harriet Beecham hurrying after them.

After they bustled out, Bri spotted Harriet Beecham's white linen gloves on her desk. Picking them up, she laughed to herself and shook her head.

"Care to share the joke? Or isn't that part of the tour package?"

Bri's gaze shifted to the open door of her office where a tall, rakishly attractive, dark-haired man stood. Her very first thought was that Matthew Sebastian did not look like an insurance agent. She quickly censored her very next thought about him.

"I'm sorry to keep you waiting," she said in her most careful, neutral voice. Even so, it had a touch of vibrato in it that made the stranger smile. An appealing smile, Bri couldn't help but note. She was also quick to note that the smile made him look even younger than twenty-eight, which was the age he'd listed on his application. And which, she reminded herself, made him nearly five years younger than she. It would be a clear case of cradle robbing.

Donning her most professional, mature demeanor, Bri gestured for him to come inside. He sauntered over to the divan that had been vacated a minute earlier by Mrs. McDermott and Miss Beecham, lowering himself into it with a lanky ease.

"Do you always interview the passengers who book your tours, Miss Graham?"

She looked across at him from behind her desk. "This is my first tour, Mr. Sebastian, and I want to start off on the right foot."

He let his eyes drop as if he somehow had X-ray vision and could see her legs through the thick oak desk separating them. Bri was glad she hadn't gone with one of those modern, clear-glass cubes the designer had tried to talk her into. Not that Bri was easily talked into anything. Except during the rare weak moment—like when she'd impulsively said yes to John Fossier's wedding proposal after a three-week whirlwind courtship.

Bri pulled herself back to the present. "I like to meet each tour member and find out if there are any special needs or requirements." She had no idea why she was blushing when this was part of her canned speech. Well, she had some idea.

"Special needs," he echoed, looking long at Bri, who dropped the ballpoint pen she was holding.

"And of course I feel it's my obligation to...get to know the passengers a bit, make sure everyone's a good...fit. I mean...match. A good match. There are only ten of us and we'll be traveling together in close quarters for a number of days."

"Ten little Indians."

She gave him an uneasy look. "I beg your pardon."

"Don't you read mysteries? Agatha Christie? The grand dame of mayhem and menace?"

Bri shook her head. "I'm not big on mysteries. I prefer..."

He quirked a brow. "Romances?"

"Biographies," she said archly, feeling a need to impress upon the young man that she was not a frivolous woman.

He merely flashed her another of his nifty smiles. "I'm crazy about mysteries. Especially Agatha Christie. *Ten Little Indians* was one of her earliest and one of her best."

"You're losing me," Bri said frankly.

"Ten travelers, *Ten Little Indians*. All held up together on a deserted island, or in this case a recreational van, and then one by one..." He let the sentence drift off, raising his index finger to his temple and miming a gunshot as a finish.

The image was vivid and sent another shiver sliding down Bri's spine.

"Then again, there's always *Murder on the Orient Express*," he said blithely. "In that one, a dastardly fellow traveler is murdered and everyone on board turns out to have had a motive for doing him in."

Despite the disquieting feeling these tales evoked, Bri gave Matthew Sebastian a no nonsense smirk. "This isn't a mystery tour, Mr. Sebastian."

He looked teasingly into her emerald-green eyes. "There's always some mystery when a group of strangers come together, Miss Graham."

Bri raised a sardonic eyebrow. "Are you sure you're really an insurance agent and not a writer yourself? You seem to have a very vivid imagination."

He grinned. "And you don't?"

"I'm too old for that sort of fantasy," she replied with a faintly condescending smile.

He leaned forward, propping his elbows on her desk and cupping his chin in his palms. "What sort of fantasies aren't you too old for?"

Bri started to bristle, but then she laughed, something about Matt Sebastian's boyish charm getting to her. "I left myself wide open for that one," she admitted good-naturedly.

Just then her phone rang. She was still laughing a bit when she picked up. A minute later the laughter was replaced by a grim, bleak look. "Yes, I understand." She swallowed hard. "Yes, I'll be there right away."

The phone went dead, but Bri hung on to the receiver. Matt Sebastian gently pried it from her hand and placed it in the cradle.

She stared at him. "That was the police. One of my neighbors called them. They're in my apartment waiting for me. I've been robbed."

He eyed her closely. "You don't sound completely surprised."

Bri compressed her lips and frowned. Matt Sebastian was right. And yet she couldn't say why precisely she wasn't surprised. Except that for the past week she'd felt a vague sense of unease and tension, feelings she'd told herself were all related to her upcoming first tour. But then why had she sometimes felt, walking into her apartment late at night, that someone was lurking in the shadows, watching her? Why, when she walked the five blocks to her office several mornings this week, did she get the edgy feeling she was being followed?

A hand was on her shoulder. "Come on. I'm parked out front. I'll take you over."

Bri looked up at Matt Sebastian who had come around the desk and was standing just beside her. And still touching her. He can probably feel me trembling, she thought, embarrassed. So much for inspiring confidence, her sacred obligation as a tour guide.

His consoling, gentle smile made her think he'd read her mind. It also made her decide to accept his offer.

Once they got outside, the bracing late-September air revived her, and Matt Sebastian's hand on her arm felt reassuring. "I don't know why I'm so upset," she muttered as he guided her over to his beat-up, vintage, red Corvette parked at the curb. "I don't have anything of value. I hocked just about everything I owned to go into business." She felt the pressure of Matt's grip on her arm increase, and she gave him a sideways glance, surprised to see a curious light in his gray-blue eyes.

He helped her into the car, and after she told him where she lived, they drove in silence the few minutes it took to get to her apartment building. He parked and came around the car for her. She was glad he intended to accompany her upstairs. She didn't welcome the prospect of walking into her ransacked apartment alone.

Bri hesitated as they got to the front door of the building.

"What is it?" he asked, concern in his voice.

A crease formed between her sharp, intelligent green eyes. "I don't know why, but I was just thinking about those books." She glanced over at him with an edgy look. "The Agatha Christie mysteries."

Chapter Two

"The croissants are great, Miss Graham. Nice touch while we're waiting for the rest of the troop," Tim Campbell said enthusiastically, swiveling in his contoured, butter-soft, gray leather window seat. The movement didn't disturb the spillproof coffee cup, filled with fresh brewed French Roast, that fit into a specially designed holder in the padded arm of the chair. The other arm was equipped with a built-in individual stereo and miniature VCR system. At the press of a button a five-inch TV popped up for viewing the latest videos, a large selection of which were shelved in the back of the van along with compact discs ranging from rap to Rachmaninoff. Bri had also stocked up on the latest best-sellers and a broad range of the current magazines—everything from *Smithsonian* to *Elle* There was even an airplane-style commode fitted into the far left corner of the van. Everything about this large, customized RV with its wide, tinted windows and shade-controlled sunroof suggested luxury. Bri had gone all out, risking everything she owned to make a go of this venture.

Tim smiled at his mother, who was sitting across the aisle from him. "This van is incredible, don't you think, Mother?"

Anna Campbell, a thin, pale, quiet woman who walked with the aid of a cane, looked up from her paperback book and gave her son a distracted look. "Very nice," she mumbled with the bored equanimity of a traveler who had seen it all. She returned to her reading.

The blond, scraggly haired Harvard student gave Bri a wry smile. "You'll have to forgive Mother. She lives for her books."

Eleanor McDermott, sitting just behind Tim, scowled. "I remember a gentleman on a bus tour we took through Mexico who insisted he could read while we were traversing a treacherous run of curved roads."

"You did try to warn him that he would end up getting motion sickness," Harriet Beecham piped in.

"Stubborn man," Eleanor muttered, her disgruntled expression accentuated by the downward curve of her thin lips.

"Yes," her sister concurred. "And so dreadful that you were sitting beside him when he . . ."

Eleanor gave her a sharp look. "We don't need the details, Harriet. Some of our fellow travelers are enjoying their pastries."

Bri took note that Eleanor McDermott had not touched her croissant.

Allison Reed, who'd wangled a seat in front of Tim Campbell's, swiveled round to face him. "I think this van's positively *narly.*" The seventeen-year-old had come to life since Tim's arrival. She'd even run a comb through her peach-highlighted blond bob and applied a bit of lip gloss.

He grinned. "*Narly?*"

"You know. Cool. Neat. Awesome. Excellent."

His grin widened. "Southern California, right?"

"A down-home Valley Girl, and damn proud of it."

"Watch your language, Allison," her grandmother chastised.

Allison threw Tim a teasing smile. "Gran hates when I say Valley Girl."

Bri carried a fresh pot of coffee down the aisle, which was carpeted in plush burgundy. She stopped first at Kyle Dunner, a portly, fifty-three-year-old, mild-mannered investor, who had told Bri when she'd interviewed him that he'd looked after his mother all her life. Now that she had passed away he'd decided to, as he'd put it, live a little.

"A refill, Mr. Dunner?"

He pursed his lips. "I really shouldn't. Mother always said caffeine was bad for the heart."

"You're drinking decaffeinated, Mr. Dunner."

He looked a bit flustered. "Oh, yes. So I am. Well, then, a second cup would be most appreciated, Miss Graham."

Eleanor McDermott hadn't touched her first cup of coffee. Reluctantly Bri asked if there was anything wrong with it.

"Bitter," she said succinctly.

"Maybe you'd prefer tea."

"I'd prefer we left on time, Miss Graham," was Mrs. McDermott's unsurprising comeback.

"We still have fifteen minutes, Mrs. McDermott. And we're only waiting for Mr. Sebastian, Mr. Weston and Miss Knight."

"One little Indian down and two to go."

Bri started at the sound of Matt Sebastian's voice, especially his reference to Indians. Regaining her composure, she turned to face him. He looked ruggedly handsome this morning in a long-sleeved navy jersey, khaki slacks and Dock-Side shoes. He had a brown leather bomber jacket slung over one shoulder and was holding a mid-sized leather suitcase. "Where do we stow our gear?"

She led him outside to the back of the van, whose rear doors opened onto a separate luggage section.

He tossed his case inside. "That was quite a mess at your place the other night. You should have let me stay to help you straighten up."

Bri shrugged, closing the doors. She'd had the feeling that night that Matt's offer included more than straightening up. "It wasn't so bad," she said with an offhandedness that didn't come easily. "As chaos goes."

"You're taking it very well."

She frowned. "No, I'm not," she admitted, hesitating. "It's an awful feeling to know someone's broken into your home, gone through your personal belongings, invaded your privacy." Bri shuddered, wanting to remove the scene from her memory.

He smiled sympathetically. "Was anything taken?"

"Not that I could tell. My TV, stereo and camera were all still there. Which isn't so surprising. The picture tube's going on the TV, the stereo only plays monaural, and the camera's ancient. Like I told you, I don't—that is, I didn't have anything of value. Whatever I once possessed is sitting in this van."

Matt scanned the shiny high-tech silver recreational vehicle with Valentine Tours emblazoned in burgundy across the side. "You must have hocked the Hope diamond for this baby."

Bri laughed. "I wish. After I hocked everything I had, I signed my life away at the bank. Tell me, do they still have debtors' prison?"

Matt smiled reassuringly. "I'll bake you a cake with a hacksaw inside if they do."

Her natural optimism took a slide. "So, you think it's likely I'll go belly-up?"

"No. I don't think that at all," he assured her. "You impress me as a very determined young woman."

"I'm not that young," she said sardonically, which served to remind her that Matt Sebastian was.

She could tell by his smile that he caught her drift, but apparently their age difference didn't seem to faze him. Maybe he didn't faze easily, she concluded. She changed her mind a moment later when she saw his distinctly *fazed* reaction to the newest arrival for the tour.

Jillian Knight, a sultry redhead, was the kind of woman who men noticed and women could only wish they didn't. She might have been a legal secretary but she would have fit in quite nicely on a Las Vegas stage in one of those titillating revues that brought down the house. Her body rivaled that of any show girl, ensconced at the moment in a snug-fitting fuchsia velour jumpsuit that showed off every inch of her to good advantage.

"Close your mouth, Mr. Sebastian," Bri whispered as she passed him and went to greet her latest arrival.

THE NATIVES were growing restless. Everyone was present and accounted for, except Andrew Weston.

"We're fifteen minutes behind schedule," Mrs. McDermott said irritably. "I understood, Miss Graham, that you were a stickler for keeping to a time schedule."

"I was so hoping we would arrive in Colport before all the antique shops closed," Harriet Beecham muttered.

"Men," Jillian Knight said with throaty ennui. "And they say women are the ones who are always late."

"Perhaps the gentleman has changed his mind," Kyle Dunner offered. "You might want to check with your office, Miss Graham."

"I've got a phone line to my office on the van, Mr. Dunner," Bri explained. "He hasn't called to cancel." Nor did she think he would. Andrew Weston's private secretary had been quite anxious to reserve her boss a spot, sending in the entire fee right off, instead of merely the required deposit. And she'd double-checked just two days ago to make sure his spot was reserved.

"He must have gotten stuck in a traffic jam. At this time of the morning the Southeast Expressway can be murder." No sooner had the word *murder* escaped her lips than Bri felt a queer sense of disquiet. She felt Matt Sebastian's eyes on her and glanced over at him.

He quirked a smile and ambled off the bus for a smoke. Bri followed, telling herself she wasn't so much seeking Matt Sebastian's company as escaping that of the others.

"Don't you pay attention to the surgeon general's warnings?" she quipped as he lit up.

"Some habits are hard to break." He turned his head away from her and let out a thin, white stream of smoke.

"Maybe you should try harder."

He smiled, his eyes measuring her. "You sound like my mother."

"Well, I'm old enough to be your big sister, anyway."

His gaze traveled provocatively from her head down to her white leather running shoes and then back up again. "You're not that big."

Bri arched an eyebrow. "That's two in your column, Sebastian. I have to stop feeding you straight lines."

"Why? Is there a surgeon general's warning against it?"

She laughed. "If there isn't, there should be."

He took another drag of his cigarette and snubbed it out. "So tell me, Bri. Do you have an real kid brothers or sisters?"

"No. I'm an only child."

He studied her for a couple of moments. "Is there still only one of you? I mean . . . are you involved with anyone?"

Bri gave Matt Sebastian a level look. "I'm presently unattached and I have every intention of staying that way, Mr. Sebastian. Especially while I'm conducting this tour."

He grinned. "You forgot to add 'And besides, Mr. Sebastian, you're much too young for me.'"

"I thought I'd already made that point."

"So you did," he said with equanimity.

Bri scowled. "Can I ask you a personal question?"

His blue eyes danced. "Do you think you should?"

Bri's frown deepened. "Really, Mr. Sebastian, why would a young, attractive man choose to go alone on a fall foliage van tour? Wouldn't a singles' weekend at Martha's Vineyard or some such place be more your cup of tea?"

"I hate tea. I hate singles' weekends." He leaned a bit closer. "And thanks for the compliment. Not the young part. The attractive part."

She gave him a long, wary look. The pieces just didn't fit. If Matt Sebastian turned out to be an ordinary insurance agent, she'd eat her hat.

His eyes sparkled. "Didn't I tell you that when strangers meet there's bound to be some mystery?"

A pink tint crept across her cheeks, and she quickly glanced at her watch, then looked anxiously up and down the street.

"You think this Andrew Weston will show up?"

"Oh, he'll show up. In his own good time. He's probably some bigwig who's used to having people adjust to his schedule instead of the other way around." Bri frowned, chastising herself for bad-mouthing a member of her tour. Especially to another member. That wasn't at all professional.

She caught Matt smiling knowingly at her. Either this guy was clairvoyant or she read like an open book. At least to someone who liked to read. She got the distinct impression that Matt Sebastian did. He was perceptive, for a kid.

"Relax." He pinched her cheek. He pinched her cheek? Kids didn't do that to their elders. It was supposed to be the other way around.

Whatever, she could hardly relax at that particular moment. Just as she was getting over the annoyance of that pinch, a shiny, white limo pulled up, and a tall, impeccably dressed, dramatically handsome, and all-too-familiar-

looking man stepped out. Leaving the chauffeur to attend
to his luggage, Andrew Weston, alias John Fossier,
boarded the van without so much as a nod in her direction.

"Close your mouth, Miss Graham," Matt whispered as
he passed her and followed Bri's soon-to-be-ex-husband on
board.

Bri had always prided herself on being able to stay cool
and calm under fire, but right now she felt under siege.

Her first instinct was to haul *Mr. Andrew Weston* right
off the van and demand to know what was going on? Why
the alias? Why was he back? Why was he pretending that
he didn't know her from Adam? Oh, there were a lot of
questions she wanted to ask him, all right. Not to mention
a few choice remarks she was just itching to make.

Bri could feel a thread of hysteria starting to bubble to
the surface. She shut her eyes. A hysterical tour guide. Oh,
that would certainly get her fledgling business off to a
grand start. Well, John, or Andrew as he wanted to be
called now, had done quite enough to mess up her life.
She'd be damned if she was going to confront John and
make a public spectacle of herself right in front of her tour
group. As hard as it was going to be, she would force herself to wait for the right moment to have her little *chat* with
her soon-to-be-ex-husband.

Needing a few minutes to pull herself together, Bri took
out her log and scribbled something in it. As she was slipping it away in its specially designed compartment in the
dash, she took a quick glance in the rearview mirror. John
had taken the last seat on the right. Across from him was
Jillian Knight. John was eyeing the luscious redhead with
appreciation as they chatted. Jillian looked equally ap-
preciative of John.

Before she pulled her eyes away, Bri caught sight of Matt
Sebastian who was sitting across from her, one row back.

Their eyes met and held for a moment. Even when she drew her gaze away from the mirror, she knew he was still looking at her. And it made her uneasy. Not because it was one of his typically seductive looks, but because it clearly wasn't. Now questions about Matt Sebastian's motives and intentions started ricocheting off all the questions about John Fossier that were whipping around in her mind.

BRI PULLED the van into the parking lot of the Skater Mill Tavern at 12:30, a half hour later than she'd scheduled for their lunchtime stopover. The tavern, located in a little village just over the border of New Hampshire, dated back to the early eighteen hundreds. While the dining room had not been exactly preserved from colonial times, the flavor of that era was there, with its worn pine floors, barn-board siding, heavy maple tables and captain's chairs. Baskets of all shapes and sizes hung from the thick oak beams that traversed the ceiling, and the lights were cleverly concealed in old train oil lanterns.

The maître d' apologized to Bri for being unable to hold one large table for the group, but he assured her he could accommodate them all if they were willing to break up into smaller groups.

"I've got two tables for four, and one for two," he explained.

Allison was quick to ask Tim to join her at their table. Tim hesitated. Ever since Jillian Knight's arrival on the scene, Bri had noticed that the college student's hormones had shifted into overdrive. She guessed he was hoping to somehow grab that table for two for himself and the redhead. But a mere college boy was no match for the suave, take-charge John. While the others were trying to sort themselves out, Bri watched her soon-to-be-ex-husband escort Jillian Knight to the coveted table. Oddly enough, she felt no jealousy. Or maybe it was just that her utter bewilderment had obliterated all of her other feelings. Even her rage and pain at having been deserted in the first place had taken a backseat to her bafflement about her husband's strange behavior now that he'd returned. She even began to consider the possibility of amnesia to explain why he hadn't so much as acknowledged her. But the coincidence of his being on her tour was simply too hard to swallow. No, she thought. There had to be another explanation.

Meanwhile, Allison got her wish. Tim joined her, her grandmother and her great aunt at their table. Bri joined Matt, Kyle Dunner and Tim's mother, Anna Campbell.

Bri deliberately placed her back to John and Jillian, knowing that otherwise she'd be too distracted to carry on a civil conversation with her lunch partners. And for some reason, she didn't want Matt, in particular, to be aware of her distress. The problem was he already seemed keyed in to it. There'd been no way of hiding the shock on her face earlier when John had showed up completely out of the blue. Still, she wasn't keen on having Matt or any of the others know her true relationship with the debonair Mr. Weston. And it seemed to her, at least for the moment, neither was John.

She picked up her menu. "I've eaten here several times and if any of you are meat eaters, I strongly suggest the lamb." She was proud of how normal she sounded.

"Too much cholesterol for me, Miss Graham," Kyle Dunner said apologetically. "I was thinking I might try the chicken salad plate. What about you, Mrs. Campbell?"

When Anna Campbell didn't immediately respond, Bri glanced over at her, half expecting to find the pallid woman still immersed in the book she'd been reading all morning. But it wasn't a book that had Anna Campbell's attention now. It was a table across the room. The table that John and Jillian were sitting at. She was watching them. And the expression on her face was grim. Perhaps, Bri thought, the woman merely disapproved of intimate associations developing between strangers on the tour. Or maybe she was just envious. Bri had to admit John looked terrific, especially with that deep tan he'd no doubt acquired on the Canary Islands or some other tropical paradise. And when it came to turning on the charm, he had few equals. Bri was sure Jillian Knight would agree.

"What are you thinking about, Bri?"

Matt's question brought her up short. She gave him a startled look.

"Will you be having the lamb?" He smiled a knowing smile that made her very uncomfortable.

"The lamb?" Bri suddenly flashed on poor little lambs being led off for slaughter and lost her appetite altogether. She must have gone pale because everyone's eyes at the table were now on her, even Anna Campbell's.

"Are you feeling all right, Miss Graham?" she asked solicitously.

Bri forced a smile. "Fine. I'm fine. Just the excitement of getting the trip underway." She glanced back down at the menu. "I think I'll have the . . . chef's salad."

They were halfway through lunch when Kyle Dunner mentioned having visited Thornhill with his mother a year back. "My mother took a real shine to the place. It's not your typical sleepy little New England town, you know. There are some very dark skeletons in its closets, a few of which have come to light over the past couple of years."

Anna Campbell, who'd been picking on her blue-plate special—turkey with stuffing and sweet potatoes—gave him a curious look. "What do you mean?"

Kyle Dunner glanced at Bri who smiled uneasily. "Mr. Dunner's right. Thornhill does have a somewhat sordid past. A couple of years back an anthropology professor from the college was murdered."

"According to what Mother heard, she was a witch."

"She was an expert in witchcraft," Bri corrected.

"But she did lead a witches' coven, didn't she, Miss Graham? If I recall, it was her adopted son who murdered her for a valuable dagger that she used in her rituals." He took a swallow of milk. "And then there was the murder of an elderly fellow at the retirement community that turned out to be linked to a Lindberg-style kidnapping almost fifty years back."

"Well...yes," Bri admitted. "But the murderer was brought to justice so it's really quite safe now, I assure you." She saw, though, that Kyle Dunner didn't seem the least bit anxious. Nor did Matt who asked her how she knew about the murder and mayhem that had transpired in Thornhill.

"I spent a few days in Thornhill a while back and had a couple of chats with the wife of the police chief." Bri smiled. "She writes a gossip column for the local paper and, believe me, she's in the right line. She also happens to be a part owner of the inn I booked for the tour group, so if any of you want to know the details of anything that's happened in Thornhill and who it happened to, she's the one to tell you."

Anna Campbell's fine-etched features tightened. "I detest those who exploit other people's misfortune."

Everyone at the table was taken aback by the vehemence of the woman's remark. "Oh, Mildred Mead is nothing like that," Bri said earnestly. "Why, in both tragedies Mr. Dunner mentioned, she actually played a part in bringing the criminals to justice."

Anna Campbell's expression turned abruptly thoughtful. "How interesting."

"She does sound interesting," Matt agreed. "I'm looking forward to meeting her."

A throaty laugh echoed from across the room. Everyone at the table but Bri glanced over at the source of that laugh—Jillian Knight.

"She's quite glamorous," Kyle Dunner commented wistfully. "Is she an actress?" he asked Bri.

"She's a legal secretary."

Matt smiled crookedly. "There's one lucky lawyer out there."

It was bad enough that Bri felt an inexplicable flash of jealousy. It was worse that she saw that Matt knew it.

"And Mr. Weston?" Anna Campbell asked in a low-pitched voice. "What does he do, Miss Graham?"

Kyle Dunner was staring off across the room, his face set. "Whatever he does, I'm sure he does it very successfully."

Bri couldn't resist a quick glance over her shoulder. Her husband and Jillian Knight were practically nose-to-nose as they leaned into each other across the small table, uncluttered by luncheon plates, both of them having opted for a *liquid* lunch of dry martinis. Well, Bri thought derisively, that much hadn't changed about him. He always had been partial to martinis. And redheads.

AFTER LUNCH Bri settled up the bill and gave the tour group a fifteen minute break to stretch and stroll around the garden area behind the tavern before the two-hour drive to Colport. When she stepped out back, Bri was surprised to see Jillian Knight teamed up with Kyle Dunner. The two were soon joined by Tim Campbell and Allison, although Bri guessed that was more Tim's doing than the smitten teenager's. Meanwhile the two elderly sisters had surrounded Anna Campbell and were bending her ear about the many joys and disappointments of gardening.

Bri searched the area for John. If he was alone, this might be her opportunity to have a little heart-to-heart with him and find out what was going on. But when she did spot her husband, she saw that he wasn't alone. He was with Matt. And he didn't appear particularly pleased about it.

Bri wasn't particularly pleased herself when she saw Matt leading John in her direction. If Matt stuck around she'd be forced into carrying on the charade that *Mr. Weston* was a total stranger. A rather formidable task under the circumstances. For an instant she contemplated bolting away, but she knew that it would only show her anxiety. So she stood her ground, a benign smile plastered on her face, determined to maintain her composure.

"Settle an argument for us, Bri," Matt said amiably. "Andrew seems to think the red maple is the best fall foliage tree and I say it's the golden oak."

Bri caught the faint twitch of annoyance at the corners of John's mouth. "I wouldn't call it an argument."

"What do you say, Bri?" Matt persisted.

"I don't know what to call it."

Matt grinned, lightly elbowing the man beside him. "She's terrific, isn't she? Of course you don't really know each other yet, but take it from me, Andrew. She's not only easy on the eyes, but sharp as a tack."

I wish I had a tack, kid, Bri thought. *I know just where I'd stick it.*

John smiled politely. "Yes, I can see that." But he really wasn't looking at her. "If you'll excuse me, I'll dash into the men's room before we take off."

"So, that's your type," Matt mused, watching his fellow tour member head back into the tavern.

Bri gave Matt a sharp look. "Don't be ridiculous," she snapped.

"Hey, why not? He's got all the qualifications: looks, sex appeal, plenty of dough, and he's an older man. That's key, isn't it?" He gave her a teasing smile.

Bri didn't smile back. "I would have thought, Mr. Sebastian, that you were at least old enough to know better."

She started off, but Matt caught hold of her arm. "I'm sorry. You're right. I am old enough to know better." His gaze held hers. "I don't really think he's your type, Bri."

"You finally got something right. He isn't my type."

He nodded, but he didn't release his grip on her arm. "But you're curious about him."

She narrowed her gaze on him. "I'm curious about all my passengers."

"How come you didn't ask him the same question you asked me?"

"What question is that?"

"Why do you suppose a guy like that joined our little fall foliage jaunt?"

"Maybe he also doesn't like singles' weekends or tca," she said dryly, extracting her arm from Matt's grip.

He grinned. "That's another one for you, Bri. You know what I think?"

She shifted her weight from one hip to the other. "I think you're going to tell me."

"I think we make a good fit." His blue eyes crinkled in the corners. "I mean, a good match."

"I think you're crazy."

His expression turned serious. "I also think you need someone around that you can trust. So, I just want to go on record that I'm the trustworthy sort. You can take my word."

"Sorry," Bri said soberly, "these days I need references."

"WE'RE STILL MISSING Mr. Weston and Mrs. Campbell," Kyle Dunner said as everyone else settled into their seats after the break.

"My mother stopped to purchase some mints at the counter," Tim explained. "Would you like me to hurry her up and track down Mr. Weston, Miss Graham?"

"No," Bri said. "I'll run in and see if she's got what she needs. I'm sure Mr. Weston will be along momentarily."

When she dashed back into the tavern, Bri was surprised to find John and Anna Campbell engaged in conversation off in a corner of the waiting area. Well, actually, John was doing the talking. Anna Campbell was listening. Which in itself wasn't so surprising; it was the look on the woman's face that Bri found startling.

If looks could kill, Bri thought, a shiver threading through her body.

Chapter Three

"Oh, dear," Harriet Beecham fretted as the van pulled into the driveway of the Colport Inn, a quaint yellow clapboard three-story country house with an old-fashioned air, just outside the center of a town popular for its quaint antique shops and old bookstores. "It's so old. I do hope the plumbing has been modernized."

"And that we have a private bathroom with a tub and a shower," Mrs. McDermott was quick to add.

"All of the rooms come with private baths that include tubs and showers," Bri assured her after shutting off the engine and opening the doors. She stepped out first, helping the other women down.

"I put you on the first floor, Mrs. Campbell," Bri said, after assisting the frail woman from the van. She hesi tated. "Next door to Mr. Weston." She looked for some reaction, but the woman's features registered no change of expression. Nor did her eyes stray to John, who was just stepping down from the van. As for John, he seemed as oblivious to Anna Campbell as he was to her. Bri began to wonder if she'd somehow misinterpreted the hostile look she'd seen on Anna Campbell's face back at the tavern. Mrs. Campbell had a solemn visage at the best of times. Maybe it was just the way the light from the window bi sected her drawn, angular face that had made her look so full of hatred for that brief moment. Or maybe it was nothing more than the product of her own overactive imagination thanks to Matt Sebastian and those damn mystery stories of his. *Murder on the Valentine Express,* indeed.

"Your son will be right across the hall from you, Mrs. Campbell. And Mrs. McDermott, her sister and her granddaughter will be sharing a suite next door to Tim," Bri went on, determined to put a lid on her runaway imagination. She had enough to contend with just making sure her fledgling business got off to a good start. Not to mention discovering to what she owed, if not the pleasure, certainly the surprise, of her prodigal husband's return.

Matt came up behind her as she went around to the back of the van to open the rear doors. "Where'd you put me?"

She started pulling out the luggage only to find Matt taking the bags from her and setting them down on the ground.

"You're on the second floor next to Kyle Dunner and across the hall from Jillian Knight." Bri hesitated for a moment. "And me."

He smiled, taking out his own suitcase. "It sounds very cozy."

"WELCOME, WELCOME," George Meadows, the innkeeper, greeted the tour group warmly as they climbed up to the porch. Meadows was a robust man in his early fifties with a bristling beard flecked with gray, receding brown hair and an air of being at ease.

"I'm sorry we're late," Bri apologized, then proceeded to introduce the group to him. She did fine until she got to John. The name Andrew Weston got stuck in her throat. Bri might have been nonplussed, but John merely smiled pleasantly and shook the innkeeper's hand as he introduced himself.

Bri found her eyes darting to the hand John kept at his side. The hammered gold wedding band he'd worn from the day they married to the day he'd walked out on her had been replaced by a ruby signet ring. She wasn't particularly surprised or disappointed, but she did feel a hollowness. This man had been her husband. She'd thought she loved him. They'd shared intimate nights together where he'd held her in his arms afterward and told her how much he cherished her.

Since that first moment she saw him this morning, she'd tried to tell herself that it didn't hurt anymore, but that wasn't true. She still felt deceived, abandoned. And, just as she didn't have the slightest clue why he'd returned, she still didn't have the slightest idea why he'd deserted her in the first place. This man—John Fossier/Andrew Weston—was a stranger to her.

Her gaze lifted to his face, in profile now, as he asked the innkeeper some innocuous questions about the history of the inn. He must have felt her observing him, because he glanced over at her as the innkeeper was responding. A bland smile curved his lips. It was that smile, more than anything else, that made Bri feel inexplicably afraid.

After helping George Meadows make sure everyone was settled into their rooms, Bri stepped out onto the porch that ran the whole width of the front of the inn punctuated with wooden rocking chairs. She took a deep breath and stood at the railing, looking out over the Monadnock mountain range awash with a golden hue, slashed here and there with clusters of ruby red and emerald green. An autumnal rainbow of colors as far as the eye could see. As wondrous a sight as it was, Bri knew that as they moved farther north where the fall foliage was at its peak, the sight would be even more spectacular.

She sat down on one of the rockers, glad for the momentary respite. First the break-in at her apartment and now John showing up without warning and behaving so mysteriously. She felt impelled to tell him at the first opportunity that she had filed for a divorce. One thing was certain. She had absolutely no desire to renew their relationship in any way. She was convinced that marrying John had been a mistake right from the first. She'd hardly known him; or very much about him. She knew that he was an importer of rather minor Middle Eastern objets d'art which he showed at a Boston gallery owned by a casual acquaintance of hers, Adam Quinn. Adam had actually introduced her to the importer at one of his gallery shows. Like Jillian Knight, she, too, had found herself immediately drawn to John. He was so charismatic, and charming, and seductive. Nor did it take very long before she discovered that he was also very passionate.

She sighed inwardly. She and John had had a few good months together, but looking back on it now, she saw that there had never been any real communication between them. There had been something shallow about their relationship. It seemed grounded on the immediacy of the moment. It was exciting, romantic, fun, but never too serious. She'd found it odd at the time that John wasn't very curious about her. Whatever he knew about her, he learned during their first few dates. Which was that she came from the Midwest, had graduated with an art history degree from Boston University and that she was bored to tears with her job as a receptionist at a Newbury Street art gallery. She quit the job with John's encouragement shortly before they were married.

John rarely asked her questions about her past or answered ones she asked him about his life before they'd met. He'd always tell her that he was a man who liked living only in the present. All during their brief courtship and equally brief marriage, John Fossier had remained a mystery to her. And now he was more a mystery than ever.

A bell jingled as the front door opened. Mrs. Beecham and Mrs. McDermott came out on the porch.

"Would you like to join us, Miss Graham?" Mrs. Beecham inquired. "We're going to walk into town to browse among the antique shops. I'm very fond of antique jewelry. Why, last year in a little out-of-the-way shop in Rockport, I came upon this exquisite ivory amulet from Egypt. It was an early nineteenth century replica of an ancient piece, or so the shopkeeper told me. I must confess I'm not very knowledgeable about Middle Eastern artifacts."

"Neither am I, but I suppose what counts is that you have a good eye, Mrs. Beecham," Bri said, thinking that John was the one who was the expert in that field. She wisely kept the information to herself.

Eleanor McDermott snickered. "If you ask me, she paid twice what it was worth. Shopkeepers see my sister coming from a mile away, and they put out all their junk." She turned to her sister. "Didn't that shopkeeper tell you the original amulet was worn by Queen Nefertiti herself?"

"Why, yes. I believe he did," Harriet replied pleasantly.

Eleanor harrumphed. "Which was when you stopped trying to bargain him down."

"Are you an expert on ancient Egypt, Mrs. McDermott?" Bri couldn't resist asking the garrulous woman, although she made sure to keep her voice sweet, her expression one of benign interest.

The large woman scowled. "Not an expert, but I lived in Egypt for a brief time with my husband, may he rest in peace. Adam worked with the state department. We traveled extensively all over Europe, Asia and the Middle East during our marriage."

"Well, not so much after the baby came along," her sister commented. "Traveling with an infant is no easy matter. I remember one time when the four of us went to Jordan..."

Eleanor McDermott gave her sister an impatient look. "If we stand here prattling all day, Harriet, the shops will be closed and you may miss out on a pair of earrings owned by Marie Antoinette. Perhaps the very ones she wore to the guillotine."

To her credit, Harriet Beecham chuckled good-naturedly. "Yes, you never know," she said, the eternal optimist.

They were halfway down the stairs when Mrs. McDermott came to an abrupt halt and turned back to Bri. "My granddaughter's lying down. Naturally I don't expect you to be a chaperon as well as a tour guide, Miss Graham, but I would appreciate it if you would make sure she doesn't get into any...trouble while we're gone."

"What kind of trouble would she get into?" Bri asked, wondering if Mrs. McDermott was worried about her granddaughter's obvious attraction to Tim Campbell.

Before Eleanor McDermott answered, Harriet Beecham tugged on her sister's arm. "Don't worry about Allison, Eleanor. She's a good girl."

"I know she's a good girl," Mrs. McDermott snapped as they continued down the stairs. The two women continued arguing as they went on their way, forgetting all about Bri.

Bri smiled to herself. Those two really were a pair of characters. But they did provide some much-needed comic relief.

After spending a few more minutes on the porch, Bri wandered inside to the cozy downstairs library at the front of the inn where she found Kyle Dunner and Anna Campbell sitting in nearby armchairs quietly reading.

"It's lovely out on the porch. You might want to read out there," Bri suggested. "Or even take a stroll before the sun goes down. It's such a beautiful day," she added, not realizing until that moment that she had an ulterior motive for making the recommendation.

Kyle took to the suggestion right off. He looked over at Anna Campbell and invited her to take a leisurely stroll with him.

"That is," he added solicitously, "if your leg won't bother you too much." Bri was surprised when the modestly handicapped woman acquiesced. Just as they were heading for the front door, Anna Campbell's son came bounding down the stairs.

"I'm off for a hike with Jillian, Allison and Andrew Weston," he announced with youthful exuberance to his mother.

"What about Matt Sebastian?" Bri asked, seeing this as her opportunity to have them all off so she could pursue a plan that had begun to take root in her mind.

"Oh, he's gone into town already," Tim said offhandedly. "He borrowed the innkeeper's bike."

MATT SEBASTIAN LOCKED up the bike to the bike rack in front of the Colport general store. George Meadows had told him not to bother since the bike had seen better days a number of years back, but Matt liked to be careful. After a quick check around, he crossed the street and headed down a small alley that led to a rundown diner, one of those tacky chrome and linoleum joints that looked out of place in the quaint town and lacked any of the charm of the tavern where the tour group had stopped for lunch. Matt guessed that tourists rarely came to the diner, but it was popular among the locals, a number of whom occupied stools at the counter and several of the booths along the windowed wall. One man sitting in the diner, however, wasn't a local. And this was the man Matt had come to see.

Matt headed straight for the booth at the far end of the diner where a middle-aged man in a gray suit sat hunched over a half-eaten donut and a cup of coffee. On first impression he passed for an ordinary local businessman type, but on closer observation he looked a bit scraggly around the edges, his graying hair in need of a decent trim, the suit dated and a little shabby, his gaunt expression world-weary. To Matt's assessing eye, Joe Holland looked exactly like what he was. An over-the-hill private eye whose two saving graces were that he was persistent and he worked cheap.

Matt slipped into the bench seat across from Holland just as the private eye was starting to dunk one bitten end of his honey-glazed donut into the black coffee. He stopped mid-dunk and gave Matt an acerbic look.

"You're almost an hour late." The dipped end of the donut broke off. A moment later the sodden mush floated to the top of the coffee. He picked up a spoon and fished it out, blithely popping it into his mouth. "Don't make 'em like they used to," he mumbled.

Matt took out a cigarette.

"No smoking," Holland said gruffly, pointing to a sign on the dingy wall. "So, what's the scoop, kid?"

Matt popped the cigarette, unlit, into his mouth for a moment, then stuck it back in his pack. "Tell me, Holland. Why does everything have to turn out to be more complicated than it should?"

The gaunt man grinned. On him, it looked like a grimace. "Yeah, she's a good-looking dame."

"That's not what I'm talking about," Matt said quickly. A little too quickly. Holland chuckled. "Okay, okay," Matt relented. "She's good-looking. A little hung up about her age, though. Or mine."

"Hey, I thought women went for younger men these days."

"Not this one." He motioned to the waitress over at the counter and pointed to his friend's coffee cup. She brought another cup of coffee right over. The cup was chipped, but she either didn't notice or didn't care. Matt didn't care, either.

"Anything else?" the waitress asked in a bored tone, wiping her hands on her apron.

"Have yourself a donut," Joe Holland suggested.

Matt shook his head. As the waitress sashayed off, Matt grabbed the sugar dispenser and poured several heaping spoons of sugar into his coffee while the private eye looked on with disapproval. "You got lousy habits for a kid," he muttered.

"Enough with the kid," Matt grumbled. "I'm beginning to feel like I should still be in short pants."

Holland chuckled. "You were never in short pants."

Matt took a sip of the muddy, sweetened coffee and grimaced.

Holland slid the sugar dispenser back over to him. "Maybe she's still hung up on her husband."

Matt looked up sharply. "Maybe that's it. Or maybe experience has just made her wary of the opposite sex."

"Can't say as how you could blame her for that."

Matt nodded. He added a little more sugar and took another sip of his coffee. It didn't taste any better, but he was getting used to it. "There's another possibility."

Holland's brow creased. The gesture made his forehead look like corrugated cardboard. "What's that?"

Matt looked over the rim of his coffee cup at the private eye. "Maybe she's scared."

Their gazes locked for a moment and then Matt pulled out a small notepad and tore off a page, sliding it across to the private eye. "Here, this should keep you busy for a while. I'd like as much as you can get for me as fast as you can get it. We'll be up in Thornhill. Meet me up there three days from now, say three o'clock, at the Mandarin House, a classy Chinese restaurant in a fashionable little mall called Thornhill Park in the center of town."

"Classy Chinese? I guess that's better than greasy donuts."

Matt smiled. "Sure. You can have some greasy egg rolls instead."

Holland looked down at the paper on which Matt had printed out a list of names. The private eye's brief good spirits vanished, his mouth drooping with skepticism. "Hey, you want checks on every one of them? In three days? You gotta be kiddin'."

"A kid can't afford to kid," Matt said dryly, but then he edged his coffee cup aside and leaned forward, narrowing his gaze on the private eye. "I have an uneasy feeling that there's more here than meets even my eagle eyes. I'm used to working in the shadows, Joe, but I don't like working in the dark."

Holland nodded sympathetically, but then he looked back down at the list of names. "This is a tall order."

Matt agreed, slipping a plain white envelope across the table. "To sweeten the task."

Holland stuck the envelope in his inside jacket pocket and gave Matt a long, assessing look. "Do your people know we're working together on this one?"

"Does it really matter?" Matt queried.

Holland dunked another piece of the donut, getting it into his mouth before he lost it to the coffee cup. "Not as long as you're happy, kid."

"I hope I'll be happy when I see you up in Thornhill," Matt said pointedly, running an impatient hand through his hair.

"I'll do my best. Just like I always tried to do for your daddy."

Matt smiled at the man he'd known since he really was a kid. "You did okay by him, Joe. I never heard him complain."

Joe Holland chuckled. "Yeah. Well, I heard him complain plenty. When he asked for the impossible and I couldn't deliver it to him. You know something, kid," he said, tapping the torn sheet of note paper, before tucking it away in his shirt pocket. "You take after your old man in more ways than one."

"You're probably right," Matt conceded with a crooked smile.

"Which is why I'm gonna tell you what I told him on more than one occasion," Joe said solemnly. "Don't go biting off more than you can chew."

Matt tapped his pearly whites. "I got strong teeth."

"Yeah, strong, maybe, but not necessarily as sharp as some others around."

BRI'S TOUR GROUP occupied nine of the twelve rooms at the Colport Inn. She'd learned that the guests who were staying in the other three rooms weren't due to arrive until the evening. Even tho innkeeper had gone off to do some errands, leaving Bri entirely alone in the place. She realized this might be her only chance to carry out her plan.

With a certain degree of guilt and trepidation, she hurried outside and around to the side of the house, stopping at the second window from the end. The one that led into John's room. Like all of the occupied rooms, the window had been opened so that when the guests arrived they wouldn't find their quarters stuffy. John had left his open.

Unfortunately the window ledge was higher up than Bri had estimated. She frowned, realizing she'd need something to step on in order to climb inside.

A minute later, as if she'd studied cat burglary as an elective, Bri was hoisting herself into John's room with the aid of a wooden milk crate she'd found out behind the house. Now that the deed was done she could only hope she had enough time to snoop around, then climb back out and remove the telltale object before anyone returned. As soon as she climbed into the room she hastily replaced the window screen so that flies didn't get in and give away the fact that someone had done precisely what she had done.

John's bedroom, like the others in the inn, was decorated with homey antiques, quilted coverlets and colorful rag rugs. The space was bright and uncluttered, furnished with a large four-poster bed, a couple of small end tables, a rust and brown tapestry print armchair and a dressing table. John's suitcase lay on his bed, unopened.

Bri stared at it, unsure of what she expected to find inside. Could there be anything in that expensive leather suitcase that would give her a hint of why John had come back so precipitously? Would she learn why he was using an alias? What he wanted?

Stealthily she crossed the room. Her heart was racing, but fear had given way to a heightened anticipation.

She felt a mixture of relief and disappointment to find the case unlocked. If there were any secrets inside, surely John would not have made the contents so easily accessible. Or had it never entered his mind that anyone, especially his once-trusting wife, would go snooping? Well, John wasn't the only one who had done some changing in the past few months.

Lightly Bri's hand skimmed the top of the suitcase. She gnawed at her lower lip as she stared down at it. *Go on,* she commanded silently, *just open it.* She sucked in a breath and lifted the lid. It made a weird squeaking noise. This was followed by a slamming sound.

Bri froze. It wasn't the suitcase that had caused the squeak or the slam. It was the front door to the inn. Someone had come back. John? Had he forgotten something? Had he had second thoughts about leaving his suitcase unlocked?

His was the second room down the hall from the main vestibule. With hardly a glance into the suitcase, a glance which took in some folded shirts and sweaters and nothing suspicious, Bri started to flip the lid closed. And then she spotted something that not only alarmed her, but made her gasp. The object was tucked under a beige cashmere cardigan. Instinctively she lifted up the sweater to reveal the large black gun fitted with a silencer. She stared at it with horror and revulsion. And terror.

It was only the sound of the footsteps starting down the hall that brought back the jeopardy of the moment. Bri's eyes darted to the open window. She'd never have time to remove the screen, climb out and replace the screen before John entered the room. And what if, on his way into the inn, he'd noticed the milk crate outside his window? Then he'd know someone was in his room. And it probably wouldn't be too difficult for him to figure out who.

Dread flooded her. She tried to calm herself by thinking that it might not be John at all but one of the other guests returning from an outing and heading for their own room. It could be Anna Campbell coming back from her walk with Kyle Dunner, or Mrs. McDermott and Miss Beecham coming back from town.

Bri held her breath as the footsteps neared the door to John's room and stopped, sending her into a fit of panic and an unceremonious dive under the four-poster bed.

Her worst fears were realized when she heard the doorknob jiggle. Any moment now John would be entering the room. Any moment now she could be discovered.

MATT STOOD outside Andrew Weston's room, debating whether this was a good time to take a peek inside. While he was biking back he'd spotted the room's occupant and three of the other tour members just turning up the road to the inn. Even walking at a fast clip it would take them about ten minutes to get here. And he'd run into Mrs. McDermott and her sister in town. That left Kyle Dunner, Anna Campbell and Bri. He hadn't seen any of them outside or in the front parlor or library. Either they'd gone off or were in their rooms.

He rubbed his jaw. He didn't have much time and he was well aware that it was a little risky, but then that was part of the fun. He smiled wryly and drew out his handy-dandy all-purpose passkey from his pants pocket. It would work like a charm on a decrepit lock like this one.

BRI PINCHED her nose to fight off a threatening sneeze and sucked in a breath as she heard the lock turn in the bolt. Terror gripped her, but she tried to reason with herself. Okay, she thought, if John discovered her hiding in here, he'd certainly be angry. He'd have every right to be. He hadn't exactly invited her in. And he wouldn't particularly appreciate her rifling his belongings. On the other hand, surely he expected her to be curious. Suspicious, even. Didn't he owe her some sort of explanation? Didn't she have the right to go looking for it when no explanation was forthcoming? Then again, maybe he was just waiting for the proper time. Maybe he was just being discreet out of consideration for her.

Then she remembered that gleaming black gun in John's suitcase. And the silencer. That was taking *discreet* too far for comfort. What little courage Bri had mustered started to slip away, accelerated by the sound of footsteps crossing the room, approaching the bed. Did he sense her presence? Did he know she was here? Would he be lifting up the dust ruffle any moment now and discover her? She squeezed her eyes shut as she imagined looking into the barrel of that silencer.

He was standing at the bed, his feet no more than a few inches from her face. Bri forced her eyes open. She gasped inwardly as she saw John's shoes, the toes pointed right at her. She stared in blind panic at the shoes. But then slowly, puzzlement invaded her panic. She realized she was looking at a pair of well-worn Dock-Sides. The shoes rang a bell. They were familiar looking. Her lips pressed tightly together and her heart slammed against her chest. Those Dock-Sides looked just like the ones Matt Sebastian was wearing today. Was it possible that John was wearing the same kind of shoes?

She shut her eyes recreating a vision of John in her mind. She pictured him stepping out of the limo that morning. Feet first. She focused in on those feet. Feet, she remembered now, that were encased, not in brown leather boat shoes, but in expensive black leather Italian loafers. Had he changed into Dock-Sides before taking off for his walk?

Muted voices drifted in from the open window. Bri immediately recognized a high-pitched youthful laugh as belonging to Allison.

"Oh, I'm a perfect clod when it comes to sports."

A huskier, sultry laugh followed. "I can say the same about some sports, but not others."

Even if Bri hadn't recognized the voice she would have known from the remark that it was Jillian Knight.

Bri's head began to swim as she then heard a familiar voice just after the front door banged shut.

"Badminton sounds like fun," Andrew Weston called out as he started down the hall. "I'll just go change into sneakers."

Moments later, just as the lock was turning in the door, Bri found herself looking into the startled eyes of Matt Sebastian as he slipped under Andrew Weston's, alias John Fossier's, bed.

Chapter Four

"We need to talk, Bri," were Matt's first words after John, now sporting a pair of tennis shoes, exited the room.

"What are you doing here?" she demanded.

"In the room or under the bed?" he replied drolly.

Bri wasn't amused. She also wasn't as afraid as she thought she probably should be. "Are you a thief?" That was all she needed. Par for the bumpy course. Hadn't she thought right from the start that Matt Sebastian didn't look like an insurance agent?

He didn't answer her question. Instead he asked blithely, "Are you?"

She glared at him, and then started to crawl out from under the bed. Matt's hand sprang out, cutting short her progress.

"Give it another minute. Let's make sure they all leave."

Bri suddenly remembered something. "Oh, no. Isn't the badminton court on this side of the house?" she asked in an anxious whisper.

Matt shrugged. "I'm not sure. Why?"

"There's a milk crate sitting right outside under the window."

He rolled his eyes.

She gave him a cutting look. "Well, I wasn't so fortunate as to possess a key to John's room."

"John?"

She silently cursed her stupidity, but then something about Matt's expression told her he wasn't all that surprised by her slip of the tongue. She stared more intently at him, but neither of them spoke as they heard voices out in the vestibule as the badminton group regathered. A few moments later, the front door slammed. Bri scrambled out from under the bed, Matt following suit.

As soon as she got to her feet, Bri brushed herself off and hurried to the window to check if she had been right about the badminton court. With a sinking sensation in the pit of her stomach, she saw the court, no more than thirty feet from this side of the house. All John would have to do was glance over and he'd spot the milk crate under the window.

But then Bri looked down, discovering with no small degree of amazement that the milk crate was gone. She turned to Matt, stopping short as she saw him methodically searching through the drawers on the small chest beside the bed.

"Okay, what's going on?" Bri demanded, taking the offense. "Who are you and what are you looking for in here?"

"My guess is, the same thing you're looking for in here," Matt replied with a faint smile. "Answers."

Bri's eyes shot to the bed. The suitcase was no longer lying there. She looked around, spotting it on a luggage rack next to the closet. The lid was open and propped against the wall.

Matt's eyes followed Bri's. Then he gave her a sideways glance. "Did you get a chance to go through it?"

Without thinking, she shook her head. Then she looked sharply at him. "That's none of your business."

He eyed her assessingly. "But it is yours, isn't it, Bri?"

She glared at him. "I think we'd better have our little chat somewhere else."

He smiled at her, but instead of heading for the door, he went straight for the suitcase across the room. Bri scooted after him.

"You have no right..." she started to argue as he began to carefully look through the contents. But she swallowed the rest of the sentence, along with her breath, as he went to lift up the beige cashmere sweater. What would Matt do when he found the gun? For all she knew, he might swipe it and use it on her. But somehow she couldn't get herself to picture Matt Sebastian as a mad gunman. A cat burglar, though, maybe.

In any event, she didn't have to worry about the gun. When Matt lifted the sweater, she saw that the gun was gone. She continued watching in silent fascination as Matt finished up his check, coming up empty-handed. Bri felt a mix of relief and puzzlement to find that the silencer-fitted gun was no longer in the suitcase. When John had come in to change his shoes he must have moved it some place else in the room or taken off with it. Wasn't it what every well-dressed man wore to play badminton?

Just as Matt was about to open the closet, they heard footsteps again. And voices drifted past the closed bedroom door. It was Anna Campbell and Kyle Dunner.

"I quite agree with you," Kyle was saying. "Boston is a much more civil place to live than New York."

"How long did you and your mother live there?" Anna inquired.

"A few years. But then the company transferred me to Boston about a year ago. Unfortunately my mother was already ill and never really got a chance to enjoy Boston as she might have."

"You must have been very lonely when she passed away," Anna said sympathetically.

"You can certainly understand, Anna. Having lost your husband, you know about the grief I suffered. How long ago did you say it's been since he passed on?"

There was a brief pause. "Oh, I didn't mean to imply before that he was...dead," Anna said, her voice taking on a strained quality. "My husband...left me. Quite a while ago."

"When Tim was a boy?"

There was another brief pause. "Yes. A small boy. He doesn't remember his father at all."

Kyle and Anna continued chatting quietly in the hall. Meanwhile from the window, Bri and Matt could hear the laughter and jocular remarks coming from the badminton group. For the moment, they were trapped inside John's room.

The situation put Bri on edge, but it didn't seem to disturb Matt who took the opportunity to quietly and meticulously go about searching through the few items of clothing John had hung in the closet.

Bri saw him remove a white linen hanky from inside the pocket of a blue blazer. He studied the initials neatly monogrammed into one corner. So did Bri. The initials weren't Andrew Weston's. They were J.F.

Their eyes met and held; Matt's eyebrows raised, Bri's lips pursed. Then he stuck the hanky back where he'd found it.

A moment later, the voices out in the hall stopped. A door closed across the way. Anna Campbell's room. Bri wondered whether Kyle Dunner had gone inside the room with his new acquaintance, but then she heard heavy footfalls go back up the hall toward the staircase that led to the second floor.

Bri and Matt made a beeline for the door. When they got to it, Bri's hand darted out for the knob, but Matt made a grab for her wrist. "Wait," he cautioned, pressing his ear to the door. Bri was sharply conscious of his hand still touching her as he listened.

No sooner had they slipped out of the room, than they saw Mrs. McDermott and Miss Beecham turn the corner and start down the hall. The two sisters regarded them curiously, as well they might since neither of them had rooms on that floor. Bri froze for a moment, but Matt smiled brightly at the pair.

"We were just knocking on your door to see if you were interested in playing bridge this afternoon," Matt said breezily.

Bri darted him a cautious look. She didn't even play bridge.

"Oh, thank you for the invitation," Harriet Beecham said, bustling down the hall, followed by her much larger, lumbering sister, "but I never was able to get the hang of playing bridge." She glanced back at Eleanor. "And you never did enjoy the game very much, did you, dear?"

"I find such pastimes to be foolish wastes of time," Eleanor McDermott said curtly. "And there's always far too much chit-chat around the table."

Bri breathed a sigh of relief. "Yes, well, I'll leave you two ladies to relax."

"Dinner at six, Miss Graham?" Harriet asked.

"Yes," Bri said. "And I'm sure you'll enjoy it The Colport Inn is noted for its fine New England cuisine."

Eleanor McDermott scowled. "Last time I was at an inn in New Hampshire, they served rabbit. I don't eat rabbit. I never have and I never will," she announced, passing Bri and Matt and marching into her room, the door already opened by her sister.

Harriet, who remained out in the hall for another moment, smiled warmly at them. "She doesn't eat venison, either. Never has, never will." She started inside but then popped her head back out the door. "Oh, and by the way,

Miss Graham, we weren't able to find a single pair of earrings that belonged to Marie Antoinette. As I told Eleanor, she probably didn't wear any jewelry at all on her way to getting her head chopped off. It would have been rather pointless, don't you agree?''

Bri nodded inanely while Matt, standing beside her, gave her a muddled look.

"Don't even ask," Bri muttered out of the corner of her mouth as Harriet Beecham disappeared.

As soon as the door to the suite closed, Matt grinned at Bri. "Good thing they turned down my offer. I don't play bridge." His grin deepened. "Never have, never will."

Bri gave him a frustrated look. "Then why did you...?"

"Hey, I had to think fast. It was the first thing that popped into my head. What if I'd said we'd stopped by to ask them if they wanted to join us for badminton? Can you just picture the four of us challenging those four out there to a game?" He laughed softly at the image.

"I don't find that very amusing. And I still want to know who you really are and what you were doing in...that room."

The answers to Bri's questions were curtailed by the dramatic arrival of Jillian Knight. Being carried by Andrew Weston. Tim Campbell was right behind them, Allison glumly tagging along.

"I feel so silly," Jillian murmured in a powdery voice. "Twisting my ankle playing badminton of all things. I guess it just isn't my sport."

Bri hurried over. Jillian's ankle did look a bit swollen. "I'd better get some ice for that. Maybe I ought to drive you over to a doctor in town and let him have a look at it."

"The ice will do the trick," Andrew Weston said with brusque authority as he started up the stairs with Jillian in his arms.

Bri hesitated for a moment, and then went to get some ice from the kitchen. George Meadows had returned from his errands and was chatting with the cook when Bri rushed in.

"One of my tour members twisted her ankle. Do you have any ice packs?" she asked hurriedly.

The cook, a buxom, late middle-aged woman, quickly made one up.

"We've got a very good doctor in town..." the innkeeper started to say, when Tim Campbell popped into the kitchen. He went straight over to the cook and snatched the ice pack from her hand.

"I'll run it up to Jillian," he said and was out the door like a shot.

By the time Bri arrived in Jillian's room, she found the voluptuous redhead being solicitously attended to by Tim, Matt, Kyle and Andrew/John. Jillian might have been in some pain, but she was also in her glory. Before making her exit, Bri checked on Jillian's status, shot a quick look at John, who resolutely refused eye contact, and then at Matt, who quirked a teasing smile before readjusting the ice pack on the redhead's ankle.

Bri found Allison downstairs in the parlor, sitting cross-legged on a window seat, looking bored and morose. She barely acknowledged Bri when she came in and sat down in one of the flowered chintz armchairs across from her.

After a few strained minutes of silence, Allison glanced over at Bri. "I think boys who chase after grown women look totally ridiculous."

For an instant Bri thought she was referring to Matt and her. She could feel her cheeks warm.

"Why, Tim's got to be five, six years younger than Jillian," Allison went on. "He's just going to make a fool of himself."

"Men have a habit of doing that," Bri muttered.

"I don't even know why I like him. He can be positively rude. I tried to get him into a conversation about Harvard, because I know a girl who goes there, and he said he hates talking about college. He wouldn't even talk about why he decided to go into biology as a major. I asked him if he was planning to go into medicine and he just gave me one of those looks." She eyed Bri conspiratorially. "I wouldn't be surprised if he got kicked out. He certainly doesn't strike me as the studious type. And, if he is in school, what's he doing on this trip?"

"His mother said he decided to take the semester off and help her. She's recovering from some sort of knee operation. That's why she walks with a cane."

Allison scowled. "He certainly doesn't seem very attentive to his mother as far as I can see. Not that I get along with my mom all that well, either."

"What about your dad?" Bri asked.

Allison glanced at her with a half shrug. "He and my mom were divorced when I was a kid. For a little while he got an apartment nearby us in Encino, then he moved away. He used to live here on the East Coast. After he left Encino though, I never really saw him much anymore. No big deal. I've had dozens of friends in the same boat."

Bri nodded, guessing that Allison's attempt at callousness was really an attempt to cover up her hurt, anger and feelings of loss. Bri knew about all those emotions, too. While her own parents hadn't divorced, they had never really gotten along. Her dad, a salesman, spent as much time away from the house as possible, which served as a source of constant irritation to her mother. But when he was home, her parents rarely did anything together but fight. Bri always had the feeling they'd stayed together because of her, but, growing up, she could never rid herself of the fantasy that one day they'd realize they really did love each other and then everything would be different. When her father died of a sudden heart attack in his late forties, that fantasy was put to rest along with him.

"What do you think of Andrew?" Allison asked, abruptly shaking Bri from her ruminations.

A pink tint crept across her cheeks. "Andrew? Well...I don't know. What do you think?"

Allison smoothed the front of her peach-tinted, blond hair to the side. "I think he's better looking than Matt Sebastian. I mean, Matt's kind of cool and sexy looking in his own way, but he seems kind of young. Now, Andrew's very mature and he's got real class. And plenty of dough. I caught a glimpse of that limo he drove up in this morning. It was hot." She waved her hand in front of her face.

"Have you spoken much to Andrew? Is he...chattier than Tim?"

Allison scowled. "He seems pretty chatty with Jillian, but he hasn't said much to me. I'm sure he just sees me as a kid. Just like Jillian sees Tim, only he's too gaga over her to notice."

Allison got up, stretched and checked her watch. "Say, it's almost time for dinner. I'll go let Tim and the rest of the Florence Nightingales upstairs know."

Bri rose, too. "Thanks. I'll gather up the others."

"Oh, don't worry about grandma and Aunt Harriet. They may complain about the meal all night but they'll show up right on time."

As if by telepathy, Mrs. McDermott and Miss Beecham appeared in the entryway to the parlor.

"I hope," Mrs. McDermott said formidably, "they serve promptly at six. There's nothing more irritating than being told the time for a meal and then being kept waiting."

ALTHOUGH BRI was relieved that dinner was served precisely at six, she felt frustrated at not getting another opportunity to pull Matt aside and get some answers from him. She felt certain now that Matt wasn't a mere insurance agent. And she was less inclined to think he was just a cat burglar. She was convinced he knew that Andrew Weston was really John Fossier, and that she was his wife. That realization made her question how he knew so much, and how much more he knew about Andrew Weston alias John Fossier. What was Matt's connection with her husband?

Bri got the distinct feeling that Matt was deliberately avoiding her that evening. During dinner he sat between Anna Campbell and Harriet Beecham, keeping up a steady banter with one or the other of the ladies. After the meal he played cards with Kyle Dunner in the library until eleven at which time he took off for his room, bidding the group a yawning good-night.

Bri debated knocking on Matt's door for a little heart-to-heart, but she was concerned about rumors spreading if anyone learned she'd paid a late-night call on him in his room. She decided that it would be wiser and more discreet to wait for tomorrow.

By midnight everyone, including Bri, had turned in for the night. For nearly an hour she lay under the covers and tried to think everything out. It got pretty full in that bed, what with Andrew, Matt and the others crowding in, demanding some room. But offering no answers. Bri finally eked out enough space for herself and fell asleep.

She was awakened by the sound of the bolt turning slowly in her lock. As the door inched open she was acutely alert. Matt, she thought. It had to be Matt. He must have used the same passkey he'd used to get into John's room that afternoon. Outrage mixed with fear as she saw a shadowy figure slip inside and shut her door. Once it was closed, the room was again bathed in blackness.

"If you're here to talk, stay right where you are and start talking," Bri demanded with a lot more defiance than she felt.

There was no response, but Bri could hear the faint creaking sounds of footsteps across the wooden floor of her room. She sat up, clutching the cover to her chest with one hand, her other hand darting out for the lamp at the side of her bed. She wasn't sure at the moment whether she meant to turn it on or use it as a weapon to strike out at her intruder.

She never got the chance to make the decision. Just as her fingers circled the lamp base, a strong hand grabbed her arm twisting it so that she had to release her grip on it.

"Matt, you're hurting me," she gasped as her hand was pulled sharply behind her back.

A dry laugh made her cringe. "Matt? You don't waste any time, do you, Bri?"

She gasped. "John?"

"Did you miss me, Bri?" His voice was low and taunting. It sounded nothing like the voice of the man who had once whispered all those words of endearment to her. It didn't even sound anything like the affable, charming tour member he'd pretended to be all day.

"What's this all about, John? Why did you come back?" Now Bri's voice was laced with fear.

"What the hell did you do with it, Bri?" His face was so close to hers she could feel his hot breath against her ear. She shivered with revulsion.

"I don't know what you're talking about. And if you don't let go of me this instant, I'll scream, John."

"No, you won't," he hissed. An instant later she felt the chilling sensation of metal against her temple. Oh, God, she thought, the gun. The gun from his suitcase. The one fitted with a silencer so that a shot could be fired and no one would even hear it go off.

Bri broke out in a cold sweat. "John, this is crazy. Why are you doing this to me?" Her voice quavered. Only now did she realize just how much of a stranger this man was—this man who was technically still her husband.

He eased the pressure of his grip on her arm, but the barrel of the silencer remained pressed against her temple, a cold reminder that he meant business. Serious business.

"I know you stuck it somewhere for safekeeping during my extended absence. And I know you didn't ditch it. You're the sentimental type. Well, now I've come back for it. I want it, Bri. And I don't have time to play games."

She could feel hysteria rising in her throat, but she used every ounce of will to keep her voice even and calm. "Listen to me, John. I don't know what you're talking about. I don't have anything of yours. I got rid of it all."

She heard the horrifying sound of the gun being cocked. Silent tears started running down her eyes.

"It's not in the apartment, Bri. So you put it somewhere else," he said quietly.

Even in her terror she felt a rush of fury as the pieces of the puzzle began to fit together. "It was you who broke into my place and ransacked it. You've been watching me in the shadows, following me all week. I thought I was going crazy. But it's you, John. You're the one who must be crazy." In her outrage, she flung her arm out wildly, knocking over the lamp. It made a loud thud as it hit the floor, startling John long enough for Bri to roll away from him in the blackness.

John was reaching out for her across the bed when there was a sharp knock on the door.

"Bri, are you okay. It's Matt. I heard a crash. If you don't answer..."

She heard John's footsteps. A moment later he opened the door. Now, in the light, Bri could see that he'd stuck the gun away.

"Sorry," John said in his affable Andrew Weston voice, smoothing back his hair. "We got a little carried away." He glanced back over his shoulder. In the soft light, his face looked almost demonic as he smiled at her. "Right, Bri?"

She sat up in bed, clutching the blanket against her, shaking with fear, outrage and mortification, but she didn't give anything away, not trusting Matt any more than she did John. She was beginning to think that trust, in general, was an emotion she could no longer afford.

"I'm fine, Matt," she said with as much calm as she could muster. Then her eyes bore in on John. "Mr. Weston was just leaving," she added in a tight voice.

Their eyes met and held for a tense moment, John's insidious smile replaced by one even more cunning. "Sleep tight, Bri. I'll see you tomorrow."

Bri stiffened as she watched John sidestep Matt as he exited, shutting the door behind him.

A minute later there was another knock on her door. She knew, even before he spoke, that it was Matt.

"Are you sure you're okay, Bri?"

"Yes," she called out from her bed, her voice resolute. "Good night, Matt."

Chapter Five

Thornhill's Sugarrun Inn was a whitewashed brick two-story colonial with a newly added, harmoniously designed white clapboard wing that sat on the corner of Clarmont and Howe Street. For over thirty years, beginning in the mid-fifties, the large old house had served as an off-campus dormitory for Dorchester College women. Eight years back, old Lucy Harris, the widowed dorm mother and owner of the house, had decided she'd had her fill of female college students with their trials and tribulations and had turned the place into a modest bed and breakfast. Her guests were most often Dorchester alumni, many of whom had actually lived in the house when they were students. There was nothing fancy about the bed and breakfast and, as innkeepers went, Lucy Harris wasn't exactly the warmest and most accommodating, but the majority of her guests knew her well enough to overlook her quirks. Many of them actually got a kick out of Mrs. Harris's inability to fully drop her role as strict dorm matron and anxious mother hen.

Two years back, seventy-five-year-old Lucy Harris, already afflicted with arthritis, suffered a stroke and had to close the bed and breakfast. For a time it looked as if she would have to sell the old place altogether, which everyone in Thornhill knew would just about break poor Lucy's heart. And a broken heart would surely be the end of her.

Lucy's longtime friend, Mildred Mead, the wife of Thornhill's police chief, Harvey Mead, and the feature writer of the *Thornhill Tab*'s What's What column, decided she couldn't let that happen. So she came up with a solution that added a few more gray hairs to her husband Harvey's thinning locks. She would go into partnership with Lucy and invest some money in order to turn the slightly dowdy bed and breakfast into the kind of upscale hostelry that would do the old town of Thornhill proud. For all Harvey's anxiety and his frantic concern about paying off the hefty new business loans, Mildred had been as good as her word. Within one year of reopening, the newly renamed Sugarrun Inn had been chosen as one of the top twenty-five inns in New England. By the end of the first eighteen months, the increasingly popular inn was, astonishingly, already in the black.

Mildred and Lucy didn't always see eye-to-eye on the running of the place, and when Mildred had first booked Bri Graham's tour group into the inn for a three-day stay during the height of the fall foliage season, Lucy had been particularly disgruntled. After a time Mildred managed to somewhat assuage the older woman's concerns about a horde of unruly comrades-in-arms overrunning the place, but she knew Lucy hadn't been completely won over.

When the day of the tour group's arrival dawned, Lucy was in a particularly crotchety mood, which, for anyone who knew Lucy in her best of moods, was saying something. By mid-afternoon, Lucy was stationed at the parlor window that looked out over the elm-shaded front lawn, on the watch for the Valentine Tour's arrival. Mildred knew Lucy wanted to look the group over before they came into the inn. She also knew she'd never hear the end of it if Lucy decided the group did not pass muster. Which, for anyone who knew Lucy, was entirely possible.

At a little after four o'clock, when the Valentine Tour van turned into the long, gravel drive, Mildred suggested she wheel Lucy out to the porch for a better look. Lucy grumbled something under her breath which Mildred took for a yes.

Mildred set Lucy near the steps of the broad porch which ran the whole front of the building. The shady spot featured groupings of comfortable wicker furniture. It was a bright, sunny day and the whitewashed brick inn glistened like a fine jewel.

Lucy absently smoothed back her white hair which she still wore in a knobby bun on top of her head. "I still say we shouldn't book tour groups," she grumbled.

Mildred, a sprightly gray-haired woman, looked down at Lucy over the top of her hallmark undersized wire-rimmed glasses. "We don't ordinarily book tour groups, Lucy," she replied patiently. "We've made an exception."

Lucy scowled. "I still don't see why."

"Of course you see why," Mildred went on in an even tone. "Because you and I both liked Bri Graham when she was here on her honeymoon last winter. And because we both felt sorry for her when we heard that her husband had walked out on her. And finally, because we both want to help her get her tour business off to a good start." As she finished her explanation, Mildred waved cheerily at Bri who was just stepping down from the parked van about thirty feet away. A faint frown crossed her face as Bri waved back.

Lucy squinted in Bri's direction. "She looks different."

"She's let her hair grow," Mildred said in a distracted voice. She, too, thought Bri looked different and she didn't think it was only the hair. Even from that distance,

Mildred could see the young woman clearly enough to detect a distinct note of tension. It was in the way she held herself, the serious expression on her face, even the lackluster manner in which she'd waved back. Mildred remembered Bri as being so energetic and effusive. Well, she concluded, the poor thing must still be getting over the pain of having been deserted.

"These tour groups can be very rambunctious," Lucy muttered. "I won't have any nonsense going on here, Mildred. There'll be no hanky-panky. I wouldn't stand for it when this was a dormitory and I won't stand for it now, even if the place has put on airs."

"I'm sure Bri's guests will be perfect ladies and gentlemen, Lucy," Mildred said in her calmest voice. "Bri told me herself when she booked the rooms that she would be personally interviewing every member of her group. I'm sure she doesn't want worries any more than we do."

Mildred was right that Bri didn't want any worries, but at that moment she was practically drowning in them. Not only was she still badly shaken by her encounter with John last night, but when she'd come down for breakfast in the morning, she'd found herself the discreet and not so discreet object of study by all the tour members. It soon became apparent that news of her tryst last night with tour member, Andrew Weston, had spread among the group. Bri would have bet it was Matt Sebastian who had spread the rumor of goings-on. She figured it was payback for having rebuffed his advances. So much for even having entertained the possibility that, for all the mystery about him, he was a halfway decent sort.

All through breakfast, Bri suffered looks from the tour members that ranged from scorn to curiosity to indignation. Jillian was especially perturbed, practically throwing daggers at her. Bri didn't blame her. She was sure, after John's flirtatious attentions, that Jillian presumed that if the man she knew as Andrew Weston was going to go bedroom hopping, it should have been her bedroom he hippity-hopped into. Allison, too, was especially expressive. She kept giving her sullen looks all during the morning meal, which were interspersed with wistful looks in Tim's direction. As for Tim, he was in high spirits. Now that Jillian had been snubbed by Andrew Weston, she seemed more receptive to his flirtatious efforts.

As for the man all the others knew as Andrew, Bri was sickened to see how perfectly calm and unruffled he was by the previous night's events. Unlike yesterday, when he'd barely acknowledged her existence, today he was going out of his way to be cordial and friendly to her. His new behavior made things even worse because now she was forced to interact with him. He'd even beat out the other tour members to the seat closest to her on the van, keeping up a steady, innocuous banter on the whole drive up to Thornhill.

"Here, let me help you with those." This time it was John, not Matt, who'd stationed himself just behind her as she started unloading the luggage from the back of the van.

"I wouldn't let you help me cross a street if I were blind," she hissed, immediately regretting the cutting retort as she caught sight of Mrs. McDermott who was standing close enough to have heard her.

"Irritability doesn't become you, Bri," John said with a sardonic smile before he slipped on his black windbreaker and sauntered off, not in the direction of the inn, but toward the street. He glanced back at her when he'd gone a few feet. "I'm going to stroll into town and see if the place has changed much since our idyllic stay last winter."

Bri gave him an icy look, but inside she felt the hot sting of outrage and hurt. Then she saw Jillian Knight make a beeline for John. Matt ambled over, edging Bri aside as he finished taking out the last few suitcases. Bri stood there watching him with a silently condemning look on her face.

Matt glanced at her. "It wasn't me, Bri," he said intuitively. "I wish you'd stop giving me the cold shoulder. We still need to talk."

For all the burning questions she'd had about Matt yesterday afternoon when they'd met so unexpectedly under John's bed, they'd folded in the wake of the questions about John that were now torturing her. She still had no idea in the world what John was looking for. What could it be that he was willing to go to such desperate lengths to get from her?

"Don't cut me off, Bri." Matt's voice was gently persuasive, but she merely gave him a wary look.

"Excuse me. I have to say hello to an old friend," she said curtly, stepping around him and heading for the front porch.

Matt watched her walk off, then headed down the driveway for the street. As he came up behind Jillian who was standing with her arms folded across her chest, staring off toward the street, he heard her mutter under her breath, "Bastard." She let out a little gasp as he passed by her. It was clear to Matt she hadn't realized anyone was within hearing distance. She did pull herself together quickly, though, and smiled sardonically at Matt. "Men. You can't figure any one of them out."

Matt's lips curved as he watched Andrew Weston turn left off the driveway toward town. "My sentiments exactly," he murmured, then continued down the gravel drive.

From her perch on the porch, Lucy Harris made a clucking sound with her tongue as she watched Bri head in their direction. "She looks a bit sickly. All we need, Mildred Mead, is for a flu epidemic to break out."

Mildred wasn't paying attention. Not to Lucy or even to Bri. Mildred's gaze was fixed on the man in the black windbreaker who was walking up the street. That's odd, Mildred was thinking. She would have sworn that tour member bore a distinct resemblance to Bri's husband, John Fossier. She shook off the notion as absurd. Surely Bri would have let her know if she and her husband had reconciled. Instead of a single room, Bri would have wanted a double. Besides, Mildred had to concede that her memory of Fossier was fuzzy at best. After all, she'd only seen the man a couple of times last winter. When he hadn't been off in romantic seclusion with his new bride, he'd spent his time in town looking up a few old pals from his Dorchester College days, graduates who'd settled in Thornhill. On many of those occasions Bri had chosen to relax back at the inn, which was how the bride and the innkeeper had become fast friends.

Mildred recalled being uneasy about one of those pals Bri's husband had visited last winter: Liz Armstrong. Liz, a graduate of Dorchester's journalism department ten years ago, had settled in Thornhill a couple of years back after putting in a stint on a New York magazine. She took over what went for the society editor's position on the *Thornhill Tab*. Rumor had it that when she and John Fossier were in school together they'd had a torrid affair. Mildred had gotten the feeling that Bri, so much in love at that time, had no idea about her husband's past involvement with the society editor. And Mildred didn't think it was her place to tell her. Besides, at that time Liz was dating John's Dorchester buddy, Steve Palmer, coach of the college track team, the Dorchester Demons. Lately, though, the romance between the two had petered out, more Liz's doing than Steve's. Then again, it had always been the general consensus among the locals that Steve's passion for Liz ran a lot hotter than hers for him.

"I tell you she doesn't look at all well," Lucy mumbled as Bri started up the steps to the porch.

The old woman's remark pulled Mildred from her woolgathering. "She's just a bit pale." A smile curved Mildred's lips as Bri got within hearing distance. "But as pretty as ever."

"Maybe her breakfast didn't agree with her," Lucy muttered even though she knew perfectly well that Bri could hear her.

Bri had to smile. Lucy was close to being right. Although it wasn't the lovely breakfast itself at the Colport Inn that had turned her stomach, certainly the circumstances under which she'd tried to eat those fluffy scrambled eggs, homemade muffins and crispy, thick sliced bacon, had caused her a definite attack of indigestion that hadn't completely subsided.

Mildred stepped around Lucy's wheelchair and gave Bri a warm embrace. "Don't pay any attention to Lucy," she whispered.

"I can hear every word you're saying," Lucy grumbled even though it wasn't true. Her stroke had left her hard of hearing as well as partially paralyzed. But she still had all her wits about her, and it wasn't hard for her to guess the gist of what Mildred had whispered.

"Well, let's get everyone settled," Mildred said in her take-charge voice. "I see that a couple of your tour members have strayed off."

"A couple?" Bri's gaze darted toward the street where she saw Matt strolling up the street about twenty yards behind John. She wasn't altogether surprised.

When Bri looked back at her, Mildred saw that the young woman looked suddenly even paler.

"That's Mr. Sebastian and Mr....Weston." Bri said, deciding on the spot that she wasn't ready to announce the true identity of Andrew Weston to Mildred or anyone else.

She was hoping that the older woman who'd only met John a couple of times over six months ago, wouldn't remember him very well.

There was something in Bri's eyes, as well as the way she hesitated over the name Weston, that convinced Mildred suddenly that her instinct about the identity of the man in the black windbreaker hadn't been farfetched after all. The local gossip columnist nodded, keeping her expression deliberately blank. She'd learned over the years that the best way to get a good scoop was to play dumb.

"They look like nice fellows," Mildred said pleasantly. "Both bachelors?"

"Yes," Bri said quickly, rubbing her hands together. "So, shall we get everyone settled?"

STEVE PALMER, a wiry former college track star turned men's track coach, blew his whistle with disgust, his team coming to a dead stop on the field.

"What is this, ladies? We're not out here for the scenery. We've got a meet in five days. At this rate we might as well phone it in. Now, let's—" The rest of the sentence fell off as Palmer caught sight of a man in a black windbreaker walking down the street a few yards from the field. Palmer's eyes narrowed. He'd only snatched a quick glimpse of the guy, but he could have sworn it was John Fossier.

"Hey, coach," one of the runners said cautiously, "you want us to run through the drill again?"

Steve Palmer turned his gaze in the direction of the questioner, but his expression was blank. "What?"

"The drill?"

He scowled. "Oh, yeah. Right." Then, to the surprise of the team, the coach tossed one of the track stars his whistle. "Ross, stand in for me. I've got to check on something."

What he had to check on was the identity of the man in the black windbreaker. If his guess about him was right, Steve had a good hunch where he'd find him . . . down the block from the practice field at the offices of the *Thornhill Tab*. Well, actually at one particular office. The one belonging to Liz Armstrong.

"A NICE, HOT CUP of tea will do you good," Mildred soothed. "Lucy is right, Bri. You do look pale."

Mildred had ushered the tour owner into her private office quarters at the back of the inn after assigning the guests to their rooms and settling Lucy in for her afternoon nap. The large, airy space which bore its original architectural features including hand-hewn beams fastened to the posts with wooden pegs and a true Rumford fireplace, looked more like a large old-fashioned parlor than an office. Mildred, who was partial to Currier & Ives prints, had several of them grouped on the walls above the hand-carved cherry wainscotting. As for the furnishings, there were several lovely Queen Anne chairs, a couple of teal-blue chintz, down sofas that faced each other on either side of the fireplace, several Early American tables and a conversation piece antique washstand. Off in one corner was an old oak desk whose top was cluttered with papers, the only hint that the room was actually used for more than just sitting, chatting and sipping tea.

Bri would have much preferred to escape to her room than accept Mildred's invitation, but there'd been no way, save for being rude, to turn the persistent innkeeper down. She accepted the steamy, aromatic cup of Earl Grey tea graciously from Mildred and sat down on one of the sofas. Mildred, a matched cup in hand, sat across from her.

"Would you like something to eat? I've got one of Paula Dubois's famous apple pies sitting in the kitchen. You met Paula, didn't you?"

"You're godmother to her little girl, if I remember correctly."

"Jessica, yes. What a little doll. She's just started first grade and she's feeling very grown-up. Paula's done a wonderful job with the child. And with her career. Besides her catering business, she's cowritten a cookbook with my daughter, Maggie."

"Oh, I'll have to pick up a copy," Bri said, although since John had left her, sticking frozen dinners in the microwave had been the extent of her cooking.

Mildred's eyes sparkled. "Maggie's pregnant. Just found out a few weeks ago. Kevin and her boys are delighted. And Maggie's tickled pink. With an emphasis on the *pink*. She's really hoping for a girl this time."

Bri attempted a smile, but didn't quite make it. Much to her dismay, she felt her eyes start to water. It was pure envy, she knew. Mildred's daughter and her husband sounded so happy, so together. She remembered how she'd told John even on their honeymoon that she wanted at least three kids, four or five would be even better. She'd always hated being an only child, spending much of her time growing up dreaming of having a houseful of siblings. John had seemed a little overwhelmed by the prospect, but he'd told her at the time that whatever she wanted he'd try to make it happen for her.

With a shaky hand she set her untouched cup of tea on the coffee table, her eyes lowered.

"Is a reconciliation a possibility?" Mildred asked gently.

Bri pressed her fingers to her eyes and shook her head. "I'm sorry," she murmured, her cheeks red with embarrassment. "I don't know what's come over me. I never...get like this."

"Well," Mildred said firmly, coming around to sit by her, "then it's high time you did."

Bri dropped her head into her hands, and Mildred soothingly patted her shoulder. "Let it out, Bri. It'll do you good. And then we'll talk."

Bri again shook her head. "I can't."

Mildred stroked her back. "You can't cry? Or you can't talk?"

"Both," she blurted out, shooting up from the couch. "You're so kind, Mildred. But I just need time to think, time to sort things out. I just don't understand. And I don't know what to do." But even as she said those final words, a voice whispered in her head *Yes, you do.* There was only one thing to do. Have a showdown with John. Convince him that she'd discarded everything in the apartment that belonged to him or even reminded her of him. She'd given most of it away to charity. Her mind came to a sudden halt. Most of it, yes. But not all of it.

"Bri, what is it?" Mildred asked, her voice laced with concern.

Bri blinked several times. "Nothing. Just something I remembered. Something that might be . . . important."

LIZ ARMSTRONG, an angular beauty in her mid-thirties, with blond hair in a becoming shoulder-length cut, cool blue eyes that held a hint of superiority and a good figure that she liked to show off, was frowning at her monitor as she tapped away at the keyboard.

"Tough story?"

At the sound of the masculine voice, Liz glanced up at the door. At first her frown deepened, but then she smoothed it out without effort.

"John."

"In the flesh."

Liz pushed herself back from the desk and gave him a long, thoughtful look. "I got a call from your wife a few months back. She was looking for you."

John Fossier smiled sardonically. "She wasn't the only one."

Liz emitted a little laugh. "Don't tell me you were naughty again, Johnny?"

He tilted his head back. His eyes came down slowly as he studied her. "Okay, I won't."

She smiled, a finely plucked eyebrow arching. "Yes, you will. You never were good at keeping secrets from me, Johnny."

"True enough," he murmured, keeping up his languid survey.

Slowly, gracefully, she rose to her feet, presenting herself to him for a better inspection. "So, how do I look?"

His smile was vaguely lascivious. But before he answered, she said, "Maybe you better shut the door before you tell me."

Two minutes later, Liz's door opened again. This time it was Steve Palmer standing there. Instead of finding his old flame pecking away at her computer, he found her in the arms of his old college buddy, John Fossier. He stood there in grim silence, just staring at them. John and Liz were oblivious of his presence. And all three of them were oblivious of the young man who walked slowly past the open door, pretending to be looking for the news editor's office.

Matt Sebastian never found the office, but he did find what he was looking for.

Neither Matt nor John showed up for dinner at the inn that night. Matt had been considerate enough to call Bri to let her know he was going to grab a bite and catch a movie in town. She wasn't exactly disappointed when he didn't invite her, but she was a little surprised. Well, she thought, maybe she'd finally convinced him she wasn't interested. Now, if she could only fully convince herself.

Bri wasn't the least surprised that John hadn't thought enough to call and let her know he wouldn't be at dinner. Being considerate wasn't one of his fine points. At the moment she was hard put to imagine any fine points he did have. As to what he was doing tonight, she had no difficulty imagining that. She was sure John was spending the evening in town with some of his old college buddies. They were probably all welcoming him back like the prodigal son.

She only hoped he'd be coming back to the inn that night. She had to talk to him. She'd remembered something that afternoon that might shed some light on this mysterious object he was so desperate to reclaim. She'd almost completely forgotten about that one small carton of items belonging to John that she'd dropped off at the Quinn Gallery after John had been gone a couple of months. Adam Quinn, the gallery owner, had been kind enough to agree to put the carton in safekeeping until John's return or until he heard from him. Bri had thought of Quinn because he, in truth, had been her only link in the Boston area to John. She'd never met any of John's family or friends, or even any other business associates. She thought now that she probably would not have met Adam, either, if he hadn't already been an acquaintance of hers and she hadn't inadvertently met John through him.

A little after eleven that night, Bri, who was standing by the window of her darkened room, saw Matt Sebastian ambling up the drive toward the inn. When he glanced casually up to the second floor, looking directly at her window, she ducked out of sight.

A few minutes later she heard him walking down the hall. Her door was the second on the right, his the last on the left. She froze as the footsteps stopped at her door. She was far too keyed up anticipating the encounter with John when he returned, to have a little heart-to-heart with Matt. Once she'd resolved matters with her husband, however, she definitely meant to attend to those questions about Matt that she'd stuck on the back burner.

She held her breath until she heard Matt continue on down the hall, then returned to her vigil at the window. By one in the morning she was thinking about giving it up for the night when she saw a car turn up the drive. After a couple of minutes the passenger door opened. John stepped out and the car began to back up. John gave a little wave in the driver's direction. As he started for the inn, Bri saw that he was weaving slightly.

She stepped back from the window, frowning. She hadn't considered having to face John while he was intoxicated. On the other hand she was desperate to have that talk over and done with so that first thing tomorrow morning, John Fossier would rent a car and head back to Boston to claim his carton at Adam Quinn's gallery. Bri knew that only after he was gone would she be able to put the pieces of her life back together and put her unhappy marriage behind her.

After debating her choices for a few minutes, Bri resolved to go ahead with her plan. With one revision. Throwing her jacket on over her jeans and sweater, she left her room and stealthily made her way outside to her van.

Her hands were trembling as she unlocked the special compartment under the dash. Inside was a little item she kept strictly for emergencies. Well, she thought, this was an emergency of a sort. She couldn't risk another unprepared encounter with John. That silencer-fitted gun was still emblazoned on her mind. She could practically feel the pressure of the barrel against her temple.

Well, she decided, resolutely sticking her hand into the compartment, this time she would show him that he couldn't intimidate her. Or abuse her. This time she'd be the one with a pistol at the ready.

HER HAND was clammy as it tightened around the grip of her gun, but she felt a lot better than she would have, knocking on John's door unarmed. She had it all planned. He would open the door, she would point the gun in his face, have him sit quietly in a chair while she said her piece, and then she'd make her exit. And that would be that.

The only problem was, the plan went utterly awry right from the get-go. Later she would see it in agonizing slow motion, the scene playing over and over in her mind. But when it actually happened, it happened so quickly that she . . . well, she hardly knew what happened.

It all fell apart with her first firm knock on John's door. Two things happened, practically simultaneously. The door instantly flew open and a shot was fired from inside the room. Instinctively Bri fired back.

The gunfire brought all of the tour members rushing out of their rooms. Everyone was in motion but Bri, who stood frozen on the spot, her smoking gun clattering to the floor as she stared in horror at the bloody body of her husband, splayed face-down on the colorful rag rug at the side of his bed.

Matt was the first one to reach Bri. On contact she collapsed into his arms. The first words out of her mouth were, "I killed him. I killed my husband."

Chapter Six

"How's Bri doing?" Mildred asked anxiously the moment the doctor stepped out of the patient's room.

Dr. Noah Bright, chief of neuropsychiatry at Thornhill's newly relocated, state-of-the-art, Harriet Michner Hospital, gave his old friend a tired look. "She's upset. Close to hysteria. But I guess any woman who'd just shot her husband would be."

Mildred frowned. "I just can't believe it, Noah. Not Bri. It's just not something she would do."

"I'm afraid Bri would disagree with you there, Mildred. She hasn't said much since you brought her in, except that she did kill this Andrew Weston or John Fossier or whatever his name really is."

"You said it yourself. The poor thing's near hysteria. She doesn't know what she's saying," Mildred persisted.

"She fired the gun, didn't she? The man is dead?"

Mildred scowled. The facts appeared irrefutable. But facts, she had come to discover over the years, weren't always as straightforward as they first appeared. She could hear sobs coming from behind the closed door. "Can't you give her a sedative to calm her down, Noah?"

"Not until I get her statement," came a familiar voice behind her. Mildred turned to see her husband, Harvey Mead, Chief of Police of Thornhill, giving her one of his solemn looks. Mildred, an expert at interpreting her husband's looks after thirty-seven years of marriage, knew that he was particularly annoyed with her. She also was fully aware why.

"I know we should have left her at the scene of the crime, Harvey," she said defiantly before he could begin lecturing her. "After all these years, I probably know proper police procedure as well as you. Or almost as well," she amended, not wanting to get him more riled up than he already was, especially right before questioning Bri.

Harvey Mead narrowed his gaze on his wife. "Then why...?"

Mildred didn't let him finish. There was no need. She could usually finish his sentences for him. "After it happened, Lucy phoned me right up. I could hear Bri in the background, and the poor thing was sobbing uncontrollably. You were staying over in Northfield, so I phoned down to the station house and then rushed over to the inn. A minute after I arrived, Bri passed right out. She looked so dreadful, actually gray. Well, we both thought she was practically at death's door herself. So naturally we rushed her over here for medical attention, which seemed the only sensible thing to do."

Harvey frowned. "Who's *we?* Don't tell me Lucy helped you bring the suspect over here?"

"No, of course not Lucy, dear. A young fellow from the tour group. His name's Matt Sebastian." She gave her husband a disapproving look. "And must you call her a suspect? It sounds so... cold and unfeeling, considering what she's been through."

Harvey rolled his eyes. It always meant trouble when his wife took it into her head to adopt a suspect. And now it sounded as if she wasn't Bri Graham's only guardian angel. "Who exactly is this Matt Sebastian? What's his story?"

"I don't really know," Mildred was forced to admit. "I haven't actually had the chance—"

"No, but I'm sure you will," Harvey muttered acerbically. The police chief glanced over at Noah Bright, who looked like a man who did not want to get caught in the middle of a family argument.

"I don't know anything about the man, either," Noah said quickly. "Except that he insisted on staying with Miss Graham, and she seemed calmer with him around so I just..."

Harvey gestured toward the closed door to Bri's room. "He's in there with her now?" He didn't sound all too pleased.

"Miss Graham was in pretty bad shape when they brought her in. And I didn't see any harm in letting him sit with her," Noah countered. "Actually I'm glad you got here so quickly, Harvey. I knew you'd want to question her first thing, so I didn't give her any psychotropic medication, but as soon as you're done talking to her, I'd like to give her a sedative and—"

"By rights she should be spending the night in jail," Harvey grumbled.

"I can't imagine what the poor thing might do at this point that would warrant putting her behind bars, dear," Mildred warned, just in case her husband took it into his head to be obstinate. "She's in a very fragile state. And physically...well, you heard what Noah said. She needs a sedative. And if she's given a sedative, it isn't very likely she'll be in any condition to pick up and take off. Anyway, I simply cannot picture Bri Graham as a woman who'd go on the lam. She's always impressed me as scrupulously honest, forthright, decent, kind..."

"Mildred," Harvey said with a mix of frustration and irritation. "You hardly know her. And might I remind you that this decent, scrupulously honest woman has already confessed to murder.''

"A confession from a hysterical woman." Mildred waved her hand in a dismissive gesture.

''A hysterical woman who fired a gun at a man who is now dead.'' Harvey added, hoping that that would be the last word on the matter.

"All right, Harvey. Since you've got all the answers already, why don't you just go right in there and drag the poor thing out of her hospital bed and off to jail? Why, you might as well pronounce sentence since you've already convicted her."

"Mildred, I hate when you do this. I am simply saying..."

"And I am simply saying..."

"Nothing you say, Mildred Mead, is ever simple."

Noah's beeper went off and he smiled inwardly—saved by the bell. "I've got to go check on another patient, but if I were you, Harv, I'd go easy on her for now."

Harvey gave him an acerbic look. "Bri Graham or my wife?"

Noah flushed, but Mildred laughed good-naturedly.

Noah cleared his throat. "I mean, she's pretty shaken up—Bri Graham."

"I'll be as gentle as a lamb," the police chief assured the good doctor, then gave his wife a saccharine smile. "I left my rubber hose at home."

Noah took off and Harvey started for Bri's private room only to be stopped in his tracks by Mildred. "I truly don't think she did it, Harvey."

"Mildred..."

"I thought I might give Noah's wife, Chloe, a call."

"Mildred..." This time his tone was sharper.

"I'm not saying Chloe's exactly a clairvoyant, dear, but you know as well as I do that she's able to pick up certain vibrations. You witnessed that whole business with that dagger that was used to kill poor Amanda Emory. Chloe saw that awful weapon and she positively felt—"

"Mildred," Harvey said very firmly, his dark eyes flinty. "Vibrations are not admissible in a court of law. And you know as well as I do that Chloe doesn't want to be dragged into these sorts of matters. As far as she and I are concerned, she's put all that behind her. She's a professor, a wife and a mother. And that's all."

"Yes, dear."

"I can do without any... meddling on this one, Milly." He reserved "Milly" for serious moments, knowing it was not a nickname she cared for...and knowing that she knew that he knew it. And knowing, finally, that if he used it, he meant to be taken with the utmost seriousness.

Mildred didn't say anything. At times like this, when she knew perfectly well she meant to go against his wishes, in this case meddling—although she certainly didn't see it as meddling—she thought it best to remain noncommittal.

His hand reached out to the doorknob, but then he looked back at his wife, who hadn't moved. "I'm likely to be here awhile. Why don't you go on home...?"

"I was thinking I should go back to the inn and see how the others are doing."

Harvey scowled. "It's one-thirty in the morning, Mildred. I'm sure everyone's turned in for the night."

"Has... he been... removed yet?"

"Len Fischer's out of town but I had Mike Gold, the medical examiner from Northfield go over straight away. A couple of my boys hightailed it to the inn as soon as you phoned the station. One of the things they were supposed to do was bring the sus—Bri Graham in for questioning. But she was already gone by the time they got there."

"The inn's only a couple of blocks from the house, dear. And naturally, under the circumstances, I drove over. I believe I heard the police sirens when Mr. Sebastian and I were a few blocks from the hospital.'' She smiled sweetly, but then turned serious. "So, you think Mike Gold's still examining the body at the inn?''

Harvey sighed. No point rehashing that she had no business taking matters into her own hands and whisking his suspect from the scene of the crime. "My guess is the body's either down at the forensics lab by now or on its way. I told my boys to check out Fossier's room, then seal it off, get statements from everyone present and let them get to bed. Roy Filmore will stay on and keep watch until the morning. And I've got George Denk coming over here to the hospital to baby-sit our... Girl Scout.''

Mildred affectionately patted his cheek. "You look tired, dear.''

Harvey fought back a yawn. He'd been at a meeting over in Northfield about twenty miles from Thornhill. The meeting ran incredibly late and it was just winding down when he got the call about the murder from one of his boys.

He finally let the yawn out, then bussed his wife on the cheek. "I suppose I'll have to take this Sebastian's statement now as well as Bri Graham's.'' He frowned. "I'm not pleased he's spent all this time with her. For all I know the two of them are in cahoots.''

Mildred smiled at her husband. "Really, Harvey, you watch too many detective shows on television.''

BRI LOOKED small and lost in the large white hospital bed. She felt weak and dizzy. Her face was still tear-stained but she'd finally stopped crying, mostly because she no longer had the strength. Matt Sebastian sat beside her in the dimly lit room, his hand lightly resting on her shoulder. They hadn't really spoken at all, except for Matt's soothing refrain that it would be okay, when she was sobbing uncontrollably.

When the door to the hospital room opened, Bri's whole body tensed, and she clutched Matt's hand with more strength than either one of them thought she could muster.

Harvey Mead announced himself at the door in a calm, quiet voice. Then he slowly approached the bed. "Do you remember me, Bri?" he asked with the kind of gentle bedside manner used by some doctors.

Bri tried to focus on the stout, pleasant-faced man looking down on her. "Yes, we met once last winter. During my—" She couldn't get out the word *honeymoon.* She squeezed her eyes shut for a moment or two.

Harvey, who stood on the opposite side of the bed from Matt, softly patted her free shoulder. "That's right. I came by to pick up Mildred at the inn one afternoon, and we all had tea together." He glanced over at Matt now for the first time. Matt met his gaze but neither man addressed the other. Harvey turned his attention back to Bri, who reached up and, like a drowning woman, clutched the police chief's sleeve.

"I . . . did it, Chief Mead. I shot him. I shot John. But I didn't mean to. I didn't realize what had happened until . . . until it was too late. Until I saw . . . him." Her hands flew to her face. "It was so awful, so horrible . . ."

"Okay, Bri. Okay, now," Harvey soothed. "I want you to get a grip on yourself. I need you to tell me . . ."

"There were two shots fired," Matt cut in, speaking for the first time. "Bri said she heard the first one before she fired back."

Harvey glanced up at the young man again, his expression thoughtful.

"I was just two doors down from Fossier's room. I was still awake. Reading. I heard two shots, too. And only one shot was fired from Bri's .22."

"Fossier?" Harvey may have been a country cop, but he wasn't a dumb country cop. And despite Thornhill's small size Harvey had gotten himself more homicide experience in the past few years than he would have liked.

"I knew that Andrew Weston was John Fossier the minute I first laid eyes on him," Matt Sebastian said without preamble. "More to the point, I was expecting him to show up for the tour. That's why I signed on in the first place. I'd been keeping an eye on Fossier ever since he resurfaced a couple of weeks ago."

Matt's statement brought Bri temporarily out of her miasma of misery and despair. She stared at him. "You were following him all along? Why?" She even managed a rueful look. "Don't tell me you wanted to sell him an insurance policy?"

Harvey was beginning to get the feeling that he was losing some ground here. "Hold on." He narrowed his gaze on Matt. "What's this about insurance?"

"I lied to you, Bri, but you already guessed that when we bumped into each other under Fossier's bed," Matt said, ignoring the police chief. "I never could have made it in the insurance game. I always had a lousy sales pitch." He smiled softly at Bri. "A lousy pitch altogether."

Harvey folded his arms across his chest, trying to push aside the craving he suddenly had for a nice crooked stogie. He was off cigars. He'd promised Mildred. Not that he hadn't promised her before and slipped up. Still, he was giving it the old college try one more time. "Look, it's very late or very early depending on how you look at it, and I admit I'm not at my sharpest at this hour of the morning. So you two are going to have to bear with me if I'm a little slow catching on here. You say you bumped into each other under Fossier's bed. I'm convinced you both had a good reason for being there. Now, suppose you share that reason with me." His gaze swept back and forth between Matt and Bri. "Unless you're embarrassed because of something...kinky."

Bri sighed. "I was snooping through John's things, and then I heard him coming into the room. So I hid under his bed."

Matt smiled rakishly. "Ditto."

Harvey just stared at them, still looking blank.

"You see, it wasn't John," Bri explained. "It was Matt."

Harvey lowered his head and eyed Matt. "It was you."

Matt nodded.

"But the second time it really was John," Bri further elucidated for the chief.

Harvey lowered his chin to his chest and switched his gaze back and forth between the pair again. "What were you both looking for, if you don't mind me asking?"

"I wasn't sure," Bri admitted.

"Ditto," Matt said.

Harvey was fast losing his patience. He pointed a finger at Matt. "Okay, you're not an insurance agent. So, who are you? What's your game?"

Matt Sebastian drew his hand into the inside pocket of his jacket. Harvey Mead made a not-so-subtle move for the gun in his shoulder holster inside his jacket. Matt grinned, pulling out a thin leather billfold and flipping it open. Both Bri and Harvey stared at the picture ID inside.

Bri raised her eyes to Matt's face. "You're an insurance investigator?"

He smiled crookedly at her. "See. It was only half a lie. Do I score any Brownie points for that?"

Bri closed her eyes, tears rolling down her cheeks. "Does it matter now? Not too many men care about scoring Brownie points with a murderer."

"Bri, at the very worst, you shot the bastard in self-defense," Matt said firmly.

Harvey looked up the ceiling, then drew his mouth down at the corners. "We don't really know that, Sebastian."

"I tell you there were two shots fired," Matt retorted. "Ask the others at the inn. I'm sure I'm not the only one who heard two shots. Your boys have Bri's gun. They can see only one shot was fired."

"You might be right, there," Harvey said in a deceptively laconic voice. "My boys did find a second gun in the room beside the body..."

"John's," Bri said in a hollow voice. "It was John's gun. He threatened me with it the night before."

Harvey zeroed in on her. "Threatened you?"

"He claimed I had something that belonged to him. Something he wanted back. And he pulled the gun on me and told me he meant business."

Harvey kept looking at Bri, but he was also watching the insurance investigator from the corner of his eye. "What was it he wanted so badly?"

Bri gave the chief a blank look. "I wish I knew. I wish I'd had whatever it was he wanted. I would have given it to him gladly. I didn't want anything of John's. Not after he walked out on me. Certainly not after he came back and treated me so—" She shivered, unable to finish the sentence. "If he'd gotten what he wanted, none of this... would have happened." Fresh tears started rolling down her cheek.

"Why'd you go to his room tonight, Bri?" Harvey asked quietly.

She looked up at him. "I remembered something." She started to go on, but Harvey made a delaying motion and glanced over at Matt.

"Wait outside, Mr. Sebastian. After I finish talking with Bri, I'll be wanting a statement from you." He gave the young man a hard look. "I assume you intend to cooperate with the law."

Matt smiled. "Absolutely, Chief." Then his eyes drifted to Bri. "I intend to do more than cooperate."

Harvey let that pass and watched the insurance investigator saunter out. Then he focused back on Bri. "What's with you two?" he asked.

Bri sighed. "He's very young, Chief," she replied, as if that was explanation enough.

Harvey nodded. "Okay, let's get back to your visit to your husband's room tonight. You said you remembered something. Something about this object?"

IT WAS ALMOST THREE in the morning and Harvey and Matt Sebastian were on their second cups of black coffee in the hospital lounge.

"The problem with Fossier's gun," Harvey was saying, "was that it had a silencer on it, so it's hard to see how you could have heard the shot."

Matt pulled out a cigarette. He knew there was no smoking allowed in the hospital, so he rolled it along his lips without lighting it. "Was there a shot fired from Fossier's gun?"

Harvey had a report on the gun from his boys on the scene. He looked at Matt, debating how much to tell the guy, then nodded.

Matt rolled the unlit cigarette over to the corner of his mouth. "So maybe I was wrong." He removed the cigarette altogether and stared thoughtfully at it. "Maybe there weren't two shots." He skipped a few beats. "Maybe there were three shots."

Harvey imagined rolling a stogie between his lips. "Three?"

Matt nodded. "The first shot from Fossier which couldn't be heard, the second from his murderer and the third from Bri."

Harvey gave Matt a dubious look. "You're reaching, Sebastian."

"It's possible, Chief. I did hear two shots. Let's say Fossier spotted someone at his open window. He takes a shot at the intruder, the intruder fires back and shoots him just as Bri's opening the door to his room. She hears the shot, naturally thinks it's Fossier firing at her and she shoots back in self-defense. You heard what she said. He'd threatened her the night before with his gun."

"Were you a witness to that?"

Matt hesitated. "Not exactly. That is, I didn't see the gun, but I was at her open door and saw her just as Fossier was leaving. She was white as a ghost."

Harvey swallowed down the rest of his coffee and grimaced at the bitter taste. "Okay, let's leave that for a minute. Go back to this rare document you claim Fossier was after. As well as you."

"Not me personally, Chief," Matt was quick to correct. "My company was hired by a representative of the Cairo Antiquities Museum to recover a very rare papyrus scroll of the *Book of the Dead* that had been stolen from the museum nine months ago. The scroll was believed to have originally been embedded in a wooden figure of the Egyptian god, Osiris circa 300 B.C. The figure itself is in the British Museum, but the Cairo museum was fortunate enough to get their hands on the scroll about a year ago. Extensive research was being done on it, and it was during that time that it was stolen from the museum's archives."

"And they believed that Fossier had stolen it?"

Matt nodded. "The curator at the museum claimed to have shown it to Fossier, who was an importer of Middle Eastern antiquities, just a few days before the scroll was stolen. Initially the curator was blamed." Matt shook his head sadly. "The poor bastard hung himself rather than go to prison. And he left a note professing his innocence and insisting that Fossier was responsible."

"So you went after Fossier?" Harvey asked.

Matt shrugged. "As soon as he got wind we were on his tail, he vanished. We figured he took the scroll with him. Until he came back looking for it."

"How much is this little baby worth?"

"The museum in Cairo is paying my company a quarter of a million just to recover it. I'm sure there are collectors who'd gladly pay a cool million, maybe more for such a rare item."

Harvey emitted a slow whistle. Then he eyed Matt. "Do you think she's got it?"

Matt hesitated. "I'd like to think that if she does, she doesn't know it."

"You like her."

Matt smiled boyishly. "She thinks I'm still wet behind the ears. I gather she goes for the more mature type."

"Like Fossier?"

A nurse came into the lounge. "Chief? Miss Graham asked if she could see you."

Harvey grimaced. "I thought the doc was going to give her a sedative."

The nurse shrugged. "I gave it to her myself about twenty minutes ago. She's fighting it, but she'll lose the battle sometime soon."

Harvey popped up and hurried into her room before she was in dreamland. Matt followed him.

Bri wasn't only still awake when the two men walked into her room, she was sitting up, looking very anxious.

"I was thinking about those shots," she said with wide-eyed agitation. Harvey guessed it was the adrenaline rush before the drug-induced collapse. "Before I fired, there was another shot. I thought at the time it was John firing at me. But now I'm not so sure, Chief Mead. John's gun had a silencer on it. I saw it the night before. There's no reason to imagine he would have removed the silencer. So, if I heard a shot, then it wasn't from John's gun. It had to be . . . from somebody else's gun."

Harvey glanced over his shoulder at Matt who was smiling. Harvey, however, wasn't. He was thinking the pair had had plenty of time to concoct this story.

"And then I remembered something else," Bri hurried on. "John was driven home by someone this morning. I was watching from my window, but it was dark and I couldn't make out who it was, but it was a light-colored sedan. White. Or beige, maybe. A new model, I think."

"I might have some ideas who brought him home," Matt said reflectively.

Harvey again looked at Matt, but didn't say anything about his remark. Instead he turned back to Bri. "You're saying this car stuck around after dropping your husband off?" he inquired.

Bri's brief good spirits waned. She fell back against the pillows. Her eyes were beginning to close and she felt light-headed. "No. I . . . I saw it back out the drive."

Matt came over to the side of her bed and squeezed her shoulder. "The driver could have come back on foot."

Bri smiled sleepily, the drug finally starting to take effect. "That's true."

Harvey Mead stood there looking more morose than usual, shaking his head. There was one thing the police chief could not abide. And that was finding himself sad-

dled with a pair of amateur sleuths who wanted to do his
job for him. Unfortunately this wasn't the first time he'd
found himself in this predicament. And the way his luck
was going, it wouldn't be the last.

Bri looked at Harvey with glazed eyes. "Are you still
going to arrest me?" Her voice was a bare whisper.

Before he answered her, she was fast asleep.

The two men stared at each other. Harvey felt a need to
make his position clear without further ado.

"Bri Graham's already confessed to the murder of her
husband," he said soberly. "And right now, everything
else is pure conjecture. Are you having any trouble following me, Sebastian?"

"None at all," Matt said sardonically.

"Good. One more thing. You're an insurance investigator not a cop. I'm counting on you not to step over the
line here."

Matt met the chief's gaze levelly. "Some lines aren't always so clear-cut, Chief."

OFFICER DENK tried to focus his eyes on the sports page,
but he kept dropping off. He repositioned himself in his
seat, hoping that would keep him more alert. But it didn't
help. Minutes later he was nodding off.

A nurse came by. Denk heard the soft squeak of the
rubber-soled shoes, and his eyes popped open. He quirked
a smile. The nurse smiled back. Then she slipped into Bri's
room to check her vital signs. A few minutes later she came
out. Denk cleared his throat.

"How's she doing?" he asked groggily.

"Sleeping like a baby," the nurse said brightly. Sure, the
policeman thought, Florence Nightingale could be cheery.
She probably had seven or eight hours of sleep before
coming on the night shift, whereas he'd been up for the
past twenty hours.

He stood up and stretched. The nurse smiled sympathetically. "Look, I'm going to be at the desk for about twenty minutes. If you want to take a break, have a smoke outside or grab a coffee, I'll keep an eye on the room."

He rubbed his jaw contemplatively.

The nurse gave him a reassuring pat on the shoulder. "Look, the sedative knocked her out. Even if she's a sleepwalker, she won't be able to budge an inch, never mind take a stroll."

George Denk knew the chief wouldn't be too thrilled about his leaving his post except for a quick trip to the men's room. The policeman also prided himself on obeying orders. On the other hand he really was beat, and he still had another three hours to go on watch before he'd be relieved by one of the day men. He rationalized that if he took a twenty-minute break, maybe a walk in the fresh predawn air, he'd come back revitalized and be that much more alert by the time the suspect's sedative started to wear off.

The nurse gave a little wave from her station as Denk walked off. Then she set about writing up her reports. She never even looked up when a figure in a white uniform passed by her about five minutes later.

The nurse behind the desk still had her head down when the nursing attendant got to Bri's door. This was going to be easier than expected. One hand turned the knob on the door, the other hand slipping into a deep pocket. An instant later the attendant was inside Bri's room, the door closing.

Bri lay motionless on the hospital bed; her breathing was shallow but even. The air in the room had a medicinal odor. The attendant cringed, never one to like paying visits to hospitals. But there were times when an exception had to be made. Besides, this wasn't exactly a sympathy call.

Ellen Jansen, the nurse at the desk, just happened to look up and over toward Bri's room as the door was closing. She frowned. That was odd. Who could be checking on the patient now? Unless Dr. Bright...

Best to look in and make sure everything was all right.

GEORGE DENK got as far as the main lobby before an attack of conscience assailed him. He realized he shouldn't have left his post like that. He could even hear the chief's lecture about responsibility, duty, service to the community at large, and on and on. He dug into his pocket, pulled out a handful of coins, bought himself a chocolate bar at the candy machine near the elevator and rode back up to the seventh floor.

The minute Denk saw that the nurse was gone from her desk, he felt very uneasy. He looked up and down the hall. It was empty. And eerily quiet. He felt a rush of apprehension as he made a beeline for Bri Graham's room and flung open the door.

He saw a figure lying in a heap on the floor. Denk cursed aloud as he rushed over to her. She moaned. "My head." She looked blearily up at the policeman. "What happened?" Ellen Jansen asked, gingerly touching the throbbing pain at the side of her head, her nurse's cap askew.

George Denk wished he could answer the nurse's question. He wished a lot of things at that moment. And as he hurried over to the hospital bed, he also prayed. He prayed that Bri would still be lying there. And in no worse shape than when he'd so foolishly, irresponsibly, unforgivably left his post.

Chapter Seven

Harvey Mead was not a happy man. Why was it, he wondered sulkily, that none of the murders he'd been called upon to solve over the past few years here in Thornhill ever turned out to be cut and dried? Why were there always complications, sneaky little twists? Why did the fates keep throwing him curve balls? It was only a couple of hours ago that he'd left the hospital convinced that he had the murderer of John Fossier *safely* tucked away in a hospital bed. Whether it was a cold-blooded killing or self-defense was up to the courts to decide. But, he'd so naively thought, here it was, a simple resolution for once. Cut and dried. That was where his head was at, only two hours ago. But a lot of things could happen in a couple of hours. And a lot of things did, the chief thought, looking glumly at his young uniformed officer.

George Denk, a lanky fellow over six feet tall, seemed to visibly shrink under his superior's moribund gaze. "I'm sorry, Chief," he said solemnly, not quite able to meet Harvey Mead's eyes. "I'll understand if you want to put me on suspension right here on the spot. I should never have left my post. I ended up putting not one but two women in serious jeopardy. Hell, Chief, if you want me to hand in my resignation..."

The chief made a dismissive gesture with his hand. "All right, George. All right. You feel rotten. You should feel rotten. This time you were lucky. You know that as well as I do. And you won't forget it any more than I will. End of discussion. Now let's get on with it."

"Yes, Chief," Denk said, gratitude infusing his voice and his features.

Harvey looked over at Noah Bright. "How is she?"

"Brianna Graham or Ellen Jansen?" There was an edge to the doctor's voice. He wasn't the least bit pleased with how the police had handled this situation, putting one of his nurses, as well as a patient, at such risk.

Harvey nodded. He got the message. "I already know about Nurse Jansen. I saw her a few minutes ago. She's got a whopper of a bump on the side of her head, but she says you checked her out and she's going to be fine. I'm greatly relieved about that. And I'm going to do my best—" he paused and glanced over at Denk "—we're going to do our best to make sure nothing like that happens again."

Noah was somewhat appeased. "The patient's vital signs are good. She never knew what hit her. What *almost* hit her," he corrected. "Luckily for her," Noah added grimly, "Ellen walked in before any damage was done. To Bri Graham, that is." Another reminder that his nurse wasn't so fortunate. "A couple of minutes later, Harvey, your murder suspect would have been your murder victim. Death by suffocation."

"Nurse Jansen told me that when she walked in she saw a figure in white that she took for an attendant leaning over the patient, holding a pillow down over her face," Harvey said. "She said it was too dark in the room to identify the assailant. She wasn't even sure if it was a man or a woman." He sighed. "Doesn't give us much to go on."

Out of the corner of his eye Harvey saw George Denk start to weave a little. He reached out and grabbed his officer's arm to steady him. "You're beat, George. Go home and get some sleep. Have one of the boys drive you in my car. You hear me?"

George Denk nodded. He started to take off, but stopped after a few steps. He looked back at the chief and the doctor. "I really am sorry."

As angry as Harvey was at the young officer, he also felt sorry for him. He'd been young once himself. He'd made a few dumb moves and, like George, he'd been fortunate enough to have had a few lucky breaks. He started to give the officer a reassuring smile, but the smile never quite made it to his lips.

"Damn," he muttered under his breath.

George Denk looked miserable until he realized the chief's expletive wasn't aimed at him, but at the young man hurrying up the hospital corridor.

Harvey Mead shook his head as the man approached. "Don't insurance investigators ever sleep?"

"Don't cops?" Matt Sebastian tossed back. "I called over to the station and was told I could find you here. What happened?" His eyes shot to the doctor and then to Bri's closed door. The coloring left his face. "She didn't try to..."

"Relax," Harvey said although he doubted Sebastian would take his advice. "She's fine. Still sleeping like a baby."

Matt eyed the police chief but saw he wasn't going to get much out of him. He leveled his gaze at the doctor. Unfortunately Noah Bright was no more forthcoming than Harvey Mead. The doctor quickly excused himself, saying that he had rounds to make before he went off duty.

Harvey looked critically at Matt. "Why were you looking for me at five in the morning?"

Matt returned the look in kind. Then he stuck his hand in the pocket of his leather jacket and pulled out a small plastic bag. Inside the bag was a bullet. Matt handed the parcel over to the chief. "It's a bullet from a .22 caliber Colt pistol. I'll lay odds it came from Bri's .22 Colt. Your boys can confirm it."

Harvey stared at the plastic bag, then raised his eyes to the insurance investigator. "What makes you so sure?"

"I dug it out of the desk in John Fossier's room. I'd say it was about a foot from where Fossier fell."

Now the two men were eyeballing each other like fierce combatants in a jousting match. "How'd you get into that room? It was sealed off. I left one of my best men . . . Damn, is my whole organization falling apart?" Harvey muttered caustically.

"Lucy told me that the closet in Fossier's room used to be a connecting door to the next room. She said it was locked up, but she had the key. Grumpy as the old gal is, she apparently has a soft spot in her heart for Bri. Doesn't think she's guilty any more than I do. So she gave me the key." He paused deliberately. "Turns out I didn't have to use it. The door was already unlocked."

Harvey Mead swore under his breath. Then he asked the only question there was to ask at that moment. "Who's staying in the room next to Fossier's?"

"A kid by the name of Allison Reed."

Harvey raised his eyes skyward. "A kid?"

"Turning eighteen this month. She's on the tour with her grandmother and her great-aunt. Quite a pair of old biddies, those two."

Harvey stared down again at the bullet encased in the plastic bag. "About an hour ago I got back the ballistics report on the bullet that killed Fossier." This time he deliberately paused, taking whatever pleasure there was to be had, which admittedly wasn't much, in keeping Sebastian in suspense. "A bullet from a .38 pierced his heart from a range of fifteen to twenty feet." He eyed Matt narrowly. "I could throw you in jail for tampering with evidence, Sebastian."

Matt smiled disarmingly. "You could do that, Chief. But it seems to me you've got your hands full already, now that you don't have a murder suspect."

Harvey gave the cocky young man a meaningful glare. "I wouldn't be so cheerful if I were you, Sebastian. You go on my suspect list along with the rest of the tour group."

Matt grinned. "Why, Chief, I'd be downright hurt if I was left out. Besides, it would be bad for my image. Any investigator worth his salt has got to raise suspicions now and again, or else folks will start thinking he's gone soft."

Harvey sighed wearily. "All I can say is, I sure as heck hope it doesn't turn out to be the teenager. I can just picture the rumpus that'll cause. I'll have her grandmother, her great-aunt, my wife and probably half the town up in arms if I've got to bring in a kid for murder one."

"She says she was fast asleep. Never heard anyone coming or going from her room once the shots woke her up." Matt's eyes strayed to the closed door of Bri's room then back to Harvey. "Something happened to Bri to have brought you back here. Are you going to tell me what it is or keep me in suspense?"

The chief mulled it over in his head. In the end he decided to tell Sebastian about the attempt on Bri's life not so much because he felt all that great about confiding in the man but because he knew that in Thornhill nothing remained a secret for very long. Even though he'd impressed upon both Noah and Nurse Ellen Jansen the importance of not repeating a word of what had happened to anyone but the authorities, he knew he was wasting his breath. One way or another, word would leak out. Word always did.

AT NINE the next morning Bri sat at the edge of her hospital bed, dressed once again in the jeans, sweater and plaid Western-style shirt she'd arrived in the night before. She was fully alert, the effects of the sedative having completely worn off. Still, she gave Matt a dazed look. "You mean it? I'm free? I . . . I didn't kill John?"

"You're a lousy shot, Bri. You missed him by a mile." Okay, so he was exaggerating just a bit. He smiled at her. A boyish smile, but at the moment Bri found it utterly enthralling. She had to fight the urge to leap up and throw her arms around him. Her gaze shifted. "Now what?"

"We go back to the inn. We've all been sequestered there until the crime's solved."

"You mean none of us can leave the inn until John's murderer has been found?"

"Well, I'm being a bit dramatic. We can come and go from the inn, but we can't leave town. Not unless we have ironclad alibis that check out. Unfortunately when a murder's committed at one in the morning, most people are asleep in their beds, which isn't exactly what the police would consider an ironclad alibi."

Bri's good spirits at learning of her freedom took a dive when she realized that this whole grisly affair surely meant the end of her fledgling tour business. Her first outing and what happens? A delightful New England fall foliage tour? No such luck. Instead of seeing colorful autumn leaves, her tour members get to be witnesses to a murder. Instead of visiting a succession of quaint New England inns for ten days, they get to be virtual prisoners in a town where a murderer is on the loose.

She gave Matt Sebastian a wan look. "It was a great business while it lasted," she said facetiously.

"Buck up, Bri," Matt soothed. "You could always claim that it's a mystery tour as well as a fall foliage tour. Hey, two tours for the price of one."

"Not funny," she muttered. "Don't you realize what this means? I'll have to return everyone's money, somehow foot the bill for the time we're forced to remain at the inn, and I can kiss goodbye any chance of getting customers to sign up for another tour."

Matt gave her shoulder a little shake. "Hey, you don't have to take this lying down. What happened to all that spunk? All that determination?"

She raised her hand up to stop him. "Please. A pep talk is the last thing I need at the moment."

"Okay," he said, pulling her up to her feet by her shoulders, "I'll tell you exactly what you do need then."

Bri was too stunned by his aggressive move to protest.

"You need to watch out for your pretty neck," he said. "And if you stop treating me like I'm still wet behind the ears, I'll watch out for it as well. Because whoever killed Fossier isn't finished."

Bri gave him a wide-eyed stare, a chill zigzagging down her spine. "Are you telling me . . . ?"

"I'm telling you that last night while you were in dreamland some creep stole into your room and tried to suffocate you with a pillow. It would have been a pretty easy job, too, except that a nurse interrupted the event in progress and suffered a mild concussion for her efforts. Unfortunately the creep got away and the nurse wasn't even sure if it was a man or a woman." He was deliberately callous in his telling because he figured that might shock her out of her depression.

It worked. She looked shocked, all right. "I'm next on the killer's list?"

Matt eyed her steadily. "Hard to figure otherwise."

"Is the nurse all right?"

Matt nodded. "She just happened to be in the wrong place at the wrong time. Which was unfortunate for her, but lucky for you."

Bri felt a rush of both fear and outrage. She shoved Matt back. "Why, damn it? Why is this happening? Who killed John if it wasn't me? Who would want to kill me?"

"It could be anyone, Bri. That's the hell of it."

She gave him a long, hard look. "No, not likely. It's probably somebody who's as desperate to get their hands on the same item that John wanted so badly. Somebody who wants what he or she thinks I have. And, damn it, I don't even know what that something is." Her look took on an icy edge. "But you know what that something is, Matt. Fact is, it's something you want, too, isn't it?"

"AN ANCIENT Egyptian papyrus scroll?" Bri shot Matt a perplexed look as they sat on a bench just off one of the paths on the Dorchester College campus.

Matt took a long drag on his cigarette as he gave her a close study. "You're saying you never set eyes on the thing?"

Bri waved off the pungent smoke that came out along with Matt's words. "That's exactly what I'm saying. If John did steal it, he certainly never showed it to me."

Matt kept up his scrutiny. "That doesn't make any sense. He certainly seemed convinced you had it."

Bri could hear the doubt in Matt's voice. He thought she was lying. She glared at him. "Well, he was wrong."

Matt cocked an eyebrow. "Dead wrong?"

Bri blanched.

"I'm sorry, Bri. That was uncalled for," Matt apologized softly. When he went to reach for her, she drew away as if his touch would hurt.

"At first I thought your only problem was that you were too young," she said in a hard voice, then rose from the bench and started off.

Matt hurried after her, forcing her to stop. "Okay, you're peeved. You've a right to be. But don't let your anger get in the way of your common sense. That scroll is worth a million or more. And people have killed for plenty less."

She flinched. "You're trying to scare me."

"You're damn right, I'm trying to scare you. Because if you're scared, you'll be careful. That was no phantom who sneaked into your room last night, Bri."

Bri's jaw went slack. She stared up at Matt. "I have never seen that scroll. I swear."

He took her hand. "Come on."

"Where are we going?" she asked warily.

"To the Asian studies library. Maybe you did see the scroll and you didn't realize it."

Ten minutes later they sat side-by-side in the library, a large tome opened in front of Bri. She stared down at the page for a long time. "I never saw anything like this."

Matt sighed with frustration. "Okay. Let's slow down and think this through."

They both slipped into silence.

"Maybe he put it in something else. Some kind of vessel or object," Matt said. "That must have been how he smuggled it out of Egypt in the first place." He turned to her, excited. "Think, Bri. Think about what he might have put it in. The scroll could have been rolled up thin enough to fit into a narrow cylinder even. Or stuck in a secret compartment in a box or..."

"I got rid of everything of John's. If there was anything I kept inadvertently, it would have been in my apartment and John went over that with a fine-tooth comb. He obviously didn't find what he was looking for."

"What do you mean you got rid of everything?" Matt asked.

Bri hesitated. When she'd confided in Chief Mead earlier about the carton of John's belongings that she gave to

Adam Quinn, he told her quite adamantly that she was not to mention it to anyone else.

"Bri?"

She stared back at the photo of the scroll in the book. "I tossed it in the trash," she said quietly, hating to lie. Especially—for some reason she didn't want to think about—to Matt. "I thought it was a bunch of...junk. Anything of value that John imported he put in...galleries." She looked over at Matt who was giving her one of his intense studies. "Importer." She laughed harshly. "That bastard was a two-bit smuggler."

"Far from two-bit. And he did far more than smuggle, Bri," Matt said quietly. "In his own way, he was a murderer as well. The curator of the Cairo Antiquities Museum committed suicide in a fit of depression after he was blamed for the theft of the scroll. From what I understand he was a man who prided himself on his integrity, honesty and absolute loyalty to the museum."

Bri cringed inwardly. She, too, had always prided herself on integrity, honesty and loyalty. She'd pledged that loyalty to her husband in a sacred vow. And now she had to face the harsh, painful reality that her husband had been a criminal, a man who lacked all those qualities she cherished. She'd been foolishly blinded by what she now realized had been infatuation, not love.

"I'm not a great judge of character," she muttered.

Matt placed his hand lightly over hers. This time she didn't reject the gesture. "Maybe all that means is that you shouldn't trust your first impressions." He grinned at her impishly. And then he leaned a little closer to her. "I get older every minute."

"So do I," she countered dryly, but she did find herself smiling back at him.

BY THE TIME Bri and Matt arrived back at the Sugarrun Inn, Harvey Mead was waiting there for them. Well, actually he was waiting for Bri, but he was beginning to get the picture that where Bri went Matt was sure to be close by. The astute police chief couldn't help wondering how much of the insurance investigator's interest in the owner of Valentine Tours was personal and how much was professional.

After a bland nod in Matt's direction, Harvey told Bri he wanted to see her alone in his wife's office. Matt didn't look pleased at being left out, but he didn't say anything. Lucy Harris, who was wheeling herself into the parlor just as Harvey was escorting Bri out, had plenty to say, however.

"You listen to me, Harvey Mead, you've gone and got everyone stirred up around here. The rumors are flying about the Sugarrun Inn being a hotbed of murder and vice and heaven only knows what else. My guests are in terror for their lives. A madman's on the loose. And what do you do? Spend your time interrogating this poor innocent young thing who looks like death warmed over." Lucy flushed. "I didn't mean to use that particular reference."

"Lucy, I only want to ask Miss Graham a few questions," Harvey said calmly.

The old woman frowned. "I won't say I've changed my mind any about not wanting to book tour groups at the inn. But we did book this group, and I intend to see to it that their stay here is not one they will deeply regret. I might add that your wife feels the same way. Granted, under such trying circumstances, this will not be easy, but neither Mildred nor I are women to shun our responsibilities no matter how difficult they may be."

Listening to the old woman, Bri was brought up short. She, too, had responsibilities. To her tour group. To Lucy and Mildred for taking her group in. To herself. Even, she supposed, to John. Whatever he might have done, whatever their lack of feelings for each other at the end, he'd been her husband and she wanted the peace of mind that could only come with bringing his murderer to justice.

She pressed her hand gently on the old proprietress's bony shoulder. "Thank you, Mrs. Harris. And I'll do my part, too, to help make the best of a trying situation." She glanced at the police chief. "Which includes answering any questions Chief Mead may have for me."

After Bri left the room with Harvey, Matt smiled at Lucy. "She's quite a woman, isn't she?"

Lucy wagged a gnarled finger at him. "A little old for you, isn't she?"

Matt threw up his hands. "What is this? A conspiracy? I thought older women were supposed to go for younger men these days."

Lucy smiled; a surprisingly girlish smile that lit up her face. "My Chester was eight years younger than I. We were married for forty-seven years, God rest his soul."

"DEAD?" Bri sank into the chintz armchair in Mildred's office. "John's art dealer friend, Adam Quinn is dead, too?"

Harvey Mead saw the color leave her face and hurriedly brought her a glass of water.

She managed a faint smile, took a sip, then pulled herself together. "When did it happen?"

"As best I can tell, about the same time as your husband resurfaced in Boston."

"Do you think John . . . ?"

"The police report I got from Boston indicates that Quinn was the victim of a holdup at a convenience store."

Bri frowned. "You mean his death was just . . . coincidence?"

The police chief shrugged. "It would seem that way." He didn't sound particularly convincing or convinced.

Bri rose and started to pace the spacious room. "If John were somehow connected in Quinn's death and still came after me, it must mean that the scroll wasn't in any of the items I stuck in that carton and gave to Quinn."

"Or at least it wasn't by the time Fossier arrived."

Bri nodded. "Quinn could have found it months ago and sold it or hidden it away."

"The Boston police have a report on file from the FBI regarding Adam Quinn. It seems the gallery owner was under investigation for receiving smuggled antiquities."

"You think John and Quinn were in cahoots?" Before Harvey responded, Bri answered her own question. "Of course. It makes complete sense." She slapped her palm against her forehead. "And I blithely handed the scroll over to him like a complete idiot."

"We don't know that for sure," Harvey pointed out. Something in his tone brought her up short.

She eyed him narrowly. "Oh, no. Not you, too."

Harvey quirked a brow.

"I don't have it, Chief Mead. If I had something worth a million bucks, would I have gone into hock starting a touring business? The answer is no. I'd be off on the French Riviera living in the lap of luxury. Now I'll be lucky if they don't book me a bunk in debtor's prison."

"When you said 'not you, too,' I take it you mean Matt Sebastian's also wondering if you might have the scroll?"

Bri scowled. "Maybe he's just frustrated over getting nowhere in his investigation. I'm sure that recouping a rare antiquity would move him up several rungs on the ladder at his company."

Harvey stared at her. His silence lasted long enough to put her on edge.

"What is it, Chief Mead?"

"Can I ask you a personal question, Bri?"

She swallowed hard, but nodded.

"Are you attracted to Sebastian?"

"Really, Chief Mead," she began in protest only to be cut off.

"I think you are, Bri. Maybe you don't want to admit it just yet."

"That's ridiculous. I can't admit something to you that I..."

"Haven't even admitted to yourself yet?" Harvey finished for her.

Bri felt her cheeks warm and frowned at the telltale sign indicating that what the chief said just might be true. "I'm not young and foolish anymore, Chief Mead."

"I'm sixty-two, Bri. And even so, on a rare occasion, I can still be young and foolish. You're all of what? Thirty-two?"

"Almost thirty-three."

Harvey steered her over to one of the sofas and sat her down, then joined her. "Listen to me, Bri. Whether or not you have the scroll, somebody around here thinks you do. If I were you, I would be careful not to trust anyone too much."

Bri felt a swift and treacherous current of fear rush over her. "You mean specifically Matt."

"It's not that I especially suspect him, but I think you're particularly vulnerable where he is concerned," Harvey said frankly.

"But you do suspect him," Bri persisted, sensing the police chief knew more than he was saying.

Harvey let out a long sigh that sounded almost like a rumble. "Sebastian's on suspension from his company. Has been for close to a month. I got the word personally from his immediate superior, Leonard Roth."

Bri felt a sudden chill, and she folded her arms across her chest. The look on her face told Harvey Mead just how young and foolish Bri Graham still was, whether she knew it or not.

"I'm not saying that means he isn't acting on behalf of his agency to reclaim the scroll, just that he's doing it on his own time," Harvey found himself saying, admonishing himself at the same time for trusting his hunch that Sebastian was on the up-and-up. The truth of it was he liked the kid, too.

Bri nodded slowly. "I wouldn't put it past him, either. But what do I know about what he would or wouldn't do. I hardly know the man."

Harvey gave her a level look. "My point is just that. You don't know what Sebastian would do, or any of your other tour members, for that matter. Don't get so caught up being wary of Sebastian, Bri, that you miss someone else sneaking up behind you."

Before she left, Harvey told her to be sure to keep her windows and door locked at night. In an effort to ease her worry, he also told her that he'd put the inn, and especially her, on a round-the-clock watch.

DINNER AT THE INN that evening was a tense affair. Mildred and Lucy did their best to liven things up with a festive meal, including entertainment from a few members of Thornhill's Doily Cart Opera Company. It was obvious to Bri that these efforts did little to distract her gloomy tour members. Only Allison seemed to respond with good spirits. Bri had a fair guess as to why. It appeared that the teenager was making some headway with Tim Campbell. Before dinner Bri had spotted the two of them walking up the path at the inn, hand in hand. And Allison talked excitedly during dinner of her plans to take in a movie with Tim later in the evening.

"A good idea. We'll join you, won't we Harriet?" Allison's grandmother said with aplomb.

Allison's mouth dropped. Much to her increased chagrin, within minutes, most of the other tour members decided to join them, as well. Only Bri, Kyle Dunner and Matt opted to stay behind.

After dinner Kyle went off to his room complaining of a headache. Bri sat outside on the porch, not surprised when Matt followed her out. He suggested a stroll into town, but after her conversation with Harvey that afternoon, she'd resolved to keep her distance from the suspended insurance investigator. Besides, she wanted some time to herself. Some time to think about all of them, Matt Sebastian and the other tour members. There was no way around it. Any one of them could very well have murdered John. And even Adam Quinn. And, as she now knew, the murderer wasn't ready to quit yet.

If Matt sensed the change in her manner toward him, he said nothing about it. He took the rejection of his offer of a stroll with apparent equanimity and quietly sat down on a rocking chair beside her.

Even though he seemed content to just sit there and not engage her in conversation, his presence made Bri uneasy, and she found herself unable to concentrate.

"You look a bit chilled," Matt said after a while. "Why don't I run in and get you a sweater?"

"Oh, no. Don't bother. I . . ."

"That's okay. I've got a quick phone call I've got to make, anyway."

When he got to the door he made way for Mildred who was stepping out.

"Well, I'm off to visit my daughter, Maggie," Mildred said brightly to Bri as she spotted her on the porch. She glanced over at the driveway, giving a little wave to the man behind the wheel of the cruiser parked there. Roy Filmore, an officer who'd been with her husband for over twenty years, waved back.

"It's going to be ladies' night," Mildred went on. "Kevin's off on a camping trip with the boys. Maggie was planning to go along with them, but she's had terrible morning sickness."

Bri smiled wistfully. How nice to be happily married and pregnant. A little morning sickness seemed a small price to pay.

"Why don't you come along, Bri?" Mildred suggested. "Paula's going to be there, too. It might take your mind off things."

"Thanks, but I'm going to turn in early. I'm still kind of shaky."

Mildred gave her a sympathetic look. "Well, of course you are." She was going to say more when her attention was drawn to a car turning in the drive. So was Bri's. She let out a little gasp as the car pulled up behind the cruiser.

Mildred gave her a curious look. "What is it, Bri?"

"Nothing," Bri mumbled as she stared at the car. "It's just that it's . . . similar to the one that brought John home last night." She gave a little laugh. "But there must be hundreds of new-model, white sedans in Thornhill."

Mildred nodded, but she was as curious as Bri to see who would step out of the car. They had to wait, though, while Roy Filmore ambled over to check out the new arrivals.

Chapter Eight

As it turned out, a man and a woman stepped out of the new-model, white sedan. An attractive couple, Bri thought, not recognizing the pair at first and thinking that they might be new guests at the inn. But then she heard Mildred mumble, "I wonder what they're doing here?" The remark had an edge to it, telling Bri her guess about the couple was wrong.

As the pair drew closer and Bri could get a better look at them, she thought they seemed vaguely familiar.

"Who are they?" she asked Mildred.

"Friends of the dearly departed," Mildred said dryly. "Liz Armstrong and Steve Palmer. Funny seeing them together again. Last I heard, she'd dumped him."

Once Mildred attached names to the pair, Bri remembered them instantly. John had introduced her to his old Dorchester College chums during their honeymoon. They'd bumped into the pair at the Chinese restaurant, and Liz and Steve had invited the newlyweds to join them. Bri remembered it as a long evening, feeling like a fifth wheel throughout dinner, the three spending much of the time reminiscing about the good-old college days. On a couple of other occasions, when John suggested getting together with them again, Bri had begged off, feeling a little hurt but trying not to show it when John went without her. Not that he'd spent all that much time with Steve and Liz, but then again, it was their honeymoon. A brief one at that.

After leaving Thornhill, Bri had had one further occasion to have contact with Steve Palmer and Liz Armstrong. About a week after John had left her, before she'd got the Dear Jane card from him postmarked the Canary Islands, she'd been so frantic, she'd phoned Liz and Steve. Other than Adam Quinn who'd seemed almost as upset and baffled by John's disappearance as she was, Bri had no one else to turn to for possible clues. Steve and Liz were the only other people she'd met who knew John. She'd asked each of her husband's old college friends if they'd either seen or heard from her husband recently. Liz had been coolly abrupt on the phone. "He never was all that reliable," she'd said sardonically. Bri felt at the time that Liz was not only unsympathetic, but that she even took some perverse satisfaction in Bri's plight. Steve, on the other hand, had been very sweet and compassionate during their brief conversation on the phone, regretting having to tell her that he hadn't heard a word from John since their honeymoon visit up in Thornhill. He'd sounded truly sorry for her. But she remembered thinking at the time that, like Liz, he was not all that surprised.

Steve looked quite sympathetic now as he approached her on the porch. As for Liz Armstrong, while she didn't look sympathetic, she certainly appeared shaken and upset. Bri was surprised by her reaction. She wouldn't have guessed that Liz and John had been all that close. Oh, John had told her about his brief fling with Liz during college, but that was a long time ago. And even though Mildred had said that Liz had recently dumped Steve, they looked as if they were on the mend today. Still, Bri thought, sometimes those old flames of youth were hard to put out entirely. And thinking back to that phone conversation she'd had all those months ago with Liz, it made sense of the woman's callousness. It was possible Liz had never quite gotten over John and resented Bri for having been the one he'd chosen to marry... however brief Bri's marriage had been. The thought that Liz might have carried a torch for John all these years was only a hop, skip and a jump from Bri's next thought. Had John ever fully gotten over Liz?

She stopped ruminating as the pair approached her, noticing that Steve had his arm around Liz. She also noticed they were both a bit surprised when she greeted them by name.

"I wasn't sure you'd remember us," Steve said.

Bri smiled, not mentioning Mildred's assistance.

"We're so sorry about John, Bri," Steve went on with appropriate gravity as he stood solemnly in front of her.

Liz's icy blue eyes fixed accusatorily on Bri. "Yes. It was such a shock."

Bri was chilled by the look. It was as if she held Bri responsible. Yet Bri knew, thanks to Mildred's fast action in getting the word out in the *Thornhill Tab*'s What's What column that day, that everyone in town knew by now that she'd been completely exonerated in the shooting of John Fossier, despite her rash confession.

"You must have had a few hellish hours there thinking you were responsible for his death," Steve said empathetically to Bri, then glanced at Mildred. "Any chance it was suicide?"

"Now, Steve, you know Harvey would have my head if I were to go around blabbing police business."

The society editor smiled sardonically at the gossip columnist. "That's never stopped you in the past."

Mildred didn't feel the remark deserved a response and gave none. As everyone in town knew, there was no love lost between the two *Thornhill Tab* columnists.

"I just can't figure out why anyone would murder John," Steve muttered.

"You can't?" The question came from Matt who'd returned from inside the inn and was now standing at the open front door, a wool cardigan folded over his arm.

Even under the dim lighting on the porch, Bri could see Steve's face had gone beet red.

Matt sauntered over and draped the sweater across Bri's shoulders. "I just thought, since word travels fast," he said laconically, eyeing the track coach, "you might have heard some things about your old college buddy that could have given you pause."

Matt had clearly caught Steve completely off guard. Flustered, he mumbled, "I mean . . . I've heard rumors these past few months that John might have been into some illegal activities, but . . ."

Liz gave him an impatient look. "Rumors are a dime a dozen in this town."

"I know that, Liz," Steve quickly assured her. "Anyway, I always make it a point of not speaking ill of the dead." He quirked an uneasy smile.

Liz gave Matt a wary look. "Are you a cop?"

Matt shook his head slowly.

She continued looking questioningly at him. "Have we met before?"

Now Steve, too, was looking at him. "Yes. You do look vaguely familiar."

Matt rubbed his jaw. A faint smile curved his lips. "Maybe you saw me in passing down at the *Tab* offices. I dropped in the other afternoon to check something out in their reference library."

Bri was astonished at the pair's tense silence that followed Matt's remark. Mildred was quite curious about it. Curious enough to delay her departure for a few minutes.

Liz, however, had no intention of hanging around to chat. She looked as if she regretted even this brief visit. "Steve insisted we stop by to pay our condolences, but we really have to get going. I have a million things to do."

"We also wanted to see if there was anything we could do for you, Bri," Steve added, regaining some but not all of his composure.

"I can't think of anything at the moment," Bri said. "But I'll be here in town for a while. Why don't we...stay in touch?" If Steve had heard rumors about John, Bri thought, he might have some clues about the missing scroll. Even about John's death.

Steve looked pleased. "Good. We'll do that. We'll definitely do that."

Bri nodded, but as she caught another of Liz's cool looks, somehow she doubted the *we* part.

WHEN THE OTHERS had left and Matt told her he was going to take that stroll into town, curiosity made Bri decide to go along with him despite her earlier intentions. She wanted to know what he'd been doing down at the local newspaper office, and just what he'd seen there that had made Steve Palmer and Liz Armstrong so uneasy.

She didn't think it wise to come right out and grill him, so she made some small talk for a couple of blocks. Not out of choice, she found herself having to do most of the talking. Matt, usually the loquacious one, was uncharacteristically quiet. When they rounded the corner to Elm Street, a block from Main Street, Bri was just about to get into a discussion of the real topic on her mind when Matt decided to get to the real topic on his mind.

"I've got a confession to make," he told her.

She stopped short, forgetting about Steve and Liz, and stared at Matt, wide-eyed with alarm. "A confession?"

"No, Bri. Not that kind of confession," he chided, a shadow of hurt crossing his face.

Bri was flustered. "I didn't...I mean..." But she couldn't hide her relief that he wasn't about to confess to John's murder.

And Matt couldn't resist commenting on it. "I'm glad you're glad I'm not the murderer."

She eyed him levelly. "But I don't really know that for sure, do I?" A pretty foolish remark, she realized, if he turned out to be. But then being foolish was something she seemed to have a propensity for, of late.

"Do I look like a murderer, Bri?"

Their eyes met and held for a moment. "No," she admitted. "But then I didn't think John looked like a smuggler," she added.

"You've got a point there," he said with a captivating smile.

A woman could get lost in that smile of his, if she wasn't careful, Bri thought. Not speaking personally, she hastily assured herself.

"I suppose if all murderers looked like murderers, the police would have a much easier job of it," she mumbled.

He kept on smiling. "That's true."

She gave him a very careful look, telling herself she was certainly thankful she was immune to his boyish charm and his enticing grab bag of smiles. "It's just that...you never know." It was a weak finish.

He stopped smiling, which gave her a measure of relief. But her relief didn't last long.

"You don't really think I murdered Fossier," he said, lighting up a cigarette. He turned his head, blew out a thin stream of smoke, then looked back at her. "But you are worried about me."

"Is that so?"

A slow smile curved his lips. "I think you're worried that my only interest in you might have to do with you being the missing link to that scroll."

"I already told you I have no idea . . ."

He took another drag, this time not being so careful to blow the smoke downwind. "But you're not so sure I believe you."

Bri gave him a defiant look, ignoring the smoke. "No. I'm not so sure."

Matt nodded, his expression one of equanimity. "And something tells me you're also not so sure my intentions are all that honorable."

She flushed. "Let's stick to a discussion of the scroll."

He smiled rakishly. "I was. I meant that maybe you're worried I might be out to nab that million-dollar piece of papyrus for myself instead of turning it over to my company. I hate to say it, but there have been some disreputable characters in my line of work. I, however, am not one of them."

Bri gave an awkward nod.

Matt's smile deepened, his eyes dancing.

"This is a ridiculous discussion," she snapped, frustrated by her own transparency.

"The thing is," he went on, deliberately ignoring her, "I do have a hard-and-fast rule about never mixing business with pleasure."

Bri knew he was deliberately trying to provoke her. The hell of it was, she felt too provoked to hide it. "I think you're very . . . adolescent, Matt Sebastian."

She started off in a huff, but he caught hold of her arm, bringing her to a halt. "I actually have two confessions to make," he said.

"I don't think I want to hear either of them," she said archly.

"If you really didn't want to hear them, Bri, you would have made a firmer statement. Once you say you don't *think*, that's a clear sign of ambivalence. Consider that your first tip if you ever get in the sleuthing business."

"Did you learn that from reading Agatha Christie mysteries?"

Matt looked deeply into Bri's emerald-green eyes. A guy could get lost in those eyes, he thought to himself. If he wasn't careful. The trouble was he never was the careful sort.

Bri was disconcerted to find that she was even more uneasy and more intrigued now that Matt had stopped smiling.

"My first confession is," he said in a husky smoker's voice, "that I've been known to break the rules—even hard-and-fast ones—on a rare occasion. This might be one of those rare occasions, Bri."

Bri self-consciously smoothed back a few wayward strands of hair from her face, as if by doing so, she could put a semblance of order back in her life and dismiss this ridiculous and even dangerous attraction she was feeling for this near stranger. "If you ask me, Sebastian, you're lousy at picking occasions."

That remark netted her a wink. "Sometimes you don't pick them, sweetheart, they pick you." He added insult to injury by then reaching out and playfully mussing up her hair.

She scowled at him. "You're regressing by the minute."

"What can I say, Bri? You bring out the kid in me." He ground his cigarette out with the heel of his Dock-Side, then leaned closer to her, giving her a look full of heat and speculation. "Now, the question is, do I bring out the kid in you?"

She knew he intended to find out the answer on the spot, right there in the middle of Elm Street, a nice, refined, tidy neighborhood of Cape Cod salt boxes and colonials. He was even being slow enough about getting to it to give her a chance to escape. But some damn invisible force held her frozen in place. When his lips landed right on target, Bri's lips not only parted, but she virtually sank against him with a light-headed weakness. Why, she might as well have swooned like Scarlett O'Hara. And there was nothing of the kid in the kiss they shared, on either of their parts. It was hard, fiery, passionate; disturbingly but excitingly adult.

Oh damn, Bri thought with a rush of despair. Chief Mead was right. She'd flipped over the guy. Temporary insanity. What else could it be? It would pass. She would see to it . . . if she knew what was good for her. Which, under the circumstances, was a moot point.

When she reluctantly broke the kiss off, she muttered into his chest, "This was a disaster waiting to happen."

He tipped her chin up, smiling beguilingly. "Was it that bad?"

"No, that good," she admitted, hating herself for her honesty. His smile deepened and she got irritated. Still, it also helped her to pull herself together and determine to set the record straight before things got out of hand. Well, more out of hand, anyway.

"Don't let it go to your head, Matt. It stops here." She wished she could sound more convincing. She wished she could feel more convinced. She thought maybe if she kept at it, the message would sink in—to her head as well as Matt's. "I want you to know I have some of my own hard-and-fast rules. And having already broken them once, I know what havoc that can wreak. I used to be naive enough to believe in love, marriage, the whole happily-ever-after fantasy. But now I'm older, smarter and tougher and I don't believe in fantasies anymore. I've just outgrown them, that's all."

"You never outgrow your need for fantasies, Bri."

She gave him a wry look. "Out of the mouths of babes?"

He grinned. "I bet even old Lucy Harris would agree with me."

"You always have a comeback."

She knew, even as the words leapt out of her mouth, that she'd opened herself right up for another one. He swept her back into his arms. "Always," he murmured before he punctuated the point with another steamy kiss.

"You've got to stop doing that," she said shakily when he released her. "I mean it, Matt. I have a murdered husband, I have someone out there wanting to suffocate me to death, I have a business in ruins before I've even got it off the ground, I'm drowning in debt, I have no idea where this damn scroll is, and . . . and I'm going to be forty."

Matt grinned at her. "Forty? When?"

She gave his chest a shove. "Five years before you."

They walked in silence, Matt matching Bri's brisk pace. When they got to the end of Elm Street they turned right onto Main Street and stood by the verandah of the stately red brick Thornhill Inn, really a colonial-style, three-star hotel, this one unique in that it was owned and operated by Dorchester College. The rest of downtown consisted of three blocks of quaint shops, upscale restaurants and boutiques, a proliferation of banks and several real estate agencies. The little stretch of storefronts sported uniform maroon awnings trimmed in white, Dorchester College's colors.

"Hey, don't you want to hear my other confession?" he asked as they started past the inn.

She shot him a wary look. "Are you kidding? If it was anything like your last confession . . ."

"I'm not just a commonplace insurance investigator like I told you," he said, not giving her a chance to finish.

Bri donned an innocent look. "You're not?"

Matt looked squarely at her. "No. I'm an insurance investigator with the distinction of being on suspension. It seems I ruffled the feathers of a local Boston politician during my last assignment. He put in a claim for some jewels belonging to his wife that he reported stolen. I was pretty sure it was a scam. I didn't have any concrete proof, but I was well on my way to digging some up. The next thing I knew, the pol withdrew the claim and ran a song and dance to my boss about my rude ways, even suggesting I'd come on to his wife—which I hadn't. Still, the pol had a lot of pull in town and would have liked my head on a silver platter. Lucky for me, my boss happens to like my head where it is. Smart politician that he is, he decided a couple of months' suspension would appease the pol and give him some time to cool his jets. Meanwhile, Fossier surfaced, and suspension or not, I was not about to let this case get away from me."

"I know. I mean, I know you were suspended. Chief Mead told me."

He looked at her steadily. "I was hoping he wouldn't beat me to it. I wanted to be first with the news. So you wouldn't trust me even less than you already do." He leaned a little closer to her. "Bri, I want you to be able to trust me. I know it won't come easy," he added, a provocative smile curving his lips, "but then I never do seem to take the easy route."

She was sorely tempted to believe him. It was downright awkward to be so attracted to a man you couldn't even trust. But the irony was perfect. You start by marrying a man you trust, who turns out to be unspeakably suspect and end up distrusting a guy who turns out to be Mr. Right.

Irony aside, Matt's confession was probably nothing more than a ploy to throw her off guard, something he definitely had a talent for. He'd figured she already knew about his suspension, anyway. It would have been dumb of him not to tell her. And whatever Matt was, he wasn't dumb.

They started strolling down Main Street. Bri turned to him, her brow slightly furrowed. "What were you doing at the newspaper office yesterday?"

"Tailing Fossier," he said without hesitation.

Bri pursed her lips. "He went to see Liz Armstrong, didn't he?"

He paused for a moment. "Yes." He checked her for a reaction, but she gave none.

"And Steve Palmer?"

"Steve Palmer spotted Fossier walking by the college track area on his way to the *Tab* offices and followed him, as well. I dropped a few paces behind Palmer." He paused, eyeing her questioningly. "You want to hear the rest?"

Again they came to a stop. This time they were standing in front of one of the storefront restaurants on Main Street, La Dolci Pomodoro, a popular pizza place in town. "For the record, I fell out of love with John Fossier a long time ago, Matt. Although it still hurt a little for having been such a fool in the first place."

They went inside the pizza place and got a small table for two in a far corner. Once they'd ordered espressos and two Italian pastries, he told her about the torrid kiss between Fossier and the society editor. It didn't surprise Bri. It even explained a thing or two. And, as she'd predicted, it did hurt a little.

"And Steve Palmer? He saw them kissing, too?" she asked quietly.

"He saw them. But they were…too busy to notice him. Palmer turned away from the door without saying a word.

I think that's when he spotted me. Although he didn't know who I was at the time. And he was so shaken up by what he'd seen that I really didn't think it registered."

Bri stared at Matt, her expression charged. "How jealous do you think he was?"

He smiled. "Well, let me put it this way, it would be ironic if Fossier's death had nothing at all to do with the million-dollar scroll."

"We've got to tell Chief Mead." And then she thought of something else. "Steve's car. I thought it was the same one I saw John get out of that night. If Steve drove John home..."

"It wasn't Steve's car. He might have been at the wheel tonight, but the car belongs to Liz." Matt hesitated. "John spent that evening at Liz's apartment. I quit watching the place close to midnight, figuring he was settled in for the night."

"Well, he spent the best part of it, anyway," Bri muttered cynically.

"The guy sure was a first-class bastard," Matt said sympathetically. "I think he did you a big favor walking out on you."

She managed a weak smile. "You must also think I'm pretty dumb."

"Pretty, yes. But definitely not dumb." He reached across the small table and touched her cheek. "Maybe just a little young," he teased lightly.

She frowned.

"Come on. That deserves a little smile," he coaxed.

Her frown deepened. "I was thinking about Steve again. If he's as in love with Liz as we think, and he also knew that John and Liz not only played kissy-face in Liz's office, but that the two of them spent most of the night at her place, it would make him that much more jealous. Which would give him even more of a motive for killing John. He could have been watching Liz's place, too. And followed them back to the inn. Oh, Matt, we've got to tell Chief Mead."

"In good time, Bri. We don't want to start tossing around accusations without any proof. It might give the murderer a chance to cover his tracks."

Bri could appreciate Matt's point.

A waitress came over with their orders and then hurried off to another table.

"By the way," Bri asked, stirring a teaspoon of sugar into the strong black Italian coffee, "how did Liz Armstrong spot you back at the newspaper office yesterday afternoon if she didn't spot Steve?"

"Steve walked off, leaving her door open. Liz must have come up for air, noticed it was open and went to close it. She happened to pop her head out and glance around the corridor first. Steve had already made his exit and I was trying to make mine. She must have caught sight of me before I succeeded."

Bri glanced across the room, noticing a familiar pair of faces. "The movie must have let out. There's Allison and Tim." She smiled at Matt. "Don't tell me they managed to ditch their bevy of chaperones?"

Matt checked his watch. "Actually, it's a little early for the movie to have ended. Maybe they snuck out of the theater to be alone for a while."

Bri observed the pair holding hands across the small table. "I guess Tim's given up on Jillian."

Matt lit a cigarette. "Allison certainly seems quite happy about it."

Bri studied Matt. "And you don't think Tim's happy?" She glanced at the college student again. "I'd hate to think he's just bored and Allison's the only available female. I'm particularly sensitive about men who use women," she added, looking back at Matt.

Their gaze held for several heartbeats. "Bri, I want to ask you something serious."

She tensed instinctively. "What?"

"What do you say we work together on this case?"

"Which case? John's murder or the missing million-dollar scroll?"

"We still don't know that the two aren't connected. Even if Palmer did do John in, we can't be sure his only motive was jealousy. Maybe he knew about the scroll."

Bri gave Matt a thoughtful look. "It's a reach, but I suppose it's even possible that Steve was in on the deal in some way and believed that John was holding out on him."

"Anything's possible. That's why I could use a partner."

"I've never read Agatha Christie, Matt. I don't know what kind of a sleuth I'd make."

"You're smart, curious, observant, and you've got a lot at stake, Bri. That'll make you a fast learner."

"I suppose that's true," she said slowly.

He gave her a shrewd look. "Anyway, you're not thinking about how good a sleuth you'll be. You're thinking, is it safe to go sleuthing with a man you still don't trust?"

"That's true, too," she said candidly. Then she gave him a challenging look. "Plus, how do I know it'll be a two-way street? I tell you what I find out. How do I know you'll tell me what you discover?"

He smiled a wry smile. "Okay. How about if I tell you something I already discovered? How about if I tell you that the murderer used a connecting door from Allison Campbell's room to get into and out of Fossier's room."

"You're not suggesting Allison . . ."

"Allison claims she didn't hear a thing."

"But if what you say is true, that isn't possible. Even if she didn't hear or see the murderer before the shots were fired, the noise would have woken her up and she would have seen the murderer come through her room then.''

''No, she wouldn't.''

Bri gave him a puzzled look.

He smiled. ''Think about it for a minute.''

Bri glanced over at Allison and Tim again. Then she looked back at Matt, excitement registering in her green eyes. ''She wasn't in her room when the murderer came and went. She was with Tim in his room.''

''Smart girl.''

She gave him a sharp look.

''Sorry,'' he said with an impish grin. ''I meant, smart woman.''

Chapter Nine

It was nearly eleven when Bri went up to her room that night. Even before she switched on the light, her senses went on alert. Her charming, picture-book room which she'd loved on first sight, was giving off an alien aura. What was it? And then, standing at the open door, the dim hall light casting the spacious room in portentous shadow, Bri realized it was the faint scent she'd picked up as soon as she'd opened the door that had put her instantly on guard. Definitely not the scent she used, yet vaguely familiar. Feminine. She was certain of that. As certain as she was that someone had been in her room that evening. Her pulse quickened. Someone might still be there now, hiding in the large antique wardrobe or in the bathroom. Even right behind her door. Terror gripped her as her mind conjured up an image of being grabbed and pinned to her bed, a large, thick pillow coming down on her face. She almost gagged.

"What is it?"

The masculine voice behind her made her practically jump out of her skin. She whirled around to find Matt there. The anxious look on Bri's face told him as much as he needed to know. Gesturing with his hand, he motioned her to step quietly away from her door.

"Matt." she whispered nervously as he placed her against the corridor wall and then started for her room.

A reassuring smile lifted the corners of his mouth.

The expression on Bri's face remained frightened and grim. Even more so when she saw his hand slip ominously into his pocket. Did Matt carry a gun on him? Was it a .38-caliber revolver? She began to tremble in earnest.

He was in her room for all of two minutes before his head popped out and he motioned her to come inside. His face registered reassurance that no one was hiding in there. However, his face did not register relief.

Bri hesitated before stepping inside the room which was now flooded in light. As she stood at the open door her eyes darted around to each corner. Then they darted over to Matt.

"It's okay," he said in a low voice.

She checked to see if he had a gun in his hand. He didn't. Instead, he was holding a folded sheet of white paper. He gave it to her once she entered the room. She was unfolding the paper as he closed her door. Bri gave him an anxious look as the door shut, still thinking of that possible gun in his pocket; still thinking that she didn't trust him. And still thinking that she wanted to.

"Read the note," he ordered quietly.

It was typewritten and brief. She read it aloud in a low, shaky voice. "Last night you almost suffocated to death. Next time you might not be so lucky. If you want to live, you will relinquish the scroll. I am giving you fair warning. I will be in touch very soon." Bri could feel beads of sweat break out along her forehead. Her underarms felt damp. The paper trembled in her hand.

Matt reached out for it, but she quickly drew the warning note away. "This is evidence. I'm turning it over to Chief Mead." Her voice sounded strange even to herself.

"I agree," he said quietly, giving her a steady look. "Are you all right?"

She wasn't, but she nodded.

She glanced over at her open window then went to close and lock it. She almost had the window shut when she abruptly drew back. "Douse the lights," she ordered in a hoarse whisper.

"What . . ."

She put her finger to her lips to silence him. Then Matt heard the faint sound of voices drifting in through the open window. He quickly shut the lights and hurried over to join Bri.

Cautiously they peered out the window, which faced the back of the inn. There were two figures having a heated conversation as they stood under a large golden oak. Unfortunately the leaves blocked a clear view of the pair, and while Bri and Matt could make out most of the conversation, the voices had a muffled quality thanks to the brisk night wind.

"I wasn't throwing myself at him," a throaty feminine voice was arguing.

"It certainly seemed that way to me," a low masculine voice countered.

"I didn't know you were the jealous type." Now the woman's voice took on a teasing note.

"It's just that you mean so much to me."

"You have to learn to be more trusting. There's nothing if there isn't trust, darling."

Bri shot Matt a look. He gave her a wink.

"We have to trust each other," the male voice responded earnestly.

The talking ended, but the pair didn't immediately move away from the tree. Matt made a low smooching sound next to Bri's ear. She nudged him in the ribs. Their playful antics came to a halt when they heard the woman's next words.

"What will we do about her?"

"Leave her to me." The man's voice held a menacing rumble. "When the time is right, I'll take care of her."

A little gasp escaped Bri's lips. Matt's arm moved instinctively around her shoulder. She was as rigid as a board.

When the couple moved away from the tree and started for the inn, they came into clear view for a moment.

Bri's eyes widened. In was the unassuming investment broker, Kyle Dunner, and the sultry secretary, Jillian Knight.

When the pair disappeared around the house, Matt silently closed and bolted Bri's window.

"If this were an Agatha Christie novel, I bet you'd be pouring me a glass of brandy right about now."

Matt smiled crookedly, pulling out a small silver flask from his back pocket. He uncapped it and offered it to her.

She laughed dryly, then took a big swallow and coughed as the strong brandy burned a path down her throat. She wasn't much of a drinker. "You certainly have enough vices, Sebastian. Smoking, drinking."

He grinned. "You ain't seen nothin' yet."

She smiled. She knew what he was trying to do. Cajole her out of her panic that she thought she was masking. Neither of them were very successful. She shuddered. He offered her another drink, but she shook her head, her green eyes clouded with fear as she stared at him.

Matt did the only thing left to do. He folded her into his arms as though she were coming unraveled and he was holding her together. She shuddered against him, not fighting his embrace, and he tucked her against his body, stroking her back until she calmed down. As soon as she stopped shuddering, he released her. He could see by the smile she gave him that she appreciated that. As well as the holding.

"I don't get it," she muttered after a long silence, trying to sort it all out. "Mild-mannered, Milquetoasty Kyle and sultry Jill, lovers?" She shot Matt a wry look. "Only Kyle isn't so Milquetoasty, is he?"

Matt touched her hand in a comforting gesture. "I thought he was making a play for Anna Campbell," he mused. "They certainly seemed a more likely pair."

"And why all the secrecy?" Bri wondered aloud as she sat down on her bed. "Why hide the fact that they're involved?"

Matt sat down beside her. "Well—"

Bri cut him off. "I'll tell you why. They didn't want someone to know. And my guess is that someone was—"

"John?" Matt managed to get in before Bri finished.

She winked at him. "I bet you're not bad at what you do."

"And you are a quick study, just as I expected."

Bri stood up. "And now they have to keep up the ruse." She unconsciously lowered her voice. "Do you think one of them killed him? That they're in it together?"

Matt and Bri stared at each other in silence for several moments, the only illumination in the room provided by a quarter moon outside.

"What's their motive?" Matt queried.

"They must know about the scroll. And they're after it." She hesitated. "And after me. They obviously think I have it, just like John thought I did. So they get rid of John and go after me themselves." She could hear her own heart pounding. "I'll bet anything it was Jillian who left that awful note in here for me."

"Why Jillian and not Kyle?" he asked.

She frowned. "I picked up the scent of a woman's perfume when I opened the door."

"You're sure it was Jillian's scent?" he persisted.

But Bri wasn't listening. "Jillian and her boyfriend, Kyle, probably wrote it together." She swallowed hard. "I wonder which one of them put that pillow over my face at the hospital. What do you think, Matt?"

Matt opened his mouth to speak, but Bri beat him to it. "I know just what you're thinking," she said. "That we're making a big jump from that conversation we overheard to Jillian and Kyle knowing about the scroll, being murderers, being the ones who are threatening me..."

"That thought did cross my mind," he said sardonically.

"I don't think so," she argued. "Look, Matt. They must have signed up for the tour because they were following John. Jillian threw herself at him to get some information from him about the scroll. When word spread that he visited my room the other night in Colport, they could have thought John and I were in the deal together. So they get rid of the stronger link—John—and figure..."

"You won't be a problem?"

Bri gave him a feisty look. "Like hell, I won't."

Matt felt a mix of anxiety and respect for her. "Okay, I grant you it certainly sounds like they're up to no good. But we're still..."

"I know. We're still filling in an awful lot of blanks from that conversation they had. But we did hear Kyle say Jillian didn't have to throw herself at him. *Him* had to mean John. We both saw her..."

"She played up to Tim Campbell a couple of times as well," Matt commented.

Bri saw that she wasn't going to win Matt over easily. "I guess we'll know more after we check out the kind of perfume Jillian wears," Bri mused, tapping her index finger against her lips. "Not that it would be concrete proof.

Someone else could have deliberately used the same scent as Jillian's. To throw us off guard. That would be clever. And not that I'm being catty here, but Jillian Knight doesn't impress me as the clever type. On the other hand, Kyle Dunner might be a different story.''

She caught Matt's smile and gave him a puzzled look. ''What?''

''I like the way you said, throw *us* off guard.''

Bri hadn't said it deliberately. The *us* had just come out. Maybe now that the focus had shifted to Kyle and Jillian as suspects, she was relaxing her guard a little. And maybe she didn't want to cope with her terrors all alone. It wasn't so easy to feel self-reliant when you were being stalked by killers.

She sat back down on the bed and slowly met his gaze. ''I'm more scared than I'm letting on, you know.''

''I know,'' Matt said softly, cupping her chin. ''You're going to be okay.''

''It's a nice thought,'' she muttered.

He smiled with a mix of tenderness and seductiveness in equal measure. ''I'm having a lot of nice thoughts about you.''

''Matt, this is no time for...childish flirtation,'' she scolded. ''Kyle Dunner said he means to take care of me. And if that's true, something tells me he doesn't mean tender, loving care.'' She looked at Matt earnestly. ''What are we going to do?'' Her voice trembled just enough to tell him she was fighting for control.

Matt had the urge to take her in his arms again, but he knew he'd be pushing his luck. Holding Bri Graham felt too good. He might not be so honorable next time around. Instead he took her hand, kissed her palm lightly, then wrapped her fingers around his flask.

Bri was both disappointed and grateful that Matt didn't take advantage of her obvious vulnerability. She took a long swallow of the brandy. This time she didn't cough. It actually felt good going down. If she didn't watch out, she'd start picking up Matt's vices.

"Here's tip number two," Matt said softly, taking a swallow of brandy after her. "A good sleuth doesn't jump to conclusions. First you were sure that Steve Palmer was our boy. And now you're sure..."

"Hold on. I'm not sure about anything just yet. And I'm not writing Steve Palmer off completely, either," Bri protested, before he finished. "The point is, you thought the same thing I thought when Kyle said he'd take care of *her* when the time was right. *Her* is me. When the time is right, he's going to take care of me. Most likely meaning, when I turn over the scroll. Which I can't very well do, even if I wanted to, since I don't have it," she said pointedly. "Everything would be a lot simpler if I did."

He playfully tapped her chin. "Tip number three, Sherlock. Nothing's ever as simple as it seems in the dirty game of murder and mayhem." He smiled enigmatically. "Except when it is."

Bri raised her eyes to the ceiling. "That's a big help. Maybe if you didn't get all your tips from mystery novels, we'd make more headway."

"Whoa," he protested. "I am a professional investigator, my dear. I've solved many a case in my day."

"How many of them were murder cases?" she countered.

"Are we going to quibble about numbers?" He took another swallow of brandy, wiped his lips with the back of his hand, then offered her the flask. She hesitated, then took another swallow. It took the edge off her terror. Or maybe it was Matt who was doing that.

"Besides," he went on, "I didn't get all my tips from dear old Agatha. I often work on cases with one of Boston's most renowned private eyes. He happens to be doing some legwork for me on this very case."

"Don't tell me. Let me guess who this famous shamus is. Spenser?"

He looked puzzled. "Who's Spenser?"

"A fictional sleuth who made it to a television series for a long stretch."

"I'm talking flesh-and-blood here, Bri. I'll even introduce you to him tomorrow. We've got a meeting set up in the afternoon over at the Chinese restaurant in town. If we're lucky, he might have some dope for us on Kyle and Jillian. And maybe even some surprises about the others." He eyed her speculatively. "So, is it a date?"

There was the briefest hesitation on her part. "You're on."

He smiled. "I think we're making some progress here," he murmured.

Bri wasn't sure just what kind of progress he meant. She began to feel edgy. And a little light-headed from all those swallows of brandy. She was also acutely aware of the fact that she and Matt were sitting here on her bed, in the dark, practically shoulder-to-shoulder...

The air was absolutely still, quiet, just their breathing. Intermingling. Their eyes met and held. They both knew they were staring at trouble.

"You must be beat. You ready to turn in?" That wasn't really what he wanted to ask.

Bri wasn't sure what she wanted to hear, but she gave him a cautious look, then nodded.

He had difficulty pulling his eyes from her face, but finally they shifted to the phone on her bedside table. "If you need me, just dial my room...103. Okay?" He was feeling very honorable, but not very happy.

She nodded, unaware that she was holding her breath.

"Any time of the night. Even if it's just a bad dream. I'll come over and . . . hold your hand."

She quirked a smile, still not breathing.

"Unless . . . ?" He gave her a questioning look.

She had no trouble interpreting what was on his mind. The same thing was on her mind, too. It might be easier if he just stuck around. Save them both the bother of a phone call.

She was tempted. The weight of a scary night alone in her room loomed over her. Maybe if that's all it was, she would have said stay, following it up with a clear set of ground rules. But she wasn't only feeling fear. She was feeling lust. And that made her as unlikely to follow any ground rules as she knew it made Matt.

Her breath came out in a whoosh. "I'll remember . . . 103. Good night."

AT A QUARTER TO SEVEN in the morning, the phone rang in Matt's room. He picked it up on the first ring.

"Bri?"

"You up, Matt?" Not even *hello,* but then Joe Holland didn't earn points as a private eye for his good manners.

Matt rubbed his face with his free hand and sat up in bed. "Yeah, I'm up."

"Then throw something on and get over here."

"Where's here?" Matt asked, tossing off the covers.

"The Grange Hall a couple of miles outside of town. Follow Main Street to the Old Fowler Road, cross an old covered bridge, and it's about a hundred yards on your right. I'll be parked around back."

"Why are we meeting way out there?"

"The Chinese restaurant ain't open for breakfast," Holland said dryly.

But Matt knew there was more going on than the private eye was saying. Holland definitely had a reason for

wanting to meet in a secluded spot. Matt guessed he was
playing it safe rather than sorry. Which meant he'd found
something out. Something hot.

"Okay. Twenty minutes. I'll have to bike over."

"I've got quite an earful for you, kid," Holland closed.
As if Matt hadn't guessed.

Within five minutes of hanging up, Matt was dressed in
a gray sweat suit and out of his room, making his way
stealthily down the corridor. As he passed Bri's room, he
hesitated. Last night he'd offered to bring her along for his
meeting with Joe. But something about the urgency and
caution in the private eye's voice, and the switch in time
and locale, made Matt decide it would be wiser and possibly even safer to leave Bri behind. Besides, she was
probably still sound asleep. He figured he'd be back before she even woke up, and she wouldn't be any the wiser.

BRI HAD BEEN UP since six. By six-thirty she began to feel
claustrophobic pacing around in her room and decided to
get dressed, go downstairs, make herself a cup of tea from
the complimentary setup in the lobby and watch the sun
rise from the front porch. The start of a new day. Hopefully a better one.

Something she'd resolved during her mostly sleepless
night did help her feel better. She was not going to simply
sit back and let others protect her. She was going to take
an active hand in getting to the bottom of this mystery. As
for teaming up with Matt, she decided that as long as she
was cautious and not overly trusting, she might get further working with an experienced investigator than going
it alone. If, in the process of working together, he turned
out to be untrustworthy, she could always turn to Chief
Mead.

Dressed in jeans and a heavy, white, cable-knit sweater,
she sat contentedly on one of the porch rockers, sipping

her tea, watching the dawn settle over the autumn-hued hills. Comforted by the sight of the Thornhill patrolman sitting behind the wheel of the cruiser in the driveway, Bri didn't have to worry about someone sneaking up on her with a pillow or anything else. Even though the policeman had dozed off, one scream and she was sure he'd be awake and out of the car, his gun at the ready.

When she finished her tea, she decided on a refill and was just about to step back inside the house when she spotted Matt coming down the front stairs. She was about to walk in and greet him, when something about his furtive manner held her back. He was looking cautiously over the banister, checking around the hall as if to make sure no one was around. He appeared to Bri to be a man who didn't want to be spotted. He appeared to be a man on a mission.

Bri instinctively ducked back from the glass-paneled front door as he looked in her direction, although she realized there was no point in hiding from him since he would see her as soon as he came out of the house.

Only he didn't come out. Perplexed, Bri peeked inside and saw him heading for the back service door at the far end of the hall. She frowned. What was he up to? She knew that she was going to have to find out the answer.

Behind the house in a small storage shed were a half dozen old bikes provided by the inn for the guests to use during their stay. Bri hid just inside the back door, peering out the window panel as Matt rode off on one of them. She noticed he avoided the path that led around to the driveway where the cruiser was parked, taking a circuitous route instead, skirting the house altogether.

Bri hadn't been on a bike in years, but the old saying was true. It was something you never forgot. Keeping a safe distance from Matt, she had no trouble following him as he rode down Main Street and then veered to the right at the cutoff for the Old Fowler Road. She maintained her distance, comforted by the fact that if he did chance to glance back, he was likely not to recognize her, since she'd donned a baseball cap she'd borrowed off a shelf at the inn and tucked all her hair under it. He would think she was just a local, out for a little exercise.

Bri knew she was going to feel pretty foolish if this mission of Matt's turned out to be nothing more than his early-morning exercise. And if that were the case, she wondered forlornly just how many miles he might bike. While she was holding her own, she wasn't exactly in marathon shape for a twenty-mile ride. After even a few miles she would certainly start to feel it. By tomorrow, she might be *sorely* regretting this excursion.

She was debating with herself about how much farther she could go, when she saw him pull off the road at the Grange Hall. Bri had been to the Grange Hall with John during their honeymoon to see a local theater company perform a mystery play. *Rockabye Baby.* The play, which was directed by none other than Mildred Mead and starred her daughter and son-in-law, was done as a benefit once a year for a local charity. Mildred had given Bri and John complimentary tickets, delighting in telling the newlyweds about the very first performance of the play a couple of years back and how a fifty-year-old murder had been solved before the curtain had come down for the final act.

The night Bri and John were at the play, the Grange Hall had been alive with activity and people and there was an air of gaiety about the place. Now, in the early-morning light, an eerie quiet dropped over the silent landscape. The large whitewashed brick building and the broad, empty parking lot beside it stood out starkly against a backdrop of a hardwood forest.

Bri waited at the other end of the Ryder Bridge as she watched Matt bike around to the back of the building. She frowned. What could he be doing at a farmer's Grange Hall cum theater at seven-fifteen in the morning?

MATT DIDN'T like it. Joe Holland had told him he'd be parked behind the Grange Hall, which Matt took to mean the private eye would be there inside his car waiting for him. But Joe's car was empty. And Joe wasn't in sight.

What really worried Matt was seeing that the key was still in the ignition. Okay, the car was no Jaguar. It was a beat-up five-year-old Ford. Still, no city slicker, never mind a private eye, would ever leave the key in the ignition, even in a deserted spot in a sleepy little country hamlet. It was like hanging out a sign on your car—Take Me, I'm Yours.

Matt glanced over at the back of the Grange Hall. The metal emergency door was shut tight. He figured it was locked, but he went over to check it, anyway.

No give on the door. He was growing more and more uneasy by the minute. Where the hell was Holland? Why couldn't a case of his go smoothly for once? He reached inside his leather jacket and pulled out his trusty semiautomatic, thinking to himself as his eyes skirted the woods behind Joe Holland's car that the only thing he felt good about at the moment was that he hadn't brought Bri along.

BRI HAD serious reservations about continuing her pursuit of Matt Sebastian. Some inner voice cautioned her to turn her bike around and ride back to the inn. But she'd resolved earlier to take an active hand in the investigation. Besides, she'd come this far and she had to see what Matt was up to behind the Grange Hall, even though she was more than a little anxious about finding out. Okay, so she wanted him to be trustworthy. At least she wouldn't do with Matt what she'd so foolishly done with John—stick her head in the sand like an ostrich and pretend that everything would work out fine.

Leaving her bike in the shrubbery off the side of the road, she made it across the old covered bridge on foot. About a hundred yards from the Grange, she decided it would be smart to cut a path through the woods that circled the parking lot so that she could maintain her cover.

She took a few indecisive steps, conscious of the crunching sound of the fallen leaves under her feet. She proceeded even more cautiously, wondering with each step about the folly of her investigation.

MATT STOPPED DEAD in his tracks a few feet into the woods and stared down at the object on the ground. He knelt and picked it up. It was a pair of nail clippers. Matt scowled. They could have belonged to anyone, but he knew for a fact that Holland always kept a pair of nail clippers on him. Coincidence? Matt didn't think so. His uneasiness gave way to out-and-out worry as he pocketed the clippers and moved deeper into the woods, trying to be as quiet as possible. It was a pretty good bet that Joe Holland was out here somewhere, maybe bound and gagged, maybe hurt... maybe worse. And maybe not alone.

Matt figured that if someone had overheard Joe's phone call or had even just spotted him in the phone booth out by the front of the Grange Hall, that someone would know Joe wasn't hanging around out here for his health. That someone would know that Joe was expecting company. Now it was up to Matt to surprise that someone before he ended up being surprised.

BRI SAW MATT'S BIKE on the ground near the beat-up sedan parked behind the Grange Hall. She noted the Massachusetts license plate, not that it afforded much of a clue. Assuming that Matt was inside the car talking with someone, she kept edging around the periphery of the woods, dodging behind tree after tree as she angled for a better vantage point so that she could see who Matt had biked here to meet.

She was behind a large oak about fifteen feet from the car. From where she was standing she had no trouble seeing inside the sedan, which meant she had no trouble seeing that it was empty.

She didn't get it. Where was Matt? Where was the driver of the beat-up sedan? Had they gone off together? On foot? Why? And maybe the most unsettling question of all—what was she doing here, quaking in her running shoes, playing amateur sleuth?

Just as she came to her senses and resolved to quit playing and get out of there she heard a piercing sound coming from the woods. An all too familiar sound. One she'd heard two nights ago as she was standing at John's door. It was the chilling sound of gunfire. Terror flooded over her, holding her frozen in its grip.

Two possibilities flashed through her mind. Matt had shot the person he'd come out here to meet. Or the p1erson Matt had come out here to meet had shot him. Neither possibility offered any comfort. And, in either case, she was likely to be the next target if she was discovered.

When she heard the second shot, Bri's survival instincts overcame her frozen fear. Keeping low, she fought her impulse to dash out of the woods, knowing that she'd be all too easy to spot racing across the flat, unprotected parking lot. As ominous as the forest felt to her now, she knew she was safer making her way back to the road moving in a stealthy, serpentine fashion through the woods.

As she inched along on shaky legs, she tried not to think of Matt lying out there under some tree in a pool of blood. Wounded. Possibly... dead. Then again, it was almost as awful imagining him as the gunman, shooting someone in cold blood. Shooting her if she wasn't very careful. And to think she'd been only a breath away from spending last night with him.

Her jaw clenched as she tried not to think about anything but getting safely away, biking as fast as she could to the police station and leaving the terrifying, seemingly endless trail of murder and mayhem in Chief Harvey Mead's lap. So much for her brief and none-too-sterling career as a sleuth.

A swooping sound of a hawk overhead made her look up for a moment, causing her to trip over a fallen log. Her hands shot out to cushion her fall. But they never hit the ground. They hit something else. Or more accurately—someone.

The scream of horror escaped her mouth before she could stop it.

The scream got knocked out of her as hard hands gripped her mouth and throat, pulling her from the splayed body lying in the fallen leaves and flattening her face-down to the ground.

She struggled, her baseball cap flying off, her auburn hair tumbling down. Abruptly, her captor's hold on her loosened. "Damn it, Bri. What the hell are you doing here? With that baseball cap on, I thought you were the character taking pot shots at me." He kept his voice to a low whisper.

Bri rolled over now that she wasn't pinned down and stared up at Matt. "I thought you were the character taking pot shots at me," she whispered back.

She still wasn't convinced he wasn't. Especially when she saw the gun gripped in his right hand.

"Stay down," Matt ordered as he shifted over to the bulky middle-aged man on the ground beside her and felt for a pulse.

"Is he . . . ?" Bri whispered.

"He's alive. But his pulse is weak. We've got to get him out of here and to the hospital." Matt didn't sound optimistic about the odds of doing that successfully.

"Who is he?"

A shadow crossed Matt's face, but Bri couldn't quite interpret it. "The private eye I told you about last night. His name's Joe Holland," he answered in a staccato voice.

Bri ran her tongue over dry, cut lips, her eyes instinctively dropping to the gun in Matt's hand.

"Don't tell me you think I shot him?" Matt gave her an incredulous look.

"Who did?"

"I don't know, but I don't think we ought to hang around to find out." He started to rise.

"Where are you going?" she asked anxiously. "You can't just leave this poor man . . ."

"I'm going to make a running dash for Joe's car and I'm going to drive as close to this spot as I can. Then you're going to help me drag him inside and hopefully we're going to make a clean getaway."

She gripped his sweatshirt sleeve. "What if you don't make it to the car?"

"That means you're at least considering the possibility I wasn't the one who shot poor Joe." He gave her a quick peck on the cheek. "See, you trust me more than you realize."

Two minutes later—minutes that felt like a lifetime to Bri—Matt managed to squeak the car between a couple of birches within a few feet of the injured man. They half dragged, half carried him to the car.

Once they all got inside and Matt started to back out, Bri breathed a sigh of relief.

Matt gave her a sideways glance and said, "We're not out of the woods yet."

As if to punctuate his point, a shot pinged against the right front fender.

Chapter Ten

"We seem to be seeing a lot of each other lately," Dr. Noah Bright said to the threesome—Chief Mead, Matt and Bri—in the hospital corridor.

"How is Joe doing, Doc?" Matt asked anxiously.

"We're going to have to perform surgery to remove the bullet. I'm afraid we'll have to wait and see how well he comes through that. Then the next forty-eight hours will be crucial."

"Is it possible to talk with him just for a minute or two before you wheel him in for surgery, Noah?" Chief Mead asked.

"He's already on his way. Best in those kinds of cases not to waste any time. Every second counts."

Bri glanced over at Matt. His expression was stoic but she could see pain in his eyes. Or was it . . . fear?

"Did he say anything to you or anyone else here?" the chief inquired.

Noah shook his head. "He was out cold when Mr. Sebastian and Miss Graham brought him in. He didn't regain consciousness. Sorry, Chief. I really have to go. I won't be performing the surgery, but I'll be assisting."

Before Noah took off, he gave Bri a careful look. "I'm not so sure we should have released you yesterday. You still look shaky." His eyes narrowed. "And you've got some bruises."

"I tripped over...a log," Bri muttered. "I'm fine, Doctor. Really."

As Noah started off, Matt stopped him to ask how long the operation was likely to take.

"About four hours. And then another couple of hours in recovery. I can give a call over to the inn to let you know how he's doing. But I should also contact a relative."

"Like I told the nurse when we brought him in, Joe has nobody," Matt said. "No relatives, that is. I'm probably as close to kin as he's got."

Noah nodded, gave Matt's shoulder a squeeze and hurried off.

As Matt and Bri turned to go, they found Chief Mead wedged between them. "Not so fast, you two. We need to have a little chat over at the police station."

BRI SIGHED. "I told you, Chief Mead. I saw Matt take off on his bike and I decided to follow him. I was...curious."

Matt scowled. "You weren't just curious, Bri. You were suspicious."

She glared at him. "If you recall, you'd invited me to come along to meet your private eye friend. Why'd you change your mind? Why'd you decide...?"

"Because I was worried that exactly what happened would happen."

Chief Mead held up his hand. It was almost as hard getting a word in edgewise with these two as it was with his wife and his mother. He focused his frustrated gaze on Matt. "What made you suspect there'd be trouble?"

"I heard it in Joe's voice when he phoned me at the inn this morning," Matt said. "We were supposed to meet in town in the afternoon. I knew something was up when he wanted me to meet him posthaste in an out-of-the-way spot. My guess is someone saw the two of us talking down in Colport, found out Joe was a private eye, got nervous that he might dig something up, then spotted him up here in Thornhill and tailed him out to the Grange Hall.''

"Did your pal dig something up?'' Chief Mead asked quietly, scrutinizing Matt.

"I never got a chance to find out.'' Once again Matt went over his movements from the time he got to the Grange Hall. "I knew someone was out there in the woods besides Joe. Joe didn't disappear without help. So, I went looking for him. I'd just . . . stumbled upon Joe when I heard footsteps, so I ducked behind a tree trunk and when I saw this figure in a baseball cap . . .'' He glanced at Bri who still didn't appreciate his football-style tackle. Nor did she like the fact that Matt didn't mention his gun.

"See anyone else?'' the chief persisted.

"No, but we heard someone else,'' Matt said. "Whoever shot Joe hit his car as we were pulling out.''

Chief Mead folded his hands together on the desk. "It certainly does seem like somebody thought your private investigator friend knew something and was anxious not to have him share it.''

"That's what I've been saying,'' Matt said, a hint of irritability and strain in his voice.

"Any ideas what he might have found out?''

Matt shrugged. "No.'' He stared down at his scuffed shoes. "And I'm worried that we may never find out,'' he finished in a low, husky voice. He went to light a cigarette but then he saw the small No Smoking sign on the Chief's desk.

Harvey smiled regretfully. "Mildred. She and the former surgeon general are a good match.''

Matt nodded, sticking the cigarette back in the pack.

"It's a bad habit, anyway,'' Bri muttered.

Matt's irritability was getting the best of him. "So is sticking your nose where it doesn't belong," he snapped. "You could have gotten yourself killed out there in the woods today. I almost took a shot at you myself."

Bri glanced over at the chief to see if he would pick up on Matt's mention of his gun, but he didn't.

"What gives with you, anyway?" Matt went on angrily. "You're not a cat, you know. You don't have nine lives."

Bri glared at him. She was about to argue, but then she stopped short. "No," she said quietly.

At first, both men thought her response was in answer to Matt's remark, but they were wrong.

"I don't think I would have gotten killed this morning," she said, surprising the two men.

"Bri, what are you talking about?" Matt countered.

She looked calmly at him, although inwardly she was anything but. "Whoever was out there in the woods this morning had plenty of opportunity to take aim at me before we all got in the car and were pulling out. I think that the car was shot at just as a scare tactic. Someone wants me scared enough to come up with the scroll."

She looked at the chief. "What with everything that happened this morning I almost forgot to tell you about the note."

Matt nodded. "Right, the note."

Harvey had to contain his frustration. Why was it that he was always the last to know, when he was the one supposedly in charge. "What note?"

"Last night Matt and I found a note in my room." But almost immediately Bri amended her statement. "Well . . . that is, Matt found it." She shot a glance at Matt, a shiver zigzagging down her spine. It was possible, she realized, that Matt had planted the note there himself. Maybe he thought that if she was scared enough, she would turn to him, confide in him, even tell him where the missing scroll was hidden. With that suspicion came one that was even worse. She still wasn't sure that it wasn't Matt who gunned down his supposed friend, private eye Joe Holland, in the woods this morning. Even if another shot did hit the car as Matt was pulling out. He could be working with an accomplice. Or accomplices. Say, for instance, Jillian Knight and Kyle Dunner. What if Matt had arranged that encounter between the two to help build her fear to a fever pitch? Why, he could even have been the one who'd put that pillow over her face in the hospital. She certainly knew how to pick them, she thought morosely.

"Bri?"

The chief's sharp voice jolted her back to the present. "Yes?"

"I asked you if you had the note on you?"

"The note?" She gave the chief a vague look. "Oh. No. No, I left it back in my room at the inn. I was going to bring it over to you this morning, but then . . ."

"I know," Harvey Mead intoned. "You decided to go bike riding instead."

"I can give you the gist of the note, Chief," Matt said.

I bet you can, Bri thought cynically.

Matt not only did a good job of reciting the note practically word-for-word, but then he went on to do the same regarding the conversation they'd overheard the previous night between Jillian Knight and Kyle Dunner.

Bri wasn't sure whether Matt sensed her suspicions, but when he was done, he looked over at her and saw fit to add, "I happen to have a photographic memory. One of the pluses in my line of work."

Chief Mead raised a shaggy salt-and-pepper eyebrow. "When you're not on suspension, you mean."

Matt scowled. "I'm sure once I give my boss the lowdown on what's happening—which I intend to do as soon as we're finished here—he'll rescind my suspension, Chief Mead. Recouping that scroll is worth a bundle to my company. And it would be a professional coup for me. Maybe even keep me from getting suspended again at the whim of some sleazy politician.''

The chief took a moment to frame what he wanted to say next. "I've got a lot more worrisome things going on here in Thornhill than a missing scroll, Sebastian. I've got a murder and a couple of attempted murders. Now maybe this million-dollar piece of paper is at the root of my problems and maybe it's not. But my job is to track down the murderer and see to it, to the very best of my ability, that no one else gets hurt.''

"Joe Holland happens to be someone I care a lot about, Chief,'' Matt said carefully. "I want to find the person who shot him as much—if not more—than you do.'' He gave Bri a swift glance. "And I don't want anything bad to happen to anyone else, either. I intend to see to that, to the best of *my* ability,'' he said firmly. Then, he rose from his seat, placing his hands palms down on Harvey's desk. "Now, unless you've got any more questions for me at the moment, Chief, I'd like to get out of here and have a smoke.''

"I FOUND OUT a couple of things that might interest you,'' Harvey Mead said to Bri after Matt took off. "In the light of what Sebastian told me this morning, it helps me begin to fit some of the pieces together.''

Bri waited expectantly.

"It's about Adam Quinn,'' Harvey went on after a pause. "Before he died he was dating a young woman. A very pretty redhead. From the police report I got sent up from Boston, it seems she was the one who identified the body because his next of kin, being his elderly mother, was away on a trip and couldn't be reached.''

Bri remained silent, but her gaze was fixed intently on the chief.

"Care to take a guess who the pretty redheaded girl-friend is, Bri?"

She nodded faintly, but it took a couple of moments for her to get the name out. "Jillian Knight?"

There was a ghost of a smile on the chief's face.

Bri hardly noticed. Her mind began to race. "Adam Quinn must have known about the scroll and mentioned it to Jillian."

"Or she might have overheard him talking to someone else about it," the chief commented.

Bri acknowledged the possibility with a nod and went on. "When John skipped town, Quinn must have thought John had run off with the scroll."

"So, I imagine, did Sebastian."

Bri frowned. "Only they were both wrong. Otherwise John wouldn't have come back looking for it, certain I had it." But then she had a thought.

"What is it, Bri?"

"I was thinking of that carton of junk I left with Adam Quinn. What if the scroll was hidden in one of those items? What if he found it?"

"You think maybe Quinn didn't just happen to be in the wrong place at the wrong time when he was gunned down? You think it was a setup?"

"Was the gunman who held up the convenience store ever found?"

"No. And unfortunately it's likely to end up another of Boston's unsolved crimes."

Bri sighed wearily. "There's only one problem."

Harvey gave her a sardonic look. "Only one?"

"If Adam had unearthed the scroll, why did Jillian and Kyle Dunner sign up for the tour? Why do they think I have the scroll?"

"Maybe Quinn didn't let Jillian know."

"If our theory is right that he was killed because of the scroll, then somebody knew. And Jillian was certainly close to him."

"Hold on. You're going too fast here. It isn't *our* theory yet."

But Bri waved off the chief's remark. "And having seen Jillian in operation, my bet is there wasn't much Adam would have or could have kept from her."

"So, you're saying if she knew he had it, there would have been no point in her coming on the tour and threatening you. If she is threatening you, that is?"

Bri's brow creased. "What I haven't figured out is where Kyle Dunner fits in."

"Maybe Jillian was two-timing Quinn," the chief suggested.

"He doesn't exactly seem her type."

Harvey rubbed his jaw. "Maybe he isn't exactly the type he seems to be."

Bri smiled. "How true, Chief. You're very astute."

Harvey grinned. "For a country cop?"

Bri flushed.

"Well, Bri, I think you're very astute, too. For a young city gal who's unwittingly got herself caught between a rock and a hard place." He gave her a sympathetic smile, but it didn't last long. "Astute enough, I sincerely hope, to leave this ugly and dangerous business in my hands."

Bri made no response.

"I've got too few men to keep up this round-the-clock surveillance, Bri. Not to mention that my boys keep falling asleep on the job. But I do think you need some protecting."

"I know what I did this morning was stupid, Chief Mead. I should have phoned you the minute I saw Matt take off."

"None of us always does what we should do, Bri. We get swayed by curiosity, by fear, by suspicion." He deliberately paused, giving her a particularly meaningful look. "And by desire."

Bri could feel her cheeks heat up. "There's nothing going on between me and Matt, Chief."

Harvey smiled crookedly. "My guess is not for want of trying. On Sebastian's part, I mean."

"Yes," she muttered cynically. "And I think we both know why."

Now it was the chief's turn to blush.

"Oh," Bri said hurriedly, "I didn't mean...I meant he's trying to get close to me because he still thinks I'm holding out on the scroll." She had some other troubling suspicions about Matt Sebastian, but she couldn't bring herself to say them aloud. When she glanced at the shrewd police chief, she had the feeling he was having some similar suspicions.

He gave her a close look. "You aren't holding out on me, are you, Bri?"

She thought he was talking about Matt, and she hesitated.

Harvey sighed. "If that scroll were turned over to the rightful owner, meaning that museum over in Cairo, Bri, it could very well save some lives."

"If I had the scroll, Chief, believe me, I'd turn it over to you on the spot," Bri said earnestly. "I know perfectly well that one of those lives that could be saved is my own." The strain and fear showed on her face.

He tended to believe she was telling the truth. That didn't mean he was always right about people. That only happened in ten-cent novels. She could surprise him. In fact, he had a feeling there were more than a few surprises yet in store for him on this case—a realization that did not please him one iota.

Bri was at the door when Harvey called to her.

"Like I said before, Bri. I can't give you personal round-the-clock protection from my small force. However, and I'm not saying as how I like it particularly, it seems my wife, Mildred, has taken it into her head to keep a personal watch out for you. For the next few days she's planning to camp out over at the inn. In the room next door to you."

"Really, Chief Mead . . ."

"Just so you know, my Mildred's a real light sleeper. And if she thinks anything's amiss, she won't waste any time phoning me." What he didn't add was his irrepressible wife probably also wouldn't waste any time sticking her nose in where it didn't belong. But after thirty-seven years, he knew it would just be wasting his breath to try to stop her.

"I really don't think that's necessary," Bri protested. "I intend to be very careful to lock my door and windows every night. And not to have any guests in my room."

Harvey caught the import of that remark as she knew he would, but he merely smiled. "Then Mildred will sleep like a baby and so will you."

Bri sighed. "Fine."

"As for during the day, Mildred will be around the inn. And I strongly suggest you stick close by it yourself. For your own protection."

"I don't really see how that will protect me, Chief, since it seems to me some person or persons staying at the inn are the very ones who intend to do me harm." She looked at him wearily. "But then, wherever I go, I suppose I won't really be out of harm's way. Not until this is all over."

Harvey went to his window and looked down at the street after Bri walked out. He hated to admit it but he had to agree with her there.

MATT WAS LEANING against a lamppost in front of the police station when Bri came out. He snubbed out his cigarette on the post and tossed it in a trash can as she started down the steps.

Bri had hoped Matt would have taken off. Her head was swarming with suspicions about him at the moment, and she was in no condition to pretend that nothing was troubling her.

"We need some breakfast," he said, coming up to her and slipping his hand through her arm.

"I'm not hungry."

"Then I'll eat and you can watch."

"Really, Matt. I'm...drained. I just want to go back to the inn and crawl into bed."

"I suppose we can have breakfast in bed if you prefer," he bantered.

She looked over at him. Did he really have no idea of her suspicions about him?

"Hey, that was a joke."

"Your friend's life is hanging on a string. Do you really think this is a time for joking?"

He grabbed her by the shoulders right there in front of the police station. "Look, Bri, you want to have it out with me, then let's just get it over with. You think people never joke when they're hurting? Well, you're wrong. Sometimes you've got to joke to keep from crying."

As abruptly as he'd grabbed her, he let her go and stormed off down the street. Bri, more shaken by his words than his actions, stood there and watched him cross the street to a small coffee shop that was part of a new strip mall.

WHEN SHE SLID into the booth across from him, there was a cup of coffee and a muffin waiting for her.

"Are you always so sure of yourself?" she asked.

Matt was buttering his muffin. He stopped, licked his fingertip and glanced up at her. "No. But I'm still young enough to hope."

"I wouldn't hope for too much," she said pointedly.

He took a long and very slow breath. "Okay, you're having some serious second thoughts about me since last night. You're thinking I stole off this morning and took that shot at poor old Joe. With malice aforethought. Motive and opportunity."

He blithely resumed buttering his muffin in a studied, meticulous fashion. Bri watched the process with silent attentiveness. "You figure Joe wasn't working for me, at all. Maybe, even, that my company hired him to investigate the missing scroll after they suspended me. And Joe got wise to me. Maybe dug up some proof linking me to Fossier's murder. So I had to do him in."

She looked up at him.

He broke off a piece of the buttered muffin and popped it into his mouth. "You could put in a call to my boss, Leonard, Bri. He can tell you Joe wasn't working for them. To tell you the truth, he's not all that crazy about Joe Holland. Sometimes Joe's methods are a bit...unorthodox, and I happen to work for a company that plays it by the book. Leonard's not going to be pleased to know I've hooked up with Joe again. But then he's probably not going to be too pleased that I'm working on company business while I'm on suspension."

"I thought you were going to phone him and he was going to be only too eager to take you off suspension now that he knows you're hot on the trail of the scroll," Bri countered.

He took another bite of the muffin, following it with a swallow of coffee. So far, Bri hadn't touched her breakfast. Matt said, "I did call. Leonard's out of town. He'll be back in a few days."

"How convenient."

He finished off his muffin and eyed hers. "Are you going to eat yours?"

"No."

"I can order another one for myself if you want it."

"I don't."

"Maybe you prefer an English muffin. Or some eggs?"

"I don't want anything." She slid the plate with the muffin across the table to him and started to rise, but Matt grabbed her wrist.

"You've got it wrong, Bri. You've got it all wrong. I hope to God Joe comes through and he'll tell you just what I'm telling you. What worries me is that while we're waiting and while you're so busy not trusting me, something bad could happen to you. And making sure nothing bad happens to you is beginning to mean a lot to me."

Bri sat back down and frowned. "We've got company," she muttered just before Eleanor McDermott and her sister, Harriet, got to their table. The two women were dressed in walking suits, Eleanor's a serviceable gray gabardine, her younger sister looking slightly more festive in burnt umber, a lovely silver scarab pinned to her lapel. Eleanor went bare-headed, but Harriet was wearing a rather comical black velvet beret which she chose to wear flat on top of her head instead of at a more typical angle.

"I hope you don't mind if we join you," Eleanor said, slipping into the booth beside Bri before getting a response, at the same time motioning impatiently to her sister to slide in beside Matt.

"Are the rumors true?" Eleanor began almost immediately.

"What rumors?" Bri asked cautiously.

"Another man's been shot dead," Harriet said in a hushed voice.

Bri glanced at Matt, who had gone practically white. "Dead?" he asked harshly.

"Well, we don't know for certain if he's dead," Eleanor corrected. "But we did hear a man was shot in the woods behind the Grange Hall."

"How did you hear it?" Bri asked.

Both elderly women shrugged. "Why, it's all over town. Everyone at the inn is talking about it," Harriet offered.

Eleanor scowled. "Everyone but my granddaughter and that con artist of a young man she's taken up with."

Bri and Matt both stared at Eleanor. "You mean Tim Campbell?" Bri asked.

"I do," Eleanor asserted firmly.

"Now, now, Ellie," Harriet cautioned. "Just because he lied about school..."

"Lied about school?" Matt cut in.

"He's no more enrolled in Harvard—" Eleanor McDermott's pronunciation sounded more like *Hahvahd* "—than my Aunt Margaret, who's been dead for twenty years."

"How do you know?" Bri asked.

"I made some discreet inquiries," Eleanor said superciliously.

Bri frowned. "But I'm sure Chief Mead checked..."

"Oh, there's a Tim Campbell registered at Harvard. Even majoring in biology. And he's on leave for the semester."

"Well?" Matt gave the old woman a puzzled look.

"Well," Eleanor said contemptuously, "the Tim Campbell who attends Harvard happens to be five foot six with a bad case of acne. I have an acquaintance in Boston who paid a visit to his roommate." She gave Bri and Matt a smug look. "I've just come from the office of the chief of police and presented him with my findings. As I've learned in my many travels, one cannot always rely on the local constabulary to acquire all the facts. There was that time a couple of years back when Harriet and I were touring some of the gardens of Louisiana and we were in this small town when one of the tour members discovered her brooch had been stolen . . .''

"And another thing," Harriet remarked, quite ignoring her sister's saga, "he's not very attentive to his mother. Why, they hardly ever say more than two words to each other."

Eleanor did not seem to mind getting back to the topic at hand. "I don't believe for one minute that they're related. If those two are mother and son I'll eat my hat. My sister's hat, that is. It's atrocious, anyway, as I've already told her," Mrs. McDermott announced and then motioned for the waitress. "Now, Harriet, shall we try the oatmeal or the pancakes?"

WHEN BRI AND MATT arrived back at the inn half an hour later, they found Mildred Mead and Anna Campbell sitting side-by-side on rockers on the porch. It was clear from the look on both women's faces that they were aware of the morning's events.

"Terrible business," Anna Campbell muttered. "Was the poor man who was shot at the Grange Hall really a friend of yours, Mr. Sebastian?"

"We knew each other," Matt said noncomittally. He looked over at Mildred. "No word yet from the hospital, I suppose?"

Mildred gave him a sympathetic look. "No. But he's in excellent hands. Especially with the move of the hospital to the new buildings this year, we've got the most up-to-date surgical facilities in the world. Even better, Harvey told me that Dr. Arnold is operating on Mr. Holland. And he's one of the very best."

Anna fidgeted absentmindedly with her cane.

"Is your son up yet?" Bri asked her nonchalantly.

"My son? No. No, I don't think so."

"Oh, a late sleeper," Bri commented blithely.

"Yes. Yes, he is. Was there something you wanted to speak to him about?"

"It's just that I thought he might enjoy seeing Thornhill's science museum. Being a biology major..."

"I'll be sure to mention it to him," Anna said abruptly.

"It looks like you'll have that opportunity sooner than you expected," Mildred commented, her gaze focused on a much awake Tim, dressed in running shorts and a cutoff sweatshirt, jogging up the front path.

Anna Campbell's mouth quirked. "I forgot. He did tell me last night that he might take a morning run." She waved to him as he came up the stairs. "Did you eat any breakfast yet, dear?" she asked her son solicitously.

"I never eat before a run." There was a slight hesitation. "You know that, Mother."

She smiled uneasily. "Yes, I suppose I'm just getting absentminded in my old age."

Tim bussed her cheek. "You're not old, Mother. But you do look tired. Maybe you ought to take a nap. You know what the doctor said."

Again Anna quirked a nervous smile. "You're right. I didn't sleep very well last night."

As she went to rise, her cane fell. Bri bent to pick it up and gave it back to her, then helped her stand, surprised by how little help she needed. But the woman's strength wasn't all that took Bri aback. There was something else. Tim seemed to notice the subtle change in Bri and a shadow of concern crossed his face.

"Here, Mother. Let me help you up to your room," he said solicitously.

When the screen door shut, both Mildred and Matt fixed their gaze on Bri. Those two didn't miss much, either.

"What's wrong, Bri?" Matt asked quietly.

She hesitated. Even with all her suspicions about Matt, something kept drawing her to him. Mildred's gaze remained expectant. She didn't seem to think there was reason for Bri to keep her counsel in Matt's presence.

Bri looked from one to the other. "It's just... Anna Campbell's perfume. It's the scent I smelled in my room last night." And then she flashed back on that incident between John and Anna Campbell a few days back at the Skater Mill Tavern. She remembered the look of hatred on Anna Campbell's face while John was talking to her. Her pulse quickened. Could she have been wrong about Jillian and Kyle masterminding that note? Could Anna Campbell have written it? Was Tim not only not a Harvard student, but not her son, as well? And if so, why the pretense? Who was Tim Campbell? And what was Anna Campbell's real story?

"The note," Bri muttered more to herself than to Mildred and Matt. She dashed into the house.

Matt followed her up to her room and shut her door. She went directly to the bureau where she'd stuck the note last night after Matt had left. She opened the top drawer. After a moment, she began rifling through it, but she knew even as she did it, that it was a waste of time.

The note was gone.

Bri wasn't really surprised. And when she looked over at Matt she saw that neither was he. The first person that came to both their minds was Anna Campbell. Anna had had plenty of time earlier that morning to slip into her room and remove the evidence.

Bri sat down wearily on the bed. So much for that.

Matt came toward her. As Bri watched him approach, she crossed her arms over her chest in an unconscious gesture of self-defense. She was defending herself against herself far more than she was defending herself against Matt. Her crossed arms might possibly keep her attraction to him from getting totally out of control. Despite the insane circumstances, the doubts, the suspicions, the always niggling reminder that he was practically five years younger than she—none of this seemed to get her over the hump of desire.

He was only inches from her when her phone rang. They both jumped, Bri actually getting to her feet.

The call was for Matt. She handed him the receiver. He said hello, listened for a few moments, thanked the caller and hung up.

He glanced at Bri. She was startled to see tears in his eyes.

"He pulled through the operation," he said huskily and went to light a cigarette.

Maybe it was the tears, the vulnerability he dared to expose to her; maybe it was that the intensity of her passion had finally gotten the best of her; maybe she just wanted to help out Mildred and the surgeon general who believed that smoking was harmful to one's health. Whatever, the reason, she took the unlit cigarette from between his fingers, tossed it over her shoulder and put her arms around his neck.

His mouth curved up.

"You have a great smile," she muttered. "And you use it to such damn good effect."

His great smile deepened to even better effect. "Are you trying to tell me that despite everything you find me irresistible?"

"You're too young, too cocky, and I don't trust you any farther than I can throw you. That's three strikes against you, Sebastian."

He grinned crookedly as his arms slipped around her waist. "I can work on the cockiness and I can definitely work on winning your trust. But, I'm afraid, sweetheart, there's not much I can do about the age thing."

She bit her lower lip. When her words finally came, they weren't what she'd planned, what she'd told herself she should say.

"Well...two out of three. I guess it could be worse," she whispered. Their gazes locked.

His hand reached out, floated toward her face. His fingertips skimmed her lips, her cheek, slid around to the back of her neck. She tilted her head up, leaned into him. They kissed and something inside Bri exploded.

She pressed her face against his chest. "This is risky, Matt."

He stroked her hair. "But you and I are risk takers, Bri."

"And look where it's gotten us."

He smiled, pressing her closer. "I can't complain."

She looked up at him, shaking her head ruefully. "What am I going to do with you?"

Before he could answer, she pressed her fingers to his lips and laughed softly. "You think I don't know what answer you'd give?"

He grinned, parting his lips, drawing in her fingertips. A bittersweet agony of longing rolled through her.

His hands slipped under her sweater and T-shirt. His fingers were cool and gentle on her bare back. When he got to the catch of her bra, he undid it with dexterity. Bri was trembling as he lifted her arms high over her head, slipping both the sweater and T-shirt off together. When she dropped her arms, her bra straps slipped from her shoulders, the lacy undergarment falling to the floor.

Matt drew her away from him, boldly admiring her firm, high breasts with their already-hardened, rosy tips. Bri's cheeks were almost the same color. "I wish you wouldn't..."

"You're beautiful, Bri." Slowly his palms moved down from her shoulders until they cupped her breasts. He smiled tenderly. "A perfect fit."

"I'm not . . . in great shape," she muttered. "I looked a lot better five years ago."

His hands were at the catch of her jeans.

Bri's blush deepened. "It's so . . . bright in here." He undid the catch. "Maybe we could draw . . . the curtains." He slid down the zipper. "Wouldn't it be wiser . . . ?" He was drawing her jeans down over her hips, his thumbs looping under her bikini panties so they were coming off along with the jeans. "Oh Matt, I don't know if I'm prepared . . ."

He smiled enticingly. "I am." He slipped a foil packet out of his back pocket.

That wasn't the kind of prepared she was talking about, but she realized it was of equal importance.

She hesitated. "Were you that certain we'd end up in bed, or are you always prepared?"

His smile deepened. "Both. I believe in taking risks, but not foolish ones."

"And you're so sure this . . . isn't foolish?"

"Yes," he answered with unhesitating confidence, letting his gaze travel slowly, provocatively down her body.

Her jeans and panties were scrunched around her ankles, above which she was stark naked. In broad daylight. With a man five years younger and probably in a hell of a lot better shape than her. Feasting on her as if she was the playmate of the month. Maybe even the playmate of the year.

He lifted his sweatshirt over his head. He was bare-chested beneath it. A fine, well-muscled bare chest.

"You work out," she blurted inanely.

He smiled. "More since my suspension. Time on my hands."

She swallowed hard as he slipped off his sweatpants and jockey shorts at the same time, his movements unhurried, deliberate, tantalizing and remarkably uninhibited. Bri fixed her eyes to his sinewy chest as if they were being held there by the force of a giant magnet. She felt too embarrassed to look either up, at what she was certain were his dancing eyes and provocative smile, or down at the rest of his body. She might have moved, turned away, but her ankles were still shackled by her jeans. If she took a step, she would stumble and fall flat on her face. Which she'd already done once that morning.

The image of that fall in the woods, the sight of Joe Holland's bleeding body flashing across her mind, made Bri suddenly shiver. Matt tilted her head up and caught a glimpse of the fear and terror there.

"Bri," he whispered so softly tears immediately sprung to her eyes. She had no idea if he'd read her mind, but when he drew close, their naked bodies pressed together, the shivering abated and he brought her winging gratefully back to the present. As he captured her lips, she responded with an almost savage desire which stunned her. Never before had she felt such an intense overwhelming pull as she did with Matt. Not with any man. Not even with John in the very beginning when she was so sure she was in love.

The room almost crackled with electricity as Matt lifted her in his arms and carried her over to the bed, her jeans and panties slipping off somewhere along the way. She knew she could lose a few pounds, but he seemed to carry her with utter ease, as if she were light as a feather. Maybe she was. She sure felt as though she was floating.

He fell on the bed with her and they both laughed as they bounced against each other on the springy mattress.

But the laughter faded, quickly giving way to a shared trembling desire.

"Oh, Matt," Bri whispered, "this isn't at all the way I planned this fall foliage tour."

His smile sent a throbbing sensation radiating through her body. "The best-laid plans..."

He let the sentence float off as he began to stroke her body, telling her that she was entrancing, beautiful, that she drove him wild. Bri's pulse pounded. She felt light-headed. And nervous. She may have been five years older than Matt, but she was certain she wasn't five years more experienced.

She felt shy, clumsy, anxious. But Matt kept caressing her with long, sinuous strokes, guiding her hands to his body, urging her to feel free to explore, openly expressing his pleasure as she did. Soon she began to relax a little. Touching him and being touched by him felt so good. She was even beginning to enjoy the bright sunlight that streamed into the room, warming their naked bodies. She felt less exposed now, and she delighted in looking at Matt's firm, muscular body.

He was a wonderful lover. Giving and receiving with so much passion and absorption. At some point—she was too enthralled to know when—her inhibitions, wariness and fears vanished. Their bodies shuddered as they boldly caressed each other, her legs entwining around him now as he moved on top of her in slow, erotic motions that drove her wild. And just when she thought she couldn't bear it any longer, his motions intensified, and they both cried out in release at almost the same instant.

For long moments afterward they lay beside each other, not speaking, not wanting to delve too deeply into the irrevocable meaning of the intimate act they had just shared with such abandon.

Chapter Eleven

"What do you think about Anna Campbell?"

Matt rolled over onto his side and grinned at Bri. "Shouldn't we wait to discuss this case until the afterglow wears off a little?"

Bri tucked the blanket modestly over her breasts as she sat up against the pillows. "It was definitely her perfume."

Matt sighed. "And, as you said last night, Jillian or anyone else for that matter, could have swiped some of that perfume to deliberately throw you off track."

"True. But what about what we learned from Mrs. McDermott? If Tim Campbell isn't Tim Campbell . . ."

"It doesn't mean he isn't Anna Campbell's son. There is a slight family resemblance. Both of them have fair hair, they're both tall, thin. They both have blue eyes."

Bri smiled at Matt. "You're very observant."

He grinned, tugging the blanket down from her breasts. "It's both my business and my pleasure."

She pulled the blanket back up, blushing. "I'm not good at this, Matt."

"You're not good at what?"

"Sexy afterglow banter. It . . . embarrasses me. You can make me feel very . . . self-conscious."

"I know," he said softly. "But that's not all I can make you feel."

"See, you're doing it again. Please, Matt."

He smiled contritely. "Okay, we won't talk about probably one of the best sexual experiences of our lives. We'll talk about the Campbells or whoever they are."

Bri nodded. "Good. Now let's consider for a minute the possibility that the two aren't related."

Matt rolled over onto his back, folding his arms behind his head. "Okay. We can consider that possibility."

"So, they each must have had a reason for the ruse. They each..." She stopped abruptly and leveled her gaze on Matt. "What did you mean? *One* of the best sexual experiences?"

A sly smile curled his lips. "I figure we'll get even better with practice."

Matt expected a smile back, but Bri's expression took a very solemn turn. "I don't think so," she said quietly.

"You don't think it will get better?"

"That's not what I meant."

"I know it's not, Bri."

"I have enough...complications in my life, Matt."

"I don't have to be a complication. Maybe I can make life simpler for you."

"Believe me, you can't."

"What if I told you I'm in love with you."

She shook her head.

"What if I told you that I think you're in love with me."

She shook her head even more fiercely.

"Okay, maybe I'd be exaggerating," he admitted. "The kind of love I think we both want takes time. It takes care and nurturing. And trust. But it starts somewhere. I think it's starting here. Right here." He leaned over and lightly kissed her lips before she could protest.

MATT RETURNED to his room to shower and change. Bri did the same in her room. As she was about to head downstairs, there was a knock on her door. She greeted her visitor with a look of surprise.

"Steve."

The track coach looked concerned. "I thought I'd see how you were doing after this morning's . . . incident."

"How did you . . . ?"

"You don't show up at the ER with a man suffering from a gunshot wound in Thornhill and expect that it'll be a secret."

Bri smiled faintly. "He's pulled through the operation, but I suppose you know that, as well."

"I thought you might like to go out for lunch. There's a terrific Chinese restaurant in town."

"Yes, I know. John and I ate there with you and Liz last winter," she said quietly.

Steve's ruddy cheeks got a little ruddier. "I'm sorry, Bri. I should have remembered. We can go somewhere else. I just thought you might like to . . ."

"The Chinese restaurant is fine, Steve. Let's neither of us pretend I'm in deep mourning for John. I feel awful that he was killed, and I want to see whoever did it brought to justice. But whatever feelings I had for him died a long time before he died."

"Do you know why he was . . . murdered?"

She gave Steve a curious look. "You said the other day you'd heard he was into illegal activities. What exactly did you hear?"

Steve hesitated, glancing up and down the corridor. "Why don't we talk over some Hunan beef and wonton soup?"

THE MANDARIN HOUSE was a popular lunchtime spot among the Thornhill locals and the college crowd. When

Bri and Steve got there a little past noon there was already a wait for tables. Steve suggested they try another spot, when Bri spotted Tim Campbell sitting alone at a table for four in the far corner of the main dining room.

"Just a sec. Maybe we can share a table," Bri said to Steve and then took off across the dining room.

"Hi," she said, approaching Tim who was gazing in a lackluster fashion at the menu.

He looked up and gave her a somewhat guarded look. At least that's how Bri interpreted it. "Oh. Hi, Miss Graham."

"Are you meeting some people for lunch? Your mother?"

"No. No, not my mother. She isn't feeling well. She decided to stay back at the inn and rest. The old lady in the wheelchair said she'd fix her something when she got up." As he spoke to Bri his eyes strayed toward the reception area where about a dozen people had gathered waiting for tables. Something in his eyes flickered and then he looked back at Bri.

"I thought Allison was going to join me, but we must have gotten our signals crossed."

"Then would you mind if a friend of mine and I joined you?" Bri asked, knowing that there was no way the young man could politely refuse.

When Bri turned to wave Steve over she wasn't surprised to spot Mildred Mead waiting for a table—and keeping an eye out for her. What did surprise Bri was seeing that Steve Palmer was no longer alone. Both he and newly arrived Liz Armstrong came over to the table together.

Liz shrugged off her jacket. "Lucky break running into Steve. I hope you don't mind if I join the three of you?"

Bri acknowledged the irony of her not being able to refuse Liz any more than Tim had been able to refuse her.

Liz slid in beside Tim, introducing herself to him. They shook hands politely.

"Tim's a biology student at Harvard," Bri commented, noting an edginess in the young man.

Liz smiled disinterestedly.

"You majored in bio for a while at Dorchester, Liz," Steve commented.

Liz opened a menu. "For a short while. Then I switched to journalism."

"What area of biology were you interested in?" Bri asked Liz.

Liz shrugged. "Marine biology."

"Hmmm." Bri glanced over at the young man beside Liz. "What about you, Tim? What area of biology are you studying?"

He gave her an uneasy look. "I'm not really sure yet."

"But aren't you a junior? Surely you've picked an area of interest," Bri persisted.

"I keep changing my mind," Tim answered distractedly. "You know how it is."

Bri was about to say she didn't really, but Liz came to Tim's defense. "I bet you'll end up premed. That's where bio majors usually end up."

"Right. That's probably what I'll end up doing. Nothing wrong with being a doctor."

"Hey, you ought to see our new hospital facility if you're thinking about medicine. It's phenomenal. The locals have dubbed it the Miracle Mile Mall because it's like its own little city," Steve said enthusiastically.

"Speaking of the hospital, how's that private eye doing?" Liz asked Bri.

Bri gave Liz a curious look. Had the rumor spread that the man who she and Matt had brought into the hospital with a gunshot wound was a private investigator? Or did

Liz have some sort of an inside line? "He's still alive, but the doctors say the next forty-eight hours are crucial."

"I wonder if Harvey Mead figures the same guy who shot John shot this investigator," Steve mused.

Tim scowled. "I don't know why we're all being kept in the dark. Does this cop even have any ideas? I mean, are we supposed to be stuck up here for weeks, months...?"

"If Joe Holland regains consciousness," Bri said, "he might be able to shed some light on the mystery."

Steve arched an eyebrow. "You think he knows who killed John?"

The track coach's question made Bri suddenly uneasy. "No. No, I'm sure he doesn't know or he would have contacted Chief Mead from Boston. I just thought he might have... some clues, that's all."

Liz looked around the crowded room and then checked her watch. "It's going to take ages to order. I'm never going to get back to the office on time. I think I'll just head out and grab a sandwich over at Red's."

Bri did not miss the look of disappointment on Steve's face.

"Will I see you tonight at the town meeting?" he asked Liz as he rose and helped her on with her jacket.

"No. I've got a date," she said offhandedly, reaching for her purse.

"I don't blame you for passing up the meeting," Steve muttered, then glanced over at Bri. "How about I skip it, too, and maybe we can take in a movie and dinner instead?"

Bri gave a noncommittal shrug, feeling embarrassed for Steve. His invitation seemed a pathetic attempt to make Liz think he was interested in another woman. Liz didn't even lift an eyebrow. She looked as if she couldn't care less.

Steve sat back down, his expression glum. Bri was certain Steve was still hopelessly in love with Liz. And the question again popped into her mind. Was he jealous enough of Liz's liaison with John the other night to murder him? And what about her date tonight? Was Steve a crazed psychopath who would kill any man that dared to get intimate with his ex-girlfriend? It was, Bri conceded, a little farfetched. But she couldn't rule it out.

When the waiter came over, Tim abruptly decided not to stay for lunch, either. "I guess I'm just not hungry, after all." He gathered up his knapsack without another word and took off.

Steve scowled. "Strange kid."

"He may be upset because he got stood up," Bri muttered, but then she chanced to spot a group of familiar faces at a table across the room. Eleanor McDermott, her sister, Harriet, and her granddaughter, Allison, were finishing up their lunch, Mildred Mead just joining them. Now, isn't that interesting, Bri mused. Allison was in the restaurant all along. So Tim wasn't waiting here for her. Who then, she wondered, was he waiting for?

BRI AND STEVE were halfway through lunch when Bri broached the subject of the rumors Steve had heard about John's illegal activities.

Steve looked uneasy. "This town is renowned for rumors, Bri." He hesitated. "Do you remember when you phoned me last winter? After John . . . disappeared?"

Bri nodded.

"Well, a few weeks after your call, I received a visit from a colleague of John's."

Bri set down her chopsticks. "A colleague?"

"I don't remember his name offhand. A middle-aged fellow, distinguished looking, well dressed."

"Quinn?" Bri asked. "Adam Quinn?"

Steve brightened. "Yes. Now that you mention it, I think that was his name."

"What did he want?"

"He said he was checking into John's disappearance and he was looking up old friends of his, trying to see if anyone had information about him. I asked if he'd gone to the police. You know, to report John missing. I even mentioned that you might have already done that and maybe the police had some information."

"And what did he say?"

Steve frowned. "He said he didn't think you'd gone to the police, nor could he. He believed that John had stolen off with some very valuable relic— I think he said it was something from Greece or...?" He scratched his cheek.

"Egypt?"

"That's it. Egypt."

Bri looked closely at Steve. "You don't remember if it was early April that Adam Quinn came up here?"

He ran his tongue across his bottom lip, thinking. "You know. I think it was sometime early on in April. I remember because I was getting my taxes done when he came over to my office at the college. I'm always doing things like that at the last minute." He gave her a puzzled look. "Why do you ask?"

Bri merely shrugged. "Just curious."

"I'D SAY that proves conclusively that the scroll wasn't in the carton of John's things that I gave Adam Quinn," Bri said, sitting across from Chief Mead in his office. "Quinn must have gone through the carton, come up empty-handed, and then went up to Thornhill to see if he could gather some clues to John's whereabouts."

"So, now you're thinking that Quinn's death was unrelated to the scroll?" the Chief queried.

Bri fidgeted with the small metal No Smoking sign on his desk. "I don't know." She sighed. "I'm confused," she confessed.

"I don't blame you," he admitted. "We've got Jillian Knight, Adam Quinn's ex-lover who's apparently now involved with Kyle Dunner who, it turns out is under investigation by the IRS for tax fraud. Then there's this young man, Tim Campbell, who says he's a Harvard undergrad, but bears no resemblance whatsoever to the real Tim Campbell enrolled at Harvard. So if he isn't Tim Campbell, it puts into serious question whether the woman calling herself Anna Campbell really is Anna Campbell. And if she isn't, who is she? And does she, too, have a deadly interest in acquiring this million-dollar scroll?"

Bri told him about the perfume.

The chief nodded glumly and continued. "Then we've got a teenager who wants to grow up too fast and those two old biddies . . ."

"Don't let them hear you call them that or they'll bite your head off. Especially Eleanor McDermott."

"She's a piece of work, all right. Can you believe her getting a friend from Boston to question Tim Campbell's roommate?"

"I'm sure she'd check out any young man her granddaughter was interested in. She's very protective."

"Reminds me a little of Miss Marple," the chief mused.

"Miss Marple?"

"The detective. From those Agatha Christie mysteries. You've read . . ." He stopped abruptly. "What is it, Bri? You look like you've just seen a ghost."

She gave him a queer look. "No. No, it's just when you mentioned Agatha Christie it reminded me of a book of hers Matt mentioned." She stood up. "Well, I should get back to the inn. I don't want your wife worrying about me."

"Mildred?" He smiled. "She's waiting downstairs to drive you home."

Bri smiled back, then started for the door.

"Speaking about Matt," Chief Mead said as her hand reached for the knob.

She stood there silently, not looking back.

"He can't be ruled out, you know. He had the means. And the motive."

"I don't believe Matt would commit murder," she said quietly, but her whole body was trembling.

"Maybe not. But he does want that scroll. How much he wants it—how far he's willing to go to get his hands on it—that remains to be seen."

Bri closed her eyes. She felt dizzy.

"Are you okay, Bri?"

She pulled herself together. "Yes, I'm okay."

"Good. I want you to stay that way."

She shot the chief a quick look and exited his office.

"ARE YOU SURE you're all right?" Mildred asked with concern as she drove Bri back to the inn. "Maybe it was the Chinese food. It was awfully spicy today. I ended up sharing a table with Eleanor McDermott and her family. They were just finishing up, but they were kind enough to keep me company while I ate."

"Yes, I noticed you'd joined them," Bri murmured.

"Her granddaughter seemed quite glum. I gather Eleanor's put the kibosh on her seeing Tim. Or whoever he is."

"I suppose your husband will be bringing him in for questioning. And Jillian Knight and Kyle Dunner. I don't really understand why he hasn't..."

"He will. In due time," Mildred said confidently.

Bri looked over at her. "What do you mean?"

Mildred smiled conspiratorially. "Sometimes it's best not to give your hand away too quickly. Not let on that you're wise to someone. You don't want to put them on their guard."

Bri nodded. "I see."

"This is quite a complex case," Mildred said excitedly. "Hasn't been anything like it since the *Rockabye Baby* caper. We had our hands full on that one, too. So many suspects."

"Yes," Bri muttered distractedly. "So many suspects."

As they pulled into the driveway of the inn, they spotted Matt hurrying over to the car. At first, when he pulled open the passenger door, Bri thought he was helping her out. Instead he shoved in beside her.

"We've got to get over to the hospital. The chief just phoned. Someone tried to kill Joe."

"Again?" Mildred gasped with astonishment.

"Again," Matt said huskily.

THE CHIEF and Noah Bright both confirmed that Joe Holland's condition hadn't deteriorated. Fortunately a nurse came in minutes after his IV had been tampered with.

"He's still comatose," Noah said soberly. "But his vital signs haven't deteriorated. Which is all we can expect at the moment. He's no better than he was an hour ago. But at least he's no worse."

"How long ago did this happen?" Matt asked.

"No more than twenty minutes," Noah said, checking his watch.

Harvey looked at Bri. "I got the call from Noah just after you and Mildred left the station house. I called straight over to the inn to let Matt know."

And, Bri thought, to see if he was at the inn. Not that Matt couldn't have raced back from the hospital in time to receive the call from the chief. But Bri had seen the look on Matt's face when he'd jumped into Mildred's car. There was anger and grief. But not guilt. Either Matt was a superb actor or he was as innocent as she so desperately wanted to believe.

"We're keeping a close, round-the-clock watch on Holland," the chief said.

Noah gave Harvey a bleak look. "I'm afraid the hospital is going to start to get a bad name if there are any more...incidents."

All eyes turned to Bri, and she felt the blood drain from her face.

"AGATHA CHRISTIE?" Matt looked at Bri from across her bedroom. He was sitting on her bed. She was standing near the door. It was nearly 10:00 p.m.

"It was something you said the first day we met. You mentioned one of her books. About a group of passengers aboard a train all having a motive for murdering someone."

"*Murder on the Orient Express,*" Matt said. "Yes. That's true. After some digging by the great fictional detective, Hercule Poirot, it was discovered that none of the passengers were who they claimed to be. As it turned out, they not only all had a motive, they actually all took part in the murder. If I remember the book correctly there were multiple stab wounds."

Bri frowned. "Well, there was only one bullet in this case. So everyone here didn't take a shot at him. But at this point I'm not so sure about any of them being who they say they are. Maybe everybody on the tour is involved in some way with John or with the missing scroll. We already have Jillian and Kyle. And then there's Tim or whoever he is." She shot Matt a look. "Does my theory sound crazy?"

Matt motioned to Bri to sit down beside him, but she stayed put. Last time she'd sat beside Matt on her bed, she'd succumbed to uncontrollable longing. She doubted her control was back in top form and she wasn't taking any chances. Not until this whole ugly business was settled. Or at least not until she could put her suspicions about Matt fully to rest.

Finally he came over to her and put his hands lightly on her shoulders. "I guess this could be one of those times when truth is even stranger than fiction. I, for one, don't trust any of our fellow passengers, except maybe for the two old gals and their granddaughter. Although, sometimes it's the ones that look the most innocent that prove to be guilty."

"I suppose that's true."

Matt gave her a long look. "And the other way round, Bri. Sometimes the ones who seem most suspicious are getting a raw deal."

"Matt...I—"

He pressed a finger to her lips. "It's okay, Bri. I know what you're going through. I know you wish you weren't going through it. And so do I."

She thought at first he was putting his arm around her, but instead he merely reached around for the doorknob. "Lock your door when I leave."

Bri nodded. "Good night, Matt."

"Sleep tight, Bri."

SHE WAS IN BED and just beginning to drift off, when she heard the muted sound of metal against metal. Someone was unlocking her door with a key. Panic held Bri frozen for a moment, but then she quickly reclaimed her wits and reached for the phone. Dial Matt? Or Mildred?

She never got to make the choice. As soon as she lifted the receiver, she realized that the phone was dead. Paralyzed with fear, she watched the door open.

No light came in from the hall. Whoever was entering her dark room had also turned out the lights in the corridor. The door quietly shut.

Scream, Bri told herself. She opened her mouth, but no sound came out. She was too terrified.

She lay there in bed hearing the sound of footsteps crossing her room. She clutched the receiver of the phone like a weapon. Who was it? Who was inexorably drawing nearer and nearer to her?

And then she picked up the familiar scent. A distinctive perfume. The perfume worn by Anna Campbell. She huddled under the covers, the receiver hidden from view. Once again she imagined a pillow coming down over her face. But this time she wouldn't be caught *sleeping*. This time she would strike back.

Chapter Twelve

Bri was poised to strike out at her intruder, but the brilliant beam of a flashlight suddenly blinded her. Instinctively she flung an arm over her eyes to block out the harsh, glaring light. An instant later the flashlight went out, and within seconds—too few for Bri to recover—two strong hands were at her throat.

"I am not a patient woman, Miss Graham. I have waited long enough. You know where the Osiris scroll is hidden and now you will tell me. You pretend to be all sweetness and virtue, but I know the truth about you. I know you're cold and heartless. And we both know you are responsible for the death of an innocent man."

The hands tightened around Bri's throat as Anna Campbell's harsh voice hissed through the darkness. Bri's heart was pounding. For a moment a blend of panic, pain and shock made her forget the makeshift weapon clutched in her left fist.

"His death will not go unavenged. And I will not allow his memory to be forever disgraced. He may have been a fool, but that was all. That was his only crime." Here Anna Campbell's voice loosened slightly. Enough to make Bri realize that the woman must be mad... and enough to bring her survival instincts to the fore.

Bri's grip tightened on the telephone receiver. She'd had just about enough of her disreputable band of tour members threatening her, accusing her, attacking her. What did they all think, anyway? That she would just crawl into some corner, whimpering? Well, they were sorely mistaken. As Anna Campbell was about to find out.

Still, Bri hesitated for an instant. She had never before struck anyone. Violence was something Bri abhorred. She never even went to movies that were too violent.

"You will give me back the Osiris scroll, Miss Graham. You will give it to me or I—"

Bri didn't give the woman a chance to complete the threat. She slipped her hand quickly out from the cover and raised it. The mouthpiece end of the telephone receiver rapped sharply against the side of Anna Campbell's head, just below and behind her ear. She fell limply sideways beside Bri on the bed and lay still.

Bri screamed. Moments later, the door burst open. The hall lights were back on, and she saw Matt come rushing into her room, Mildred hot on his heels. Bri sprang out of bed and stared down at the limp body of Anna Campbell, just as everyone else came running out of their rooms, crowding into Bri's. For all of them, there was a horrifying sense of déjà vu as they saw the prone body.

Bri pulled herself together and reached for Anna Campbell's pulse. "She's all right," she announced with surprising calm. Surprising her as much as the others. "She's coming around."

The rest of the tour members stared at Bri with silent accusation. She stared back defiantly at them. "I guess I just don't take kindly to being assaulted."

Matt had to smile. Bri Graham was something, all right.

Mildred picked up the telephone receiver. There was no dial tone. A moment later she saw that the phone jack had been pulled from the wall and cut. She looked across at Mrs. McDermott.

"Call the police and an ambulance."

Mrs. McDermott nodded, exiting without a word.

Harriet Beecham followed her sister out. "I'll go downstairs and tell poor Lucy what's happened. All this commotion must have woken her and she'll be frantic with worry."

Mildred gave her a grateful smile, then looked at the others. "I doubt if any of us can go back to sleep now. I think it would be best if everyone went down to the parlor and waited for my husband."

She zeroed in on Tim Campbell who had not made a move toward the woman who was supposed to be his mother. Only now, when Mildred's gaze was focused on him, did he make a step in Anna Campbell's direction.

Matt stopped Tim's forward progress with his free hand. "Mrs. Mead is right. Everyone should go downstairs until the police arrive. Under the circumstances, it would be a really dumb move for the chief to find any of us missing when he gets here." He might have been addressing the group, but his gaze was fixed on Tim Campbell.

The young man merely shrugged, did an abrupt about-face and strode out of the room. The others meekly followed.

Bri gazed up at Matt, her usually shimmering emerald eyes slightly glassy. "I was scared for a minute there that I'd hit her harder than I meant to," she confessed.

"You hit her just hard enough to get the message across," he said with a tender smile, smoothing back her tangled hair. "And not just to Mrs. Campbell."

Bri smiled back weakly, the shock and terror of her experience having taken its toll despite her best efforts to remain cool, calm and collected.

"I've still got some brandy left in the flask in my room," Matt murmured.

Bri nodded.

Matt put his arm around her shoulder and they headed for the door. He glanced back at Mildred as Bri stepped out of the room. "When Harvey gets here, we'll come down to the parlor."

Mildred smiled faintly. "I'll stay here with Mrs. Campbell." She looked down at the woman who was almost fully conscious now, but not speaking. "Or whoever she is."

LATER, after the paramedics had attended to Anna Campbell's head and she'd refused to be taken to the hospital for observation, Harvey Mead escorted her into the downstairs parlor of the Sugarrun Inn where the rest of the Valentine Tour members were already assembled. Mildred and Lucy, also present, sat quietly on the sidelines. A minute earlier, a revived looking Bri had entered the room with Matt. They sat side-by-side on a two-seater sofa.

All eyes turned to Anna Campbell as the police chief guided her to a comfortable armchair. To most everyone's surprise she no longer used her cane and showed no sign of having a limp. Anna Campbell kept her eyes downcast until she was sitting, and then she looked directly across the room at Bri.

The look was so chilling that Bri shivered despite the warmth from the fire that Mildred had started in the large brick fireplace. There was no one in the room who failed to notice the unmasked hatred radiating from the older woman's pale gray eyes.

"It is all her fault," Anna hissed in much the same voice she had used earlier in Bri's room.

Bri stared at her in confusion, recalling the older woman's earlier charges. "You must be crazy," Bri said. "Why would you want to avenge John and wipe away his disgrace? Whatever could make you think he was simply a fool and that I was the...mastermind of this despicable crime? Don't tell me you were in love with John, too?''

"In love with your husband?" Anna spit out malevolently. "I spit on your husband. As I spit on you. You may fool the others, but I know the truth. I know that you and that bastard of a husband of yours planned the theft together. How clever of him to leave the country for several months, making you out to be the poor, deserted wife. An innocent."

Anna Campbell laughed harshly. "And now that he's conveniently out of the way, you stand to reap all of the wealth. Oh yes, I have no doubt you have the underworld connections to sell the scroll for hundreds of thousands of dollars, perhaps more. But I swore on my husband's grave that I would not rest until I..."

And suddenly it all made sense to Bri. Everything Anna Campbell had said. Even her rage and thirst for vengeance. And the excruciating pain just beneath the surface of her words. "You're the curator's wife from the Cairo museum. Your husband was the one who...committed suicide." Bri saw the tears brim in Anna's eyes.

Bri spoke more softly now. "Matt told me about your husband. I know that he was originally blamed for the theft of the scroll even though he swore his innocence." She also remembered the rest of the tragic tale of the curator's suicide.

There was silence in the room. Harvey Mead looked at the woman who called herself Anna Campbell. "Is your real name Anna Khaffir, wife of the deceased Cairo curator, Selim Khaffir?"

She stared at him defiantly, no more the meek, retiring American widow, Anna Campbell. "Yes, that is my true name. I met Selim twenty-five years ago when he was studying at New York University. We were married six months after we met, and for the past twelve years we lived in Cairo where Selim worked his way up to curator of one of Egypt's most celebrated museums. He was a great curator. A great man.''

Tim Campbell popped up from his seat and pointed a finger at her. "Now that you've gone this far, tell them the rest of the story and get me off the hook," he demanded. "I'm getting real tired of having everyone around here looking at me like I'm some sort of criminal."

She shrugged and looked at the police chief. "This young man is not involved in any way. He isn't my son. Selim and I weren't able to have children. I hired this young man through a New York theatrical agency. I thought it best to give no hint of my true identity. A crippled widow with a son. I thought it wise."

"I knew there was something fishy about the two of them the whole time," Eleanor McDermott muttered, elbowing her granddaughter who looked sullenly at both her grandmother and the college student imposter.

"That was a lot to go through, Mrs. Khaffir," Harvey Mead commented. "Why the charade?"

Anna Khaffir's gaze remained fixed on Bri, her features muted. "I didn't know how much her husband might have told her about me. I met John Fossier briefly in Cairo on two occasions. Not that he took notice of me. But I couldn't take any chances."

"How did you know John was going to join the tour?" Bri asked.

"I didn't. I believed he was still out of the country waiting for the heat to die down. I meant to deal with you. I thought I had a better chance . . . with you."

"And when he arrived?" Bri asked.

A shadow crossed Anna's face. "He didn't recognize me at first. Just to be on the safe side I'd changed my hair color, my way of dressing. I had a limp, a son." She laughed harshly. "He walked past me in the van that first morning without so much as a glimmer of recognition."

"But later that day, when we stopped for lunch at that tavern, he recognized you then," Bri countered. "I saw the two of you arguing. I saw the look of...hatred on your face."

She laughed harshly. "Even then he wasn't certain who I was. Merely that I looked vaguely familiar. He couldn't place me, but it was clear that I made him nervous. He made some veiled threats. And then he went off to carry on his flirtation with the young, lovely Miss Knight."

She smiled contemptuously at Bri. "He loved beautiful women. In Cairo, he always had a beautiful woman, sometimes two, on his arm. I doubt he was ever faithful to you." Her gaze took in Matt. "But then, maybe it was the same for you, Miss Graham. A business arrangement, pure and simple between you and your larcenous husband."

Bri gaped at her. "You're sadly mistaken. I had nothing to do with John's business affairs, legal or illegal. He never shared a word with me. I wasn't aware he knew you or your husband. Or even that he'd spent any time in Cairo. I never knew a thing about this scroll until John showed up again a few days ago. You still believe I was his...his accomplice?"

Anna Khaffir's silence was accusation enough. Bri glanced around the room at the others. It was clear from the looks on Jillian's and Kyle's faces that they, too, shared Anna's belief that she was in on the heist. That she knew where the Osiris scroll was hidden. Even the expressions on the faces of Mrs. McDermott, her granddaughter, Allison, and her sister, Harriet, revealed, if not certainty of her culpability, the possibility.

As for Tim Campbell who had not as yet given his true name, he seemed merely curious. And relieved to be out of it. There went Bri's enthusiastic theory that everyone on the tour had some connection to John or to the stolen scroll. Tim, at least, seemed exempt. And she was still short on a connection that would tie Mrs. McDermott, Harriet Beecham and Allison to her theory.

Mildred and Lucy both looked as though Anna Khaffir's accusation was ludicrous. Bri could only smile gratefully in their direction. The chief, maintaining his professional stance, remained poker-faced, giving off no clue as to his inner thoughts or suspicions about her.

The only person left in the room was Matt. He was seated beside her, but Bri had deliberately avoided looking at him. She was afraid. Afraid to discover that he, too, might think her guilty as charged. Here, all this time, she'd struggled with her ambivalence over his guilt or innocence in this whole awful mess. How ironic if he, all along, had been struggling with the very same issue about her. Was his intent, the entire time, to unearth her as John's accomplice as well as to recover the Osiris scroll? Had this been the real reason for his grand seduction? It was almost too painful a thought to tolerate.

And then she felt his arm move lightly around her shoulder. Just his touch brought tears to her eyes. It flooded her with a sense of warmth and safety, no matter how temporary. She dared to look at him then. He smiled tenderly at her. A trusting smile. And she knew then that she was in love with him. Or at least as he had said, it was the beginning of what could be love. It was funny. All this time she'd anguished over Matt being close to five years younger than she. And now she felt that, despite his chronological age, he seemed a lot older and wiser than she felt at this point.

The silence in the room lasted all of a minute, but it was a long minute for everyone present. Chief Mead turned to Anna Khaffir and he fixed her with a no-nonsense stare. "I'm a country cop, Mrs. Khaffir. And I don't have much taste for draggin' things out. You had both the motive and the opportunity to kill John Fossier. A confession would sure save us a lot of time, expense and unnecessary grief."

Anna Khaffir did not bat an eye as she stared up at the chief of police. "I'm sorry to say that someone else beat me to it. And, believe me, that is my only regret."

"Very well, Mrs. Khaffir. For the moment I have no proof of your guilt in Fossier's death, but I am bringing you in on assault charges against Bri Graham." As he began telling her her rights, Anna Khaffir broke down at last and began to sob.

"Wait," Bri said, cutting him off. "You can't arrest her if I don't press those charges, can you, Chief Mead?"

"Bri, are you crazy?" Matt gasped in amazement. "The woman nearly choked you to death."

"And I nearly clobbered her to death," Bri countered.

"Really, Bri," Mildred broke in. "You mustn't be foolish about this. This woman has made it clear that she meant to harm you. There's no reason to believe she won't assault you again. Don't be deceived by her tears."

Bri couldn't help it. Her heart went out to Anna Khaffir. "You can't lock her up for having loved her husband so deeply that she was driven to avenge his tragic fate. She truly believed I'd hidden the scroll, and she was just so hurt and angry."

"You've had one shock after another to your system, physically and emotionally," Matt argued. "You're in no condition to make a decision like this tonight."

Mildred concurred. "You aren't thinking clearly, my dear."

Bri walked over to Anna Khaffir and knelt down beside her. "I know that you struck out at me in desperation and despair. But you must trust me, Anna. I'm as innocent as your husband was. And if that scroll is ever unearthed, I'll do everything in my power to see to it that it's returned to the Cairo museum where it belongs. Please believe me."

Anna Khaffir held Bri's gaze for long moments. Slowly the hostility radiating from her features softened.

"Was it you who put that note in my room the other night?" Bri asked quietly.

Anna shook her head. "No, but I wrote it. And I was not the one at the hospital who attacked you. But we'd all heard about it and I decided to use the incident to my advantage. I intended to put the note in your room, but then I lost my nerve. It disappeared from my desk before I had a chance to decide what to do." She glanced over at the young man who'd played her son. "Did you take it?"

Tim looked astonished. "Me? No it wasn't me. Why the hell would I swipe your stupid letter? What would I want with it?"

"I had told you earlier that day that I would need a favor from you and you agreed, after extorting a hundred dollars from me."

He jumped up from his seat. "Baloney. I wasn't extorting anything. I had a sneaky suspicion you were up to no good, and if I was going to be taking any risks I damn well was going to see I got paid extra for my efforts."

"And did she also pay you extra to almost suffocate Bri with a pillow at the hospital?" Matt challenged, grabbing the young man by the collar.

"You're nuts," Tim snapped, struggling out of Matt's grasp.

"He's telling you the truth," Anna said listlessly. "I neither paid Tim nor was myself in any way involved in that attack. I swear that's true," she added, looking only at Bri.

Matt still had a fistful of Tim's shirt. "What is your real name, anyway? And how'd you come to take over this college kid Tim Campbell's identity?"

Harvey frowned. That was supposed to be his question. Then again, this was supposed to be his investigation.

"I don't have to tell you anything. You're not a cop," Tim grumbled. "In fact, if you don't let go of me, you creep, I could bring assault charges against you. Couldn't I, Chief?" he demanded, glancing over at Harvey.

Harvey looked sternly at Matt. Matt reluctantly unhanded the actor.

"Now suppose I ask you the same question my friend here asked you," the chief said quietly to the garrulous young man.

"What? You want my vital statistics? Sure. I'm happy to cooperate with the *police*. My name's Keith Baron. I'm an actor, although I make ends meet by bartending. I live at 132 West 11th Street in Manhattan. I happened to bump into Tim Campbell while I was tending bar at a Greenwich Village hangout one night. We got to talking and he told me about how he was a Harvard student majoring in biology and that he was taking a semester leave to look after his mother who was recovering from a heart attack. A few days later I heard through the grapevine that there was a lady casting for a young man to play her son. I looked her up, gave her a résumé, suggested I could play Tim Campbell and she liked the idea. She thought it was a good cover."

"And you never questioned her about why she wanted this cover?" Bri asked him.

He shrugged, smoothing down his shirt. "For a thousand bucks and what I thought was going to be nothing more than a breezy little fall foliage trip, I didn't question a thing, sweetheart.'' He scowled dramatically. "I certainly never bargained for any of this, though, or my price for this gig would have been a hell of a lot higher." He started to leave the room, but Harvey motioned for him to take a seat. Reluctantly the actor sat.

As the chief surveyed the small gathering, he pressed his palms together in front of him and rocked back and forth slightly on his heels. "Now I know it's late and everyone's tired, but since a couple of you have begun exposing your true identities, I think we may as well continue to set the record straight here."

There was dead silence in the room. If anyone was even breathing, it couldn't be heard. Harvey smiled inwardly. He had center stage at last. And then he thought to himself, better take advantage of it because chances were he wouldn't be there for very long with this cast of characters vying for the limelight.

He leveled his gaze on Jillian Knight. The young woman turned scarlet. "Me? Me? Well, I'm not an imposter, I assure you. My name *is* Jillian Knight. I'm exactly who I...I claim to be."

"How well did you know the deceased, John Fossier?" the chief barked at her. This was not a tone the group was accustomed to hearing from the mild-mannered police chief. Even Mildred looked a bit surprised.

"I...I didn't. I didn't know him very well at all. I just...met him. We...we had an innocent—completely innocent—flirtation."

"Let's skip that one for a minute," the chief said caustically, the late hour and the frustrations of this case adding to his irritation. "How about Fossier's partner in crime?" He deliberately paused for a moment, letting his gaze bear down on the trembling, pallid redhead. "Adam Quinn."

There was a faint hiss coming from someone in the room, but as all eyes were so sharply focused on Jillian Knight, no one seemed to know to whom the hiss belonged.

Jillian looked wanly at the chief, then glanced over at Kyle Dunner who was seated on the couch beside Harriet Beecham. Kyle's expression remained mildly befuddled and sympathetic. Jillian looked away. "I knew Adam Quinn." Her voice was a bare whisper, but because the room was still so silent, everyone heard her without any difficulty. "But I have no idea what you mean when you say 'partner in crime.' "

"In fact, you and Adam Quinn were lovers," Harvey said, the edge still in his voice.

Jillian Knight began to cry softly. "Yes."

"And you now have a new paramour," the chief went on in a softer tone, a tone that did not deceive anyone, least of all Jillian Knight.

She gazed wanly up at the police chief, but made no confirmation.

It wasn't necessary, Bri thought. It was written all over her face.

Harvey Mead shook his head, his gaze shifting from Jillian to Kyle Dunner. "Are you going to put the whole burden on her, Kyle?"

Kyle Dunner gave the chief a shocked look. "What?" He blinked several times. "Surely, you aren't suggesting . . . Why, that's ludicrous. I hardly know Miss Knight. Certainly I find her to be a most attractive woman, but she's got to be a good fifteen years younger than me. I prefer a more, shall I say, mature woman, Chief Mead."

Matt left Bri's side and sauntered over to the investment broker. "Tell me if this conversation between you and Jillian rings a bell, Kyle?" And just as he'd done once before, he replayed, verbatim, the little talk between the pair that he and Bri had overheard from her bedroom window.

Kyle Dunner's complexion went from red to ashen in a split second. "How could you...? How did you...?" And then realizing his stammering was an admission of guilt, he stiffened and eyed Matt defiantly. "I may have had a brief discussion the other evening with Miss Knight, but you obviously misheard, or misunderstood most of what was said."

"I seriously doubt that two people could have misheard or misunderstood what was said, Mr. Dunner," Bri cut in. "I was a witness to that same conversation between you and Jillian. And I remember it exactly as Matt remembers it."

Kyle recoiled in his seat. "If this is some kind of veiled allegation— Well, it's absolutely absurd. I never met John Fossier in my life. And as for my relationship, if that's what you want to call it, with Miss Knight, I would certainly not characterize myself as her paramour. I will admit we met shortly before the trip and dated a few times. Indeed, she was the one who told me about the tour. But we both agreed that it would be... inappropriate for us to travel as... to travel together, as it were, and I happen to have certain moral standards—"

"That don't apply to paying taxes apparently," Harvey commented, figuring this was as good a juncture as any to bring that up. "You made yourself quite a bundle in the market these past couple of years, and the government is a little miffed it didn't get its rightful share, isn't that so?"

The measure of the real man was glimpsed for an instant. Cold, calculating fury flashed across Kyle Dunner's face. And not for the first time since this merry little jaunt began, Bri thought to herself, *If looks could kill.*

The investment counselor was quick to compose himself. Quick enough, Bri was sure he hoped, not to have revealed too much about his true personality to the police chief. Harvey gave nothing away, but she was equally sure the police chief was a quick study. Bri was more and more impressed with the local constabulary, as Mrs. Mc-Dermott might have put it.

"I have every confidence that the IRS and my lawyers will iron out what is most assuredly an error on the government's part," Kyle said in an even voice, folding his hands together on his lap.

Harvey smiled pleasantly. "You are a confident man, Mr. Dunner. I'll give you that."

Jillian, who had finally stopped sniffling, dabbed demurely at her eyes. "I don't care what anyone heard. Kyle and I are completely innocent. Why, the night John Fossier was murdered, we were together in my room. I know how Kyle feels about...about certain improprieties, and since neither one of us had any reason for murdering the man, I didn't feel there was any reason to mention that we both had solid alibis." Her gaze shifted to Kyle for corroboration.

Kyle gave her a sharp look. It was apparent to everyone in the room, except possibly Jillian, that her admission of a sexual dalliance with the investment broker on the night of John's murder turned Kyle's earlier statement about their *virtuous* relationship into a lie. And why would he have stopped at only one? Unless, of course, Jillian was lying now.

Bri cast Matt a rueful look. He winked at her.

"Anyone else here care to fess up about anything?" Harvey asked laconically. "Anything at all?" He looked over at Harriet Beecham who nervously clutched the lapels of her flannel robe.

"As I already told you, Chief Mead, I was asleep in my room on the night of Mr. Weston's—that is Mr. Fossier's death. And so was my sister. Weren't you, Eleanor?"

"I most certainly was," her older sister said supercili- ously.

"And what about you, Allison?" Bri asked quietly.

"Me? Are you asking me about my alibi again? I al- ready told the police that I was fast asleep in my room."

"Did you know before the murder," Matt broke in, "that your room had a connecting door to that of the murdered man's?"

"Really," Mrs. McDermott snapped. "This is going too far. My granddaughter is barely eighteen years old. She never met this John Fossier before in her life. She hasn't the slightest motive on earth—"

"I didn't mean to imply that she walked through that connecting door and shot Fossier, Mrs. McDermott," Matt said calmly.

"Then what exactly are you implying?" she demanded angrily.

Before he could respond, Allison sprang up and fled the room in a sudden torrent of tears.

"Now see what you've done?" Mrs. McDermott snapped, hurrying after her granddaughter.

"Yes," Harriet Beecham said, mimicking her sister, "see what you've done now?"

The young actor stood up and stretched. "Well, folks, I haven't seen anything this good in acting class or even on stage in ages. What can a lowly actor like me say, except that I'm humbled by the experience." With that review, Keith Baron, alias Tim Campbell, sauntered out of the parlor. Jillian Knight and Kyle Dunner followed close on the actor's heels.

"Well, I declare," Lucy muttered. Those were the first words that evening from the usually loquacious old woman, who had been surprisingly quiet. But then this was certainly a night for surprises.

"WILL YOU BE ABLE to sleep?" Matt asked Bri solicitously as they got to her bedroom door. "You sure you won't worry about another visit from *the strangler?* I still agree with the Meads. You should have let the chief stow Mrs. Khaffir in the pokey. It would be one less worry on your mind."

"I don't know if Anna Khaffir believes me, but she'd have to be very crazy to make another move on me," Bri replied. "I admit, for a while there I thought she might actually be crazy, but not anymore. Except maybe crazy with grief. I feel sorry for her, Matt."

She opened her bedroom door. Matt made no move. "I suppose you know that you have too trusting a nature," he murmured.

She turned back to him. Their eyes met and held. "I know."

"It's gotten you in trouble before."

"I know that, too."

"You need someone to keep an eye out for you."

Bri smiled, gesturing toward the room next door to hers. "Mildred's on the job." But even as she said that, she remembered that it was Matt, not Mildred, who was the first one to respond to her screams earlier that evening. He was clearly not only keeping an eye but an ear out for her.

"Well . . ." He gave her an ingenuous smile.

Caution lights flashed in her head, but she sped right through them. "Now that I think about it, maybe I will have trouble sleeping. My mind's churning."

"Mine, too."

"So much to figure."

"It's certainly confusing."

"Matt?"

"Yes?"

"I'm not one hundred percent trusting. I can't completely shake some of my suspicions."

He smiled. "I know."

"If this were as much about the scroll as it was about me, would you tell me?"

His gaze held hers. "If I said, yes, would you believe me?"

"Yes, that it is as much about the scroll? Or yes, that you would tell me?"

His hand cupped her chin and he kissed her lightly. "Which do you think?"

She was instantly aroused. "Do you want to come in and...talk for a while?"

He shook his head slowly.

"Do you want to come in, anyway?"

He smiled, let his eyes close ever so gradually and kissed her again.

They were still kissing on the other side of her door, his hands laced into her hair, hers wrapped around his neck.

Bri could still see the caution lights flashing in her mind, but they were murky at best. There were danger and caution signs at every turn she made. Was this a more dangerous turn than the rest?

As he pressed her up against her closed door, lifting her and curving her legs around him, both of them groping, fumbling, burning, wanting, the caution lights inside her head were expunged by the urgent intentions of her body. And her heart.

BRI STOOD by the window later in the darkened room, looking up at the moon, watching wisps of clouds curl around it.

"It's really beautiful up here in the fall. This was going to be such a special trip."

"It is special," Matt murmured from her bed, where he lay studying her.

She looked over at him and smiled. "I know." Then she turned back to the window. "But what happens when this is over? I put everything I had into this tour business, never dreaming my first jaunt was going to be my last."

"It doesn't have to be. You might be surprised. There are a lot of folk looking for a little adventure out there..."

She shot him a look. "A *little* adventure?"

"Bri, can I ask you something?"

She was immediately alert to the change in his tone. She wasn't sure what it meant, but she braced herself, nonetheless. "What?"

"Did John ever show you the scroll?"

She stiffened. "No." After a pause she asked, "Don't you believe me?"

Any hesitation on his part would have been a bad sign. When he didn't respond at all, Bri was devastated.

He swung his legs over the edge of the bed and sat up. "I think he did."

She couldn't believe her ears. She was too stunned by his response to even be angry. Yet.

He got out of bed and came over to her. The minute he touched her, her fury was ignited. She went to take a swing at him, finding words insignificant to express her rage.

With the ease of a man who'd had a punch or two thrown at him in his day, he caught her by the wrist in mid-swing.

"No, listen to me, Bri. You don't see what I'm getting at."

She struggled to free her arm, but Matt wasn't taking any chances.

"Man, you're beautiful when you're angry," he said with a provocative smile.

"And you're... you're..." But an apt description for what she thought of him now refused to come into her head. Maybe the word hadn't been created yet.

"I think he gave you something at some point early in your marriage..." He paused, grinning. "Well, I guess any point would have been early in your marriage since all you had was early."

She glared at him. "I think I hate you."

He grinned. "No, you don't. You think you love me a little and you hate yourself for it. But you're getting me off the track."

"What track?" she demanded caustically.

"Maybe he didn't just stow the scroll in some objet d'art. What if he gave you something, a gift he figured you'd hold on to for sentimental value."

"John gave me lots of little sentimental gifts. I tossed them all out. I threw out everything that had sentimental value," she muttered. "My sentiments underwent radical change."

"It was probably something valuable enough for Fossier to think you'd hold on to in any case. That night in Colport, did he give you any clue...?"

"No."

"You do know, Bri, that my company's offering a fifty-thousand-dollar reward for the return of that scroll. Fifty thousand bucks can go a long way when you're wondering where your next tour group is coming from."

"Matt, you aren't listening to me."

"I am listening. I'm also hoping that maybe something slipped your mind, something you forgot all about, something you never got around to tossing out, something Fossier overlooked the day he ransacked your apartment."

She looked him straight in the eye. "Are you hoping for my sake... or yours, Matt?"

He met her gaze without flinching. "For both our sakes, Bri."

She thought it a fair response. Maybe he was a fair man. Maybe even honest. Maybe even trustworthy. Her eyes fixed on him as she let go of the blanket wrapped around her naked body. With a whoosh, it fell to the floor. "Okay, I'll think about it. Meanwhile, let's go back to bed."

He smiled crookedly. "Best idea I've heard in the past twenty minutes."

Chapter Thirteen

Bri's dreams that night were punctuated with horrific visions. She was driving her tour van at top speed along a winding, narrow cliff road, a voice behind her urging her to go faster, faster. Heeding the frantic plea, she floored the gas pedal, gripping the steering wheel with all her strength, terrified that one false turn and the van would go crashing over the precipice.

"They're gaining. Hurry. You've got to go faster, Bri." It was Matt's voice. Sharp, urgent, insistent.

"I can't. I can't," she cried out.

"She can't. She can't escape. It's too late for her." Other voices joined in. A cacophony of chants. Bri's eyes darted to the rearview mirror. All of her tour members were seated as they'd been on that first morning out—Anna Campbell and her son Tim, Jillian Knight, Kyle Dunner, Mrs. McDermott, her sister, Harriet Beecham, pretty, young Allison, and there in the very back of the van was John, chanting louder than all the others, an insidious smile on his face.

"You're going to have to give it up, Bri," Matt whispered seductively in her ear as she squealed around another hairpin curve, nearly losing control, her knuckles white as she gripped the wheel. "Give me the scroll, Bri. Then you'll be safe."

"Give it up before it's too late," the others chanted. "Give it to me," they all demanded.

Again Bri's eyes darted to the rearview mirror. She gasped in horror. It was like looking through one of those mirrors in a fun house. The whole group took on weird, distorted shapes, their faces grotesque and terrifying. And they were all rising, swaying with the van, moving slowly, inexorably toward her. And now John was leading the group. He was going to reach her first. And he had a gun.

"Quick, Bri," Matt whispered in her ear. "Give me the scroll and you'll be safe. I'll protect you. I won't let them hurt you."

"I can't. I can't," she cried over and over, her hands locked on the wheel, frozen. She was paralyzed with fear as the van sped up to another hairpin curve. If she didn't turn the wheel sharply to the right, she knew they'd all go careening over the cliff. She tried. She tried with all her might. But now she discovered that the steering wheel itself had locked.

"Give the scroll to me. It's mine. It's mine. It's mine," voices pressed in on her in turn. They all wanted it. Even Matt. Even Matt.

Bri saw the road dropping off in front of her, heard the hideous demanding cries behind her, bearing down on her. And still the steering wheel would not budge. No right turn was possible.

Her mouth gaped open in horror as the van went sailing over the cliff. Down, down, down. Spinning now, faster and faster. She was so dizzy. Voices whirring, the words themselves no longer intelligible. She was caught in a vortex. Whirling. Whirling.

And then, suddenly, she stopped spinning. The voices vanished. The tour members evaporated. Even the van was gone. She was all alone on a knoll. A lovely knoll surrounded by snow-capped mountains. Not an ordinary knoll. A cemetery. An old cemetery with crumbling, crooked grave stones. She looked around, no longer dizzy. No longer afraid. But sad. She sat down on the ground. The earth was cold. Cold and white. She began to shiver. And then she began to cry.

"Bri. Bri, wake up."

She could hear Matt's voice, even feel him shaking her gently. But she incorporated him into her dream, crying harder as she pressed herself against him for solace.

"It's okay, Bri. It's okay. Just a bad dream, baby. That's all. Just a bad dream."

She never really woke up, but Matt's soothing words guided her out of the nightmare into welcome blackness.

WHEN BRI WOKE at a little after ten the next morning, Matt was still sound asleep beside her. Her terrifying dream still clung to her like a bad taste in her mouth. The whole dream was terribly upsetting, but what disturbed her the most, now that she was awake, was the knowledge that, in the twilight shadows of her mind, she still didn't fully trust Matt. The suspicion remained that he was using her to get the scroll. Was he? Did he still feel certain she had the scroll? And that she was deliberately holding out on him? Did he maybe think that she really had been John's accomplice?

Yet, earlier last night, down in the parlor, when he'd put his arm around her and given her such a trusting smile, she'd felt certain their suspicions about each other had vanished. She felt even more convinced later, when their lovemaking had been so free and spirited, neither of them holding anything back. That was a new experience for her and she even sensed that it was one for Matt. They had really connected. His feelings for her seemed as honest as hers were for him.

And then she'd had that miserable nightmare that had brought back the doubts.

She dressed quietly, so as not to wake him, and slipped out the door. Downstairs in the breakfast room Eleanor McDermott and her sister, Harriet, both dressed in their customary walking suits, were sitting over tea and freshly baked muffins. Bri sat down across from them, acutely aware of their close study of her.

"However did you manage to sleep last night?" Harriet Beecham asked with feeling.

Eleanor McDermott arched a brow. Bri was certain she'd surmised that, however well she'd slept, she hadn't slept alone. Little got past the shrewd older woman.

Harriet fidgeted with an ornate gold scarab pinned to her blouse at her throat. "The very thought of that awful woman sneaking into your room and trying to strangle you."

"She only meant to frighten me, Miss Beecham. So that I would give her back the scroll. She honestly thought I was working with John and that I knew where the scroll was hidden. I only wish I did. Next to Anna Khaffir, I'd most like to see the papyrus scroll returned to its rightful place in the Cairo Antiquities Museum. Still," she added in a sad tone, "it will never make up for the loss she's suffered."

"It is tragic what happened to her husband," Eleanor McDermott said sympathetically. "So many deaths. So much bloodshed. What fools men can be. And how greedy. If only they didn't always want so much."

Bri was a bit surprised by the elderly woman's almost wistful tone. It wasn't one Bri had heard before. Eleanor McDermott had always impressed Bri as shrewd, contentious, overbearing and more than a little intimidating. But sentimental, even maudlin? Never.

"Ouch," Harriet Beecham cried.

The two women looked over at her.

"What happened?" Eleanor demanded in her usual sharp voice.

"The clasp of the brooch opened and stuck me." As Harriet fidgeted with the scarab, trying to fasten it again, Bri observed the brooch more closely.

"That's a beautiful piece. Is it Egyptian?" Bri asked.

"Why yes," Harriet said, fixing the scarab in place again. "And quite old. Eleanor brought it back for me when she and her husband returned from Cairo."

Bri's eyes shifted to Harriet's sister who seemed to stiffen visibly in her seat. "Cairo?"

Eleanor arched a brow. "I believe I already told you that my husband and I spent time in Cairo."

"I do remember now that you mentioned Egypt. I didn't realize you'd settled in Cairo," Bri said.

"Eleanor's husband was with the state department," Harriet reminded Bri. "Cairo is where our embassy is located and—"

"Don't start babbling, Harriet. If you're finished eating, I suggest we gather Allison and take a stroll through town," Eleanor said, cutting her sister off rudely. "That granddaughter of mine has done enough moping. She needs some fresh air and activity."

Harriet, used to her sister's rudeness, merely shrugged, then smiled slyly in Bri's direction. "Maybe we'll go hunting for buried treasure this morning."

Bri gave her a distracted look, not really paying attention. She was still thinking about Eleanor McDermott and her husband having spent time in Cairo. Up until now, Bri had viewed the two elderly women travelers and their young charge as innocent bystanders. She saw no link whatsoever between them and John or the missing scroll.

Now she was beginning to wonder. Was their presence on this jaunt pure coincidence or was there more to it?

There was something else niggling at Bri's mind. Something else Mrs. McDermott had remarked in passing the other day about her stay in Egypt. At the time Bri hadn't thought there was any significance to what she was saying, and she hadn't paid close attention. But now she had this funny feeling that there was a clue there somewhere. She wished she could remember what it was the elderly woman had said.

"Have you heard the latest rumors, Bri?" Harriet Beecham was saying.

Bri gave her a puzzled look, her mind still trying to reconstruct Eleanor McDermott's conversation from the other morning. If only Matt had been with her. Matt with the photographic memory. Then again, maybe it was just as well that he wasn't with her.

"Some folk are saying," Harriet said excitedly, "that this million-dollar relic is hidden up here in Thornhill."

Bri stared blankly at her. "Why would anyone...?"

Harriet Beecham supplied the answer before Bri finished the question. "There are those who think that you and your husband were using the tour group as a front, and your real reason for returning to Thornhill was to reclaim the treasure the two of you had stashed away up here."

Bri was only half listening. She remembered. She remembered what it was Mrs. McDermott had said. Without even touching the coffee or muffin she'd served herself from the buffet, Bri sprang up from her chair.

"What's the matter?" Harriet Beecham asked, startled. "You're not angry, I hope. It isn't that my sister or I would buy into such a silly rumor. I was only telling you what's been said."

Bri wasn't listening. She gave Harriet a preoccupied nod. "I'm sorry for dashing off, but I just...remembered something. I mean...I remembered I was supposed to meet someone. For breakfast," she mumbled as she made a hasty exit.

Bri bumped into Mildred in the front hall. "Where are you off to in such a hurry?" Mildred asked.

"I need to check on something. But I'm not sure how to go about it." Keeping her voice low, Bri hurriedly explained her predicament to Mildred. Trust the wily news hound to have a solution.

They were almost out the front door when Matt, looking wonderfully rested and rugged in his jeans, navy turtleneck sweater and leather jacket, came barreling down the stairs two at a time. "Wait for me."

"I think that young man's lost his heart," Mildred murmured.

Bri looked sardonically at the older woman. "And his mind."

Matt caught up with the two women and followed them outside. "So where are we off to?"

"Barker Library," Mildred informed him. "We're going to do a bit of research in the reference room."

IT WAS WELL into the afternoon when Bri hit pay dirt. Rubbing her strained eyes from having pored over the small newspaper print on the microfiche screen for hours, she read the article over again, just to make sure. Then, eyes dancing, she nudged Mildred, who was sitting on her right, and Matt, who was sitting to her left, each at their own microfiche station.

"Eureka," Bri said excitedly. "Listen to this." She leaned a little closer to the machine. "Adam McDermott, his wife, Eleanor Quinn McDermott, and their twelve-year-old son, Adam, Jr., returned from a six-month stay in Cairo where Mr. McDermott, a state department official with a background in Egyptology, had been advising an international group of archaeologists on ancient Egyptian life."

When Bri finished she stared expectantly at her two cohorts. "That's it. That's the connection. Mrs. Eleanor Quinn McDermott. Quinn. And a son named Adam. She's got to be Adam Quinn's mother."

"The murdered gallery owner? The man that Harvey thinks was John Fossier's partner in crime," Mildred queried.

"It makes sense," Matt said. "Quinn could have easily dropped his last name when he opened his Boston art gallery. Or even before."

"Exactly," Bri said breathlessly. "And I wouldn't be at all surprised if we discover that Adam Quinn is Allison's father. She once mentioned to me that her parents were divorced and she lived out in California with her mother and that her dad used to live back East. I never did pick up the *used to*. I just figured at the time it meant he'd moved and she no longer knew where he was located. But it could also mean that he'd died."

"It certainly could," Mildred said enthusiastically. And then she gave Bri a pat on the back. "A fine piece of work, my dear. Dr. Bright's wife, Chloe and my daughter, Maggie, have a new rival in the amateur sleuth department."

Bri blushed. "Really, I should have figured this all out sooner. Eleanor McDermott gave her hand away a few days ago, but so many other things were going on, I just didn't think. But this little discovery does make my theory almost one hundred percent accurate."

"What theory?" Mildred asked.

Bri smiled at Matt. "Matt was the one who started it. With his talk about the Agatha Christie mystery, *Murder on the Orient Express.*"

"Why I read that years ago. And I saw the film," Mildred recalled. "Ingrid Bergman was wonderful. And so was Lauren Bacall. What marvelous actresses." Mildred gave her head a little shake and pushed her wire-rimmed spectacles back up the bridge of her nose. "But, that's beside the point. I see the point you're making. Almost everyone in your tour group is in some way involved in this mystery. Either they were after your husband, or they want to get their hands on the scroll."

"Or both," Bri pointed out, then looked over at Matt who appeared thoughtful. "What are you thinking about?"

"There's a third possibility," he said slowly. "Mrs. McDermott might be along for the ride for much the same reason as Anna Khaffir."

Bri stared at him. "To avenge her son's murder? You think Adam Quinn's murder during that convenience store holdup was a setup? You think his murder and John's are connected? Maybe even that the same person murdered both men?"

Matt cast Mildred a rueful smile. "Tell her she's an ace sleuth and look what happens." He shifted his smile to Bri.

"She could have thought John murdered her son," Bri said.

"Or that someone else on the tour did," Matt pointed out.

Mildred frowned. "What reason would anyone other than John have for killing Quinn? We know Quinn didn't have the scroll."

"The murderer might have thought he did," Bri said, on a hot roll now. "Or that Quinn knew where it was. Especially if John and Quinn were partners in the heist."

Matt grinned. "She took the words right out of my mouth."

Mildred smiled, but then her expression turned pensive. "What about Harriet Beecham?"

"What about her?" Bri asked.

"Is she really Harriet Quinn?"

"I can't believe the two aren't sisters, or at least related," Bri said. "I can't imagine any other reason why Harriet would put up with Eleanor."

"The two could be half sisters. Different fathers," Mildred suggested. "Unless we've got another pair of world-class liars on our hands. Easy enough for Harvey to check," she said, printing out a copy of the McDermott article from the microfiche machine. "I'll bring this right over to him. And tell him all about your brilliant work, Bri. Do you two want to come along?"

"No," Matt said. "I'm going to head over to the hospital and see if there's any change in Joe's condition. I'd like to be there with him when he regains consciousness." He smiled crookedly a determined, optimistic smile. "He's sure to start swearing like a trooper when he comes to."

Bri gave Matt's shoulder a supportive squeeze. The more distance she was getting from her awful nightmare, the better she was feeling about Matt again.

"Do you want to come over to the hospital with me?" he asked her.

Bri had had her fill of hospitals for a while. "I think I'll stick around here and do some more checking. I'd like to reread all the articles from the Boston *Globe* on Adam Quinn's death. Maybe I'll pick something up."

Matt kissed her lightly on the top of her head, and he and Mildred took off.

ABOUT AN HOUR LATER Bri was slipping another microfiche card into the viewing machine when she felt a hand
on her shoulder. She jumped.

"Sorry," Steve Palmer said apologetically. "I didn't
mean to startle you."

"I startle easy these days."

"What are you doing?"

Bri wasn't about to tell him. "Just researching some
travel tips. But I'm ready to hang it up for the day."

"Bri, could we go for a little stroll and . . . talk?"

His edgy expression told Bri the track coach had something specific in mind. "Sure. I could use a little exercise," she said, gathering up her jacket.

They strolled along a path on campus that took them
past the famous row of Greek-revival, white brick buildings that formed the original structures of Dorchester
College and then wound by the field house and track. They
turned up the path at the north end of the track where
there was a small clubhouse and the soccer fields. The path
curved at the clubhouse, winding up to a hilly knoll. Bri
suddenly flashed on the knoll from her dream and held
back.

"It's beautiful up here. Come on," Steve urged, his first
words since they'd begun walking. "Great views. Second
only to the one atop the Barker Library clock. But that's
closed for repair of the bell." Although his remarks were
innocuous and pleasant enough, she saw that his features
were strained. And, despite the cool autumn breeze, Bri
noted that his sweatshirt was stained with several damp
patches.

"I wish John had never come back," he suddenly
blurted out, walking on ahead of her.

Bri felt compelled to follow. "Because of Liz?" she
asked gently, catching up with him.

His pace quickened, and she had to practically run to keep even with him as they wound their way up the steep spruce-shaded hill.

Perspiration erupted on his brow. "The minute I saw him that afternoon I knew there'd be . . . trouble." A vein throbbed in his temple.

Bri realized, too late, that it was more than a little dumb of her to have allowed Steve Palmer to lead her off to such a desolate spot. Her heedless curiosity again. What if Steve was the killer after all? And what was to say he wasn't? She checked her watch, noticing that her hand was trembling. She hoped Steve didn't notice.

"Why don't we head back toward the inn, Steve? Mildred's waiting for me," she lied.

Steve's gaze bore down on her. "He didn't care two hoots for her. He was just using her. Like he used you. Like he used everyone."

She told herself to stay calm. "He wasn't a very nice man," she muttered inanely, concentrating only on escape. She took a few steps back down the path only to be grabbed by the coach's powerful grip.

"Damn it, Bri. Do you have that scroll?" Bri's heart leapt into her throat. Steve's hand tightened around her arm. "You're the only one who can put an end to this, Bri. I'm desperate." He gave her a pleading look, but his eyes looked hollow. "You do understand." His free hand slipped menacingly into his jacket pocket.

Her lips felt numb with fear, but she somehow managed to get out the words, "I understand."

He shook his head morosely. Maybe she wasn't convincing enough. Maybe he wasn't listening or didn't care.

She forced her lips to work. "Mildred's waiting for me at the inn, Steve. I'm late already. She'll be worried."

"I'm worried, too," he snapped back irritably. "That's what I'm trying to tell you. If you don't give up that scroll, your life isn't going to be worth two cents. This isn't a game, Bri. And if you don't believe that, you'd better believe that you're not going to come out the winner.''

He gripped her harder, a cold glint of determination in his eyes now. Chills rippled down her body. She wanted to cry, to shout, to plead with him, but his expression was so fierce, so frightening. If only she'd gone with Mildred or Matt.

Matt. If only he were here. He *would* protect her. He *did* love her. There could even be a future for them. If only Steve would release her and she could dash down the hill to safety. But the thought of getting away from him, even given the opportunity, was laughable. Talk about not coming out the winner. There was no way on earth she could hope to outrun the Dorchester College track coach.

Humor him, she told herself. It was her only hope. ''I suppose you're right, Steve. I can't win. I . . . do have the scroll. I don't want any more trouble. I'll give it to you. You can come with me to get it. I'll put it in your hands.'' She used every ounce of energy she had left to try to sound convincing.

He stared at her. She could see him visibly weighing the truth of her words. She waited, holding her breath. *Please believe me. Please, please, believe me.*

And then, at the very moment Steve's features softened and she thought she'd won this round, she heard a whistling sound and the coach's face suddenly contorted. At first she thought it was rage that had twisted his features, but when he released her abruptly and gripped his arm she saw the blood. He'd been shot. Bri wasn't the least bit sure whether that shot had been meant for Steve or for her, but she certainly wasn't going to stand around and try to figure it out.

She spun and tore through the spruces, nearly tumbling on the steep decline. She zigzagged. She weaved. She couldn't hear footsteps behind her, but the wind and the chirping birds could have camouflaged the sound. The assassin was out there and maybe a wounded, enraged Steve, as well. She couldn't take any chances. She just kept running, right, left, right again so she wouldn't be an easy target.

Darting to her left, she slipped on a pile of wet leaves and went tumbling forward, wrenching her ankle. Grimacing in pain, she forced herself quickly back on her feet and kept running.

She was almost at the small, deserted clubhouse when she realized she just couldn't run anymore. Her ankle was throbbing badly, she had an excruciating stitch in her side and just about no wind left. Besides, an open, deserted stretch lay before her with no place to hide.

Hide. She had to hide. Just for a few minutes. Just until she could catch her breath. Until she could run for help. But then, eyeing the clubhouse, she realized she might not have to run for help. If she had any luck left, she could call for help. Surely there was a telephone in the clubhouse.

She raced for the door, praying she wouldn't find it locked. There was no time to go around testing windows. Even now Steve or the gunman could be observing her going into the clubhouse. But what choice did she have? Outside she was a sitting duck.

She gasped with relief as the door to the clubhouse gave way. She practically lurched inside, literally falling to her knees. But she struggled to her feet, ignoring the pain her latest fall had caused, and shut and bolted the door.

Play for time. That was all she could do. That and find a phone. Tears of relief sprang to her eyes as she spotted a telephone on a desk in a corner of the small room. She dragged herself over to it and lifted up the receiver. She felt a rush of exhilaration as she heard the dial tone. Fingers trembling, she began to press out 911.

She never got to finish dialing. She never got to see the figure stealthily entering from the room next door and moving toward her. And as the hard object came smashing down on her head, she never got to know what—or who—had hit her.

Chapter Fourteen

Matt was still sitting vigil in Joe Holland's room, waiting for him to regain consciousness, when Noah Bright opened the patient's door and motioned for Matt to come outside.

"What's wrong?" Matt asked, the moment he stepped into the hospital corridor. Just that brief glimpse of the doctor's face had told him to be prepared for trouble.

"Steve Palmer just came in with a gunshot wound."

"Bad?"

Noah shook his head. "Grazed his arm. He's being treated down in the ER."

Matt stood there for a moment, squinting, mouth dry. He knew there was more to the doctor's story. And his gut told him that *more* involved Bri.

Noah didn't waste any time getting to it. "He says he was walking along the campus with Bri when it happened. A shot out of nowhere. He has no idea . . ."

Matt went cold inside. "What happened to Bri?"

"Steve says she took off like a scared rabbit."

"She wasn't hit?"

"Not while she was with Palmer. He says he ran after her, once the shock of being wounded wore off, but she was nowhere to be found. He was bleeding badly by that time, and he came in to the emergency room." Noah hesitated. "But he's clearly worried about her safety. I called over to Sugarrun on the outside chance..."

Matt knew the end of the doctor's sentence. "But she wasn't there."

"Harvey's on his way over here to talk to Steve. So's Mildred. She's very upset. Says she should never have left her alone over at Barker Library. Feels responsible."

"She's not the only one," Matt said, his expression grim.

VOICES WHISPERED to her, danced around her head, taunted her, jeered at her. "Look at all the trouble you've caused. Make it easy on yourself. You've got the ticket to your freedom. All you have to do is unearth it." *Unearth it. Unearth it.* Yes, Bri thought to herself. Unearth it. Of course. Her awful nightmare last night. The cemetery. The cold ground. Yes, that was it. She had to unearth it. Just like the archaeologists once did in Egypt. Digging up buried treasure.

The realization brought her fully back to consciousness. The solution to the missing scroll had been there in the back of her mind the whole time, edging ever closer to the surface. Matt had sensed there was something she was holding back from him. And now she knew it was true. But it hadn't been deliberate. In suppressing her feelings for John after he deserted her, compounded by her grief and fury toward him after his return, her unconscious had suppressed certain memories of happier times she and John had shared together. And one memory in particular probably held the key to the mystery of the missing scroll. She felt sure there was a good chance it did.

Bri's excitement gave way very quickly to pain as she felt a terrible pounding at the back of her head and found that when she went to open her eyes, there was only blackness. There was a band over her eyes. A constricting band. And then, with a rush of panic, she realized the problem. She was blindfolded. Panic flooded her. She opened her mouth to scream. But she couldn't part her lips. Tape. Her mouth was taped shut. A thick sourness coated her throat and tongue.

And what was wrong with her body? She couldn't move. Still dazed from having been clobbered, it took a few seconds for her to put together that she was actually bound. Her hands were taped behind her back, her ankles taped as well.

She tried to struggle free. Her throbbing head hit something cold and hard. And as she tried to twist around, moving her legs, a shooting pain shot up from her sore right ankle.

The pain in her ankle brought it all back. Being on the knoll with Steve Palmer. Feeling terrified that he would kill her if she didn't hand him over the scroll. She remembered she was trying to convince him to come with her, promising to give it to him, when the gunshot came whistling out from the woods. Hitting Steve.

She could picture the oozing blood spreading over his gray sweatshirt sleeve. She could recall her horror and fear. And then she could see herself racing down the knoll. Racing for her life. Feeling menace at every turn.

The last thing she remembered was being in the deserted clubhouse, standing at the phone dialing 911. And then everything went blank, and she fell into a black void.

A shiver went through her as she felt a cold gust of wind. It struck her for the first time that she must have been moved from the clubhouse. She must be somewhere outdoors. The wind and the chillness in the air led her to guess that it was dark out. Evening. How late, though? How long had she lain here—wherever she was—trussed up, unconscious?

Where was she? The woods? Was that a tree trunk her head had struck? Again, she moved her head, this time more gingerly and deliberately. She made contact with the hard, cold surface. She twisted her head a little and touched the object with her cheek.

Metallic. A metal·object. Maneuvering some more, her cheek against the cold, smooth surface, she began to explore its contours, trying to figure out what it was. Definitely not a tree trunk. But then what? She attacked the puzzle with determination. It was a concrete task. It kept her momentarily occupied. It kept the terror that was skimming just beneath the top layer of her flesh on temporary hold.

"How MANY TIMES do I have to tell you?" Steve Palmer gave Matt, Mildred and the chief a pained, hollow look. "We went for a stroll. I was showing her the view from the knoll out behind the clubhouse. We were just chatting when . . ."

"What were you chatting about?" Matt demanded.

Steve gave the chief a weary look. "I've answered that a dozen times. Why am I the one getting the third degree here, Harvey? I'm an innocent victim. I could as easily have been shot in the heart as the arm. I'm lucky to be alive."

"And we're worried," Harvey said quietly, "that Bri Graham may not be so lucky."

The track coach paled. "I know. I'm worried, too."

"Then tell us again," Matt persisted, "what the two of you were talking about when the shot rang out."

"I don't see what it has to do with—"

"Someone was out there, crouched behind a tree, listening to the two of you talking. I think that someone might have been afraid you'd say something you shouldn't be saying."

Steve Palmer stared at Matt. "You're saying that shot was meant for me, not Bri? No. No, that couldn't be. There was nothing I said..."

"But there was something you might have said," Matt retaliated, working on gut instinct now.

"You're crazy," Palmer retorted. "He's crazy," he repeated for Mildred and Harvey.

"If there's something you know, Steve, you'd best tell me now. It might mean the difference between life and death for an innocent woman," Harvey said evenly.

Steve closed his eyes and shook his head. "I don't know anything," he said huskily.

Matt looked at Harvey, who rolled his eyes.

"Okay, Steve. Go on home," the chief said. "We'll be in touch," he added pleasantly. But the remark was no pleasantry, as all four of them knew.

THE CONTOURED METAL SHAPE rung...a bell. It was a big metal bell. Under the circumstances Bri's discovery proved little satisfaction. She had a damn good guess which bell this one was. The broken one in the clock tower, high above Barker Library. The tower that Steve had told her was closed for repairs. Who would ever think to look for her up here?

The question was—who had clobbered her back in the clubhouse and dragged her up here? An injured Steve Palmer? Not very likely. The person hiding in the woods by the knoll who'd fired that shot at him? A shot she felt sure must have been meant for her. It was even possible that Steve had an accomplice out there in the woods who'd simply taken bad aim. But another possibility also made sense. What if it was Liz Armstrong out there, seeking revenge? What if Liz believed Steve had murdered John in a fit of jealousy? A conclusion Bri herself had considered. That would explain the attack on Steve. But it didn't get Bri far, concerning her own predicament.

She had plenty of time to consider a number of possibilities. To name two, there were Jillian and Kyle. They were certainly a team. There was every possibility they'd set Adam Quinn up and arranged for that *accidental* death at the convenience store in Boston. And there was Anna Khaffir. The curator's wife could still believe Bri was holding back about the scroll. How much would that actor, Tim alias Keith, do for money? Bri was starting to regret her decision not to have pressed charges against Anna. Worse still, she might not get the chance to do much regretting.

She couldn't even rule out Mrs. Quinn McDermott and her sister, Harriet. She remembered the looks on their faces when Anna Khaffir had accused her of being John's accomplice. Did they also blame her for Quinn's death?

And then there was Matt. Only that morning, waking from that awful dream, she'd realized she still had her suspicions about him. But could he ever do something like this? Could he ever treat her so despicably? Bri was convinced he couldn't. She really did think he might be in love with her. And her suspicions could just be a defense against letting herself admit how much she really cared for him. After all, hadn't she vowed never to get swept up in a whirlwind relationship again?

Of course, there was still the question of what he intended to do with the scroll if he recovered it. Now that she thought she knew what had happened to the valuable relic that question was a pressing one. Not, however, in the same league as her present predicament. Isolated, utterly helpless and defenseless. What came next? Torture, death?

She was about to find out. Her ruminations cut off in a flash as she heard the creaking sound of a wooden door opening. The misery of her contemplations was nothing compared with the terror that seized her at that moment.

She sucked in her breath, trying to ride the terror out, not let it overtake her. If ever she was going to need courage, this was it. She focused on the pain screaming from her battered head and her injured ankle. The pain made her angry. Angry was a lot better than scared.

She could hear the footsteps approaching. Her heart was pounding. Her courage was short-lived, her revived terror doing battle with her will. The terror was winning. She felt a hand on her cheek and cringed in fear and revulsion. Tears stung her eyes, but the blindfold prevented them from going anywhere.

A new scaring pain shot across her face as the tape was ripped swiftly from her mouth. She started to scream only to find a gloved hand clamped over her mouth.

A whispered "No" was breathed ominously into her ear. She couldn't even decipher whether the voice was masculine or feminine. Only that it was deadly serious.

She pressed her lips together against her captor's gloved palm. A sign of cooperation. What other choice did she have?

The hand slowly lifted from her mouth. It was a small improvement.

Bri waited for her captor's next words, hoping to at least be able to identify the voice. For several moments all she heard was steady, even breathing. Then a faint click.

"If you don't give up that scroll, your life isn't going to be worth two cents. This isn't a game, Bri. And if you don't believe that, you'd better believe that you're not going to come out the winner."

It was Steve Palmer's voice. Bri felt stunned. The very words he'd said to her up on the knoll that afternoon. Another click. *Click, click?* Of course, it wasn't Steve Palmer in the flesh, but a recording of the track coach's voice. Someone had been out there in the woods, recording their conversation.

"What . . . ?"

Again a gloved hand clamped over her face. She got the message. No questions. She also got the point. Her captor did not want to give away his or her identity by speaking. Frustrating though that was, Bri took it as a good sign. If her captor meant to kill her, it wouldn't really matter if she knew his or her identity. Then again, it could be a ruse to lull her into believing she wouldn't be harmed if she cooperated. She had to believe her life depended on keeping her guess about the scroll's location from her captor.

The gloved hand slipped away from her mouth.

"Please," Bri whispered. "My head. It hurts so much. I can't think straight."

There was no response. But then she was forced roughly back, her sore head pinging against the metal bell.

Bri moaned in pain and terror. She heard the click of the recorder. One more time she was forced to listen to the sound of Steve's recorded voice. He sounded positively diabolical.

The recorder clicked off. Silence. Several tense minutes passed. Bri knew her captor was waiting. Waiting for her to crack.

For want of any other brilliant idea, Bri tried the strategy she'd tried earlier on Steve. "Okay. You win. Untie me and I'll take you . . ." Again her words were cut short, her captor's hand once again clamping over her mouth.

Only then did she pick up the sound of voices below. Were they just college kids or was it a search party? She was sure Matt would be out looking for her. And Mildred and Harvey and the entire Thornhill police force—all four or five of them.

Here. Up here. Up in the bell tower. I'm up here. Please. Please . . .

The hand lifted from her mouth, but before Bri could even part her lips, a wide band of tape replaced the gloved hand, sealing her mouth shut once again.

Bri listened in anguish as the voices below faded.

And then that eerie, disembodied voice in her ear again. "I'll be back."

"THEY'RE ALL ACCOUNTED FOR" Lucy told Harvey, as soon as he and Mildred returned to the inn. "Everyone from the tour group is here. Word's spread that their tour guide is missing and they're all quite upset."

Harvey scowled. "I wouldn't say all," he grumbled.

"Steve Palmer called a few minutes ago and asked if Bri had shown up yet," Lucy told him. "Oh, and Liz Armstrong even stopped by a little while ago to see if there'd been any word."

Mildred snorted. "Probably looking to get a scoop for the *Tab*. She never was satisfied stuck writing the society column. Knowing her, she'd like to be running the whole shebang."

"All right, Mildred," Harvey muttered. "We all know that. Just like we all know that Liz has a personal interest in this case as well as a professional one."

Lucy tsked. "I always said that woman was nothing but a hussy. Carrying on with a married man. And then acting like she has any real concern about his widow."

"It's a pity Steve Palmer never wised up," Mildred clucked.

"How can he, when she keeps him dangling on a string the way she does? Always hedging her bets, she is."

"Do you mind, ladies," Harvey interrupted, pink spots of agitation blooming on his cheeks.

Both women stopped talking and looked contrite.

Harvey cleared his throat. "What about comings and goings over the past couple of hours?" he asked Lucy.

Lucy gave the question some thought. "Well, there's been a lot of that. Jillian and Kyle were both out earlier. Whether they were together the whole time, I can't say. They left and came back here together. But then Jillian went out again a little later with Mrs. McDermott of all people. I certainly didn't think those two would get chummy." Lucy paused. "And I was right. When Jillian came back, it was obvious she'd been crying. And when Mrs. McDermott followed her inside a few minutes later, she looked fit to be tied."

Mildred gave Lucy a sly look. "Mrs. McDermott is Adam Quinn's mother." She pursed her lips together. "I wonder if the old woman thinks Jillian was involved in her son's death."

Harvey gave Mildred a sharp look. "There are enough rumors floating around without starting any new ones."

"But it is possible, Harvey," Mildred persisted. "If Quinn was in cahoots with Fossier, Jillian could have been in on the operation from the start, too."

Harvey rolled his eyes. "Why would she kill Quinn?"

Mildred looked thoughtful. "Of course, it's equally possible John Fossier gunned his partner down, not wanting to split the proceeds of the sale of the scroll. A million dollars might have appealed to him a lot more than half a million."

"But then who killed Fossier?" Lucy queried. "Jillian? Is that why she came back crying from her walk? Did Eleanor suspect . . . ?"

"Or did Eleanor do Fossier in herself and Jillian, really in love with the murdered man and not Dunner, suspect that Eleanor . . . ?"

"Ladies, ladies. Do you mind if, for the moment, we focus on Bri Graham's disappearance instead of idle speculation?"

"I don't believe she just disappeared, Harvey," Mildred continued. "Any more than you do. I believe the poor child was kidnapped. And we all know what the kidnapper wants. An ancient scroll worth a million bucks."

"Do you think Bri really knows where it's hidden?" Lucy asked Mildred.

Mildred scowled. "She seems so sweet and innocent."

Harvey was scowling, too. But for an altogether different reason.

Mildred knew that look. "What are you thinking, Harvey?"

He hesitated. The chief, like his wife, was fond of Bri. "It is possible she hasn't come to any harm."

"What does that mean?" Lucy demanded.

But Mildred knew what it meant. She looked at Lucy. "Harvey means that Bri could have simply run off with the scroll while we're all imagining she's been abducted."

"No," Lucy said, stunned. "Why, I can't believe it."

"Okay, I don't want to believe it, either, so I'll put that theory on hold. For now, let's get back to the whereabouts of your guests," Harvey told Lucy.

"Well, there was Tim . . . I mean Keith," Lucy replied. "After Mrs McDermott took off, Allison, looking quite upset if you ask me, insisted that Tim—Keith—take a walk with her. She came back alone about ten minutes later, looking a bit soothed."

"What about Keith?" Mildred asked. "When did he get back?"

"He showed up about twenty minutes later. Right when Liz was pulling out of the driveway. Actually she practically ran him down when she was backing out." Lucy looked askance. "It was as much his fault as hers, the way he darted out from the space right behind her car. But he certainly didn't think he bore any responsibility. The way he cursed at her." She tsked a couple of times. "Young people these days. If he'd been one of my students, I'd have washed his mouth out with soap."

"Don't tell me Liz let him get away with it," Mildred said with a smirk.

"She didn't. She slammed right on the brakes, jumped out of the car and gave him what for, for a good five minutes," Lucy said. "Not that it penetrated his thick skull. Why, he came sauntering into the inn, whistling and acting just as carefree as a lark."

"What about Harriet Beecham?" Harvey asked.

Lucy considered. "No, I think you're off base there, Harvey. I don't recall seeing her leave the inn at all this afternoon. But I was busy checking on dinner preparations in the kitchen for a bit, and it's possible she wandered off briefly. I remember chatting with her about a crocheting project she was doing before I left for the kitchen, and when I went past the front parlor about twenty minutes later, she was still sitting there, crocheting."

"I guess I'd better round everyone up and get their statements," Harvey said, preparing to check in with George Denk on the progress of the search for the missing tour guide before bringing the group together in the front parlor.

"You won't get Matt Sebastian's," Lucy said as Harvey pulled out his walkie-talkie. "I haven't seen him since he left with Bri and Mildred here late this morning."

"He was at the hospital when Bri vanished," Mildred said. "Waiting for his friend from Boston to come around." But then she looked over at her husband, a worried expression on her face. "Of course, that poor unconscious private investigator can't tell us whether or not Matt slipped out of the room for a time, can he?"

Harvey had already had the same thought. Before leaving the hospital, he'd checked with the staff on Holland's floor about Matt. No one could say for sure whether Sebastian had actually been there the whole time.

Harvey had a sudden craving for a good cigar. That always happened when he was stumped.

WHEN THE RAIN STARTED, it came as a downpour. While the bell tower was sheltered by a cupola overhead, the sides of the half-walled tower were open to the elements. Thanks to the brisk wind coupled with the rain, Bri was quickly soaked. She shivered, but the cold wetness also served to revive her.

She had no idea how much time had gone by, but her head had stopped pounding so badly and, ironically, the tight tape around her ankles had even given some relief to the one that was sore. It wasn't throbbing anymore. Maybe she'd only twisted her ankle instead of it being sprained. Small blessings. But, given her situation, Bri would take any that came her way.

Her spirits rose a little as she got the idea of kicking out at the bell and summoning her rescuers. She wiggled around on her back until she had a good position with the balls of her feet against the bell. She pulled them back and struck out with all her might. No sound. Nothing but a shock wave that ran right through her spine from the impact. Only the big metal mallet that struck it from the side would do the trick and that was the part that was out for repair.

Still, she couldn't give up. If only she could tear away the tape that was wrapped around her wrists. The problem was, it was some kind of strapping tape and every time she tried, the edges seemed to cut deeper into her flesh.

She had to think of something else. Some way to cut through the tape. Crawling, rolling, dragging herself along the cold, wet wooden floor of the octagonally-shaped bell tower, she searched blindly for some solution to her problem. And as she searched, she was ever conscious of precious moments ticking away. When would her captor return? And what would happen to her then?

MATT LEFT George Denk at the clubhouse by the soccer field, where the officer was giving the place another sweep, hoping for some further clue to Bri's disappearance. The police had already ascertained that Bri had been in there. Her fingerprints were on the telephone receiver. And there were some scuff marks on the dusty floor. A body had been dragged.

Matt lit a cigarette as he started walking toward the nearest college gate. He had an idea. A long shot, but it was worth a try. Anything was worth a try. He headed down the street, angry at the downpour because it made it impossible for him to smoke. He tossed the cigarette. Maybe he should quit anyway. Bri was right. It was a bad habit. He had enough bad habits as it was. Like falling head-over-heels in love with a woman who, for all he knew had *faked* a disappearance and gone merrily skipping off with a million-dollar relic.

The crazy thing was that he almost hoped that was the case. Because the alternative was even worse. The alternative made him sick with fear.

ALLISON AND HER grandmother stayed behind after the other tour members shuffled out. Harvey was about to leave, as well, when Mrs. McDermott asked if they could have a private word with him.

Harvey nodded.

''Would you mind closing and locking the door, Chief Mead?'' Mrs. McDermott asked somberly.

Harvey obeyed her request. He had a feeling the woman was finally ready to come clean. He had given her plenty of opportunity while he was questioning the whole group, but she hadn't budged. Now he realized she probably hadn't wanted an audience.

"Chief Mead," the staunch elderly woman began without preamble. "On the night of Andrew Weston, alias John Fossier's, murder, my granddaughter was not in her bedroom. The bedroom, I'm sure I don't need to remind you, in which there was a connecting door to the murdered man's room."

Allison, sitting meekly beside her grandmother, stared down at her nails. Not that there was much of them left. She'd practically gnawed them down to her cuticles.

Harvey waited for the old woman to go on. He didn't have to wait long.

"Allison has confessed to me that she spent the night with that horrible young man who hired himself out as Anna Khaffir's son."

Allison lowered her head even further.

"As I'm sure you can well understand, Chief Mead," Mrs. McDermott proceeded, "this is not the sort of news one wishes to hear from one's seventeen-year-old granddaughter."

"I'll be eighteen in three weeks," Allison muttered.

Mrs. McDermott shrugged off the remark and continued. "As upsetting as this was to hear, I am honest enough to admit a modicum of relief that at least this provides Allison with an alibi."

Harvey raised a brow.

"As I'm sure you will find out, if you haven't already," the elderly woman said, eyeing Harvey shrewdly, "Allison is the daughter of my son, Adam Quinn."

Harvey gave Mrs. McDermott a look of admiration. One sentence to get it all out.

Tears started to roll down the young girl's cheeks. "I didn't kill him, I swear."

Harvey was taken aback, thinking for a moment Allison meant her own father. But then he realized she meant John Fossier.

"As your grandmother points out, you have an alibi," Harvey said gently.

Allison didn't respond. The tears continued to stream down her face. After a few seconds she said, "Keith says he really cares about me." Slowly she looked up at the chief. "Do you think he means it?"

There was something so sad and pathetic and desperate about the young girl that Harvey's heart went out to her. But there was something else he picked up in her look. Call it a cop's instinct, but he had the feeling Allison was holding something back. Something was troubling her. Something that could have an important bearing on the case?

BRI WOULD HAVE CRIED OUT with joy if her mouth wasn't taped shut. All of her painful searching efforts hadn't been for naught. Over in a corner of the bell tower, she'd struck gold in the form of a small screwdriver, probably left behind by one of the repairmen.

It was going to be no easy feat to use the sharp, flat edge of the tool to cut through the binding on her wrists. Nor did it help that her hands were taped behind her back, and that time was not on her side. If her captor came in before she'd completed the task . . .

But Bri pushed that terrifying thought from her mind, gritted her teeth and set to work.

Several times during her painstaking efforts, she dropped the screwdriver. One time it rolled away and she had to use precious moments to search it out again. But finally, after what felt like a lifetime, the tape began to give way. Working with renewed vigor, she managed to cut through enough of the tape to pull her wrists apart.

Wasting no time, she ripped the blindfold from her eyes, the tape from her mouth and, using the screwdriver once again, attacked the thick strips of reinforced nylon strapping at her ankles.

She had just gotten to her feet, when she heard the gut-wrenching sound of footsteps coming up to the door of what she now could see for certain was the Barker Library bell tower.

Like a cornered rabbit, her eyes darted around the tower for cover. The screwdriver was clutched in her hand. But just as Bri heard the creak of the door, she conceded she was in no condition for a face-off with her gun-toting captor. Dropping the screwdriver, she gulped in a breath and climbed over the waist-high wall of the tower just as the door swung open.

Chapter Fifteen

The wind and rain whipped at Bri as she pressed herself
flat against the wall and tried to keep a foothold on the
thin ledge that wrapped around the outer perimeter of the
tower. She shut her eyes, praying that her captor would
think she'd escaped via a conventional route, never
dreaming the prisoner would be foolhardy enough to risk
her neck in a daredevil stunt like this.

Her captor's muttered curses. Bri could hear them
faintly over the howling wind and rain. No, she thought,
not one voice but two. Two against one.

She was shivering badly now, her sodden clothes cling-
ing to her skin. And now that she'd had to put full weight
on her ankle, it began to throb again. But pain and wetness were the least of Bri's worries. Any moment now her
captors could peer over the half wall and discover her.

And even if that didn't happen, there was always the
awful possibility that Bri could lose her footing....

Don't look down. Whatever you do, don't look down.
Down, Bri knew, meant a good hundred feet to the wet
green lawn in front of the library. She'd made the mistake
of checking that out when she'd first climbed over the wall.
And the sickening thought had flashed through her mind—
What a splash I'd make!

Bri had to fight the temptation to peek over the wall and learn the identity of her captor, the person who very likely had also killed John. But sneaking a look was just too risky. She might be spotted. Her situation was precarious enough as it was.

It seemed an eternity before Bri heard the door leading from the bell tower slam shut. Although her first instinct was to immediately pull herself back up and over the wall to safety, she forced herself to wait another minute—an interminable minute—to make sure her captors had really left.

Climbing to the outside of the tower certainly hadn't been a piece of cake, but Bri discovered that getting herself back into the tower was even more of a feat. It required her to stretch her arms up and grip on to the edge of the wall and haul herself up and over. Not only did she have a problem getting a good grip on the wet edge, but so much of her strength had been drained away by injury and fear that she didn't know if she had enough left to do it.

She might not have made it had she not found a crevice in the wall deep enough for her to wedge part of her foot in, giving her the added boost she needed. Just as she was about to climb over the wall her shoe slipped off and went sailing toward the ground. Bri gasped. What if her captors were just exiting the base of the tower and spotted her shoe landing?

Instinctively Bri looked down. A bad mistake. She was struck with an attack of vertigo and nearly lost her grip on the edge of the wall. Another instant and it wouldn't have just been her shoe landing on the lawn. The rest of her would have followed.

With great relief, she managed to reclaim a firm grip. And she'd also managed in that brief glance to spot two shadowy figures hurrying across the library lawn, oblivious to her fallen shoe. As she climbed over the wall to safety, Bri heard the angry squeal of tires as a car pulled out below.

MATT WAS JUST turning down a deserted street a few blocks from campus when he heard a car come roaring around the corner after him. He looked back. The car's high beams were on, blinding him. But one thing was certain. It was making right for him, bearing down on him, a fleet mechanical beast of prey. He began running in a zigzag fashion, his arms pumping, bent at the elbows. He knew there was no way he was going to outrun the car, but he was looking sharply for some place to duck into before he was struck down.

The car was weaving back and forth, following Matt's running pattern, its windshield wipers on high speed, its engine screeching. Matt saw an alleyway just up ahead that cut between two darkened buildings. He made as if he was going to keep running straight, darting down the alley at the last minute. Unfortunately the driver anticipated his move.

Matt saw he had one last hope. Just as the car was about to barrel into him, he managed to pull out his gun and shoot. The car veered as the shot came off, but not quite enough. The next thing Matt knew, an excruciating pain was ripping into his thigh where the left front fender of the car had caught him. He went flying forward, landing in a heap on the cold, wet ground. He lay there motionless.

The car came to a stop for a few moments, then pulled back out of the alley.

BRI KNEW there was one way, and one way only, to put an end to the constant danger she was in. She had to unearth the treasure she'd buried here in Thornhill all those months ago on her honeymoon. A treasure that she prayed held an even more valuable one within it.

Her thoughts flew back to a small silver and ivory statuette of a pair of young lovers embracing that John had given her on their honeymoon. Bri had been very touched by the gift, saying she would always treasure it. They had made love and afterward, snuggling close to John, Bri had murmured that even on their twentieth anniversary she could picture them there in that very same room, celebrating their love and devotion for each other in the very same way as they had that night. John had kissed her tenderly and told her he saw the same picture.

At the close of their honeymoon, while Bri was packing and John had gone off to say goodbye to Steve Palmer and Liz Armstrong, she started to place the statuette in her suitcase when she came up with a better idea.

It had been such an innocent, romantic gesture. She'd gone off to the old cemetery not far from the inn, and on a lovely knoll, she'd buried the statuette in the ground beneath an elm tree, thinking at the time that when she and John returned on their twentieth anniversary she would take him to that spot and they would dig it up. At the time she'd thought that the statuette would symbolize the renewing of their vows. She never mentioned it to John, and completely forgot all about it herself in the painful procession of events that followed.

How ironic, she thought. Had she brought the statuette home, she would most likely have stuck it in the carton of items she'd given to Adam Quinn as it was too valuable a piece to toss. And if her guess about the statuette was right, the gallery owner would have unearthed the scroll wrapped inside it. Everything would have been different then. . . .

HARVEY AND GEORGE examined the torn strapping tape on the wet flooring of the Barker tower.

"What do you think, Chief?" George asked.

The chief spotted the screwdriver. "It looks to me as if she must have freed herself with that." He picked it up with heavy tweezers and dropped it into a plastic bag so it could be checked for fingerprints at the lab. "The question is, did she get caught in the act?"

AS BRI MADE HER WAY down the street, she kept constantly checking over her shoulder for a car. She was sure that she was being hunted. It was only a question of whether she'd end up getting caught. She stuck to the shadows, trying to ignore the pain in her ankle and the cold, raw chill that had reached right down into her bones.

There was only one thing on her mind. Getting to the cemetery and finding out if her theory was correct. Well, there was one other thing pressing on her mind. Should she track Matt down and take him with her to dig up the statuette? If the scroll was inside as she guessed, and she turned it over to him, it would be the final proof, both to him and herself, that she trusted him completely. But did she trust him completely? How could she love him and remain suspicious? Wasn't love an act of faith, after all? Did she have faith in Matt? Did she have faith in herself?

LUCY WAS JUST wheeling herself out of her office when the phone rang. Swinging around, she went back to her desk to answer it. No sooner had the caller identified herself than Lucy shrieked, "Bri? Bri, is it really you? Oh, my goodness. We all thought... Oh dear, where are you? Are you all right?"

"Please, Lucy. Is Matt there? I've got to talk to Matt. And I don't want anyone else at the inn to know I'm calling."

Lucy glanced guiltily at her open door. She hoped none of the guests had been within earshot. She decided not to worry Bri about it. Last she'd noticed, they'd all gone up to their rooms.

"Matt isn't here," Lucy told Bri. "I haven't seen him since he left with you and Mildred this morning. My guess is he's out looking for you along with Harvey, Mildred, George Denk and the rest of the Thornhill Police Force."

"Listen to me carefully, Lucy. I want you to get a message to Harvey."

Lucy did listen carefully. Unfortunately, unbeknownst to both Lucy and Bri, so was someone else at the inn.

AT LEAST IT HAD STOPPED raining. But the dark, dank, gloomy mistiness that clung to the cemetery gave Bri an eerie feeling. Somewhere in the distance, she could hear a car's engine. *It could be any one of thousands of cars,* she chided herself. No one but Lucy, and soon hopefully the police chief, knew where she was heading. And what about Matt? Where was he? Lucy had told her he wasn't with Mildred and Harvey. And she'd called the hospital to see if he was with his friend Joe Holland, but the floor nurse had told her he'd left hours ago. Bri was sure he must be out searching for her. She only prayed he hadn't run into any trouble. Little did she know what trouble had run into him!

IT TOOK SEVERAL MINUTES for Matt to manage to get back on his feet. His thigh was bruised, and the wind had been knocked out of him. Even after he was standing, he found himself having to bend forward, supporting himself by placing his palms on his knees, and trying to catch his breath.

Holding that position, he looked around and spotted a phone booth down the street.

IT DIDN'T HELP Bri's spirits any to have to make her way through the old grave stones toward the knoll. At the time she'd placed the statuette in the cold earth under the elm tree, she'd thought only that this was such a tranquil, picturesque spot. Her mind was on life then, not death. She and John had spent one delightful afternoon reading the curious, moving and sometimes comical epitaphs on the old stones here. And what would *her* epitaph read?

A GRAY-HAIRED NURSE popped her head into room 314. "Dr. Bright. The patient in 302 is regaining consciousness."

Noah Bright nodded to the nurse. "I'll be down there as soon as I finish here."

By the time Noah got down to 302, the patient was fully awake and cursing to beat the band.

Noah smiled. "Your pal, Matt Sebastian, warned us you were going to be pretty ornery when you came to."

"Where is he?" the private eye croaked, his cursing having taken the stuffing out of him.

"I'm not sure," Noah said, "but he was hanging around here most of the day. My guess is he'll be calling in anytime now to check on you. I'm glad I'll be able to give him some good news."

"Well, I've got some good news to give him, too. About one of his fellow tour members. So, you do me a favor and see if you can track him down for me before someone gets hurt."

Noah was not about to tell the private investigator, given his condition, that it was a little late for that.

MATT'S MOUTH went dry and his heart went haywire with panic, when he spotted the white sedan with the shattered windshield parked on the street in front of the old cemetery. Was he too late?

EVEN THE TINY stone marker was still in place. Bri gave it a brief wistful look as she set it aside and began to dig away the wet earth with her fingers. *A little earlier than she'd expected to be doing—namely, nineteen and a half years earlier.* At least she'd dug a shallow hole. The ground had been too cold and hard to dig deeply.

With trembling fingers she lifted out the gauze-wrapped statuette, thinking now that it reminded her a bit of a miniature Egyptian mummy. John had told her he'd purchased the lovers' statuette at a bazaar in Turkey. But what he'd conveniently failed to mention to her was that the scroll she believed was hidden inside the statuette, he'd stolen from a museum in Cairo.

Crouching on the ground, she unwrapped the statuette. The silver and ivory embracing figures were cold and clammy. A quarter moon was peeking out of a cloud, shedding a faint, hazy light. Bri was just about to rise with the statuette when a voice behind her made her freeze.

"Hand it over."

It was a masculine voice, one that was familiar, but not one that she had in any way expected.

She turned slowly around and stared with astonishment into the face of Tim Campbell, alias Keith Baron.

"You look surprised. And here I thought you'd figured it all out by now. I'm disappointed, Bri."

The shadowy male figure moved closer to her. And as he did, he smiled. And for the first time, Bri saw the resemblance not to Anna Khaffir, but to Thornhill's society columnist. Bri was willing to bet the young actor had at least one more alias. Keith Armstrong.

Bri saw it all clearly now. "That day in the Chinese restaurant. You weren't waiting for Allison. You were waiting for Liz. That's why the two of you were so edgy. You were expecting to have a private little chat. But Steve and

I spoiled the plan so you had to improvise. Something you're very good at.''

"You are good, little brother," a voice said from the shadows, confirming Bri's guess.

"If you can't count on family, who can you count on?" Keith quipped.

Liz Armstrong stepped out of the shadows and stood beside her brother.

Bri stared at her. "I thought you were in love with John. How could you go to bed with a man and then an hour later shoot him to death?"

"Give credit where credit is due," Keith interrupted. "I was the one that killed that creep. It was easy as pie. I lured that dumb little blonde, Allison, to my room so I'd have an alibi, then slipped out of the room for a couple of minutes so that she could—uh—put herself together. She thought it was real gentlemanly of me." He sneered at Bri. "And your no-good husband thought he was going to hold out on my sister, but there was no way we were going to stand for that, right Lizzy?"

"First he sends me a postcard," Liz said with a smile that didn't touch her eyes, "to let me know he was joining your tour so that he could get the scroll from you, and then we were supposed to go riding off together into the sunset."

Bri could hear the sarcasm in Liz's voice. She saw it all clearly now. "But you never intended to run off with him, did you, Liz? You wanted the scroll all to yourself. So you contacted your brother and had him join the tour as well. Has he always done all your dirty work for you, Liz?"

Keith chuckled. "I couldn't believe my luck when I heard about that middle-aged bag, Anna 'Campbell' wanting to hire a 'son.' I not only got to go on the tour, it was all expenses paid. It worked out so tidily. And once 'Momma' came clean, I was completely off the hook. No reason in the world for anyone to suspect me of anything. I had no connection to anyone. Just a lowly actor hired to play a part. And I played it great if I do say so myself."

Liz sneered at Bri. "Do you know John and I made love on your honeymoon and that he told me he realized marrying you was a big mistake? That it was me he should have married?"

"Okay, Lizzy, let's not stand around here shooting the breeze all day." Keith drew out his gun and pointed it at Bri. "The time has come, sweetheart, for a parting of the ways." His smile was positively gleeful. "You part with the statuette and we part with you."

Just when Bri was resigning herself to the terrifying reality that all was lost, that she would never even get the chance to tell Matt how much he really meant to her and that she really did trust him in the end, who should she spy creeping up behind the deadly duo, but Matt himself. He might have looked the worse for wear, but as far as Bri was concerned, he had never looked better.

Without giving herself a second to think about the consequences if her stunt failed, she hurled the statuette with all her might at the diabolical actor, then hurled herself at his sister who was taken completely by surprise.

Instinctively Keith dropped his gun to have his hands free to catch the statuette. Matt sprang into action, landing a vicious karate chop to Keith's neck, which rendered the actor temporarily out of commission. Bri and Liz, struggling with each other for the advantage on the ground, both tried to reach for the gun. Just as Liz managed to get her fingers on it, Matt caught sight of what was happening, and kicked it out of her hand. With a reserve of strength that amazed her, Bri sprang for the gun. It was just within her grasp, when all four of them were startled by a new gun-toting arrival on the scene.

Jillian Knight motioned for all of them to stand up. "That's good. Now raise your hands over your heads."

She guided all four of them away from the fallen gun and the statuette. "Keep your hands up and don't even blink an eyelash or you won't even have time to regret it." As she spoke she gathered up both the weapon and the treasure.

"I hate ending such a lovely trip on such a sour note," Jillian drawled.

"So do I, my dear," came a voice behind her that made her as well as the others jump.

"Kyle." There was no hiding the edge of nervousness in Jillian's voice, but she quickly recovered. "I was going to surprise you."

"I'm afraid, my dear, I have a surprise for you, as well," the mild-mannered investment broker said pleasantly, moving closer. "Drop the gun and set the statuette down beside it."

She hesitated, but something hard in his features convinced her he meant business. Fear and regret etched on her face, she did as he ordered.

"Join the others, Jillian."

"You're not serious, Kyle." Jillian's voice held a pleading note. "Why are you turning on me?"

"I suppose I could ask you the same question," he tossed back.

"It isn't what you're thinking, Kyle. I wasn't going to double cross you. I was doing this for both of us. I wanted you to be proud of me. I love you, Kyle. I thought . . . I really meant something to you."

"Oh you do, Jillian. You do. You mean a possible life sentence to me."

"You mean Adam? But I helped you arrange the whole thing. I got him to the convenience store so you could—"

"And I'm sure if you ever decided to turn state's evidence you could do a nice bit of plea bargaining. But where would I be? Rotting in prison while you enjoyed the fruit of all my hard labor."

"No, no, I wouldn't. You're wrong, Kyle."

"Step away, Jillian. I'll give it some thought."

But everyone, including Jillian, knew he was lying. He meant to do away with all of them. Bri felt Matt's hand clasp hers. He smiled tenderly at her. Even though her mouth was trembling, she smiled back. At least, she thought wistfully, they'd go together.

And then they heard the sirens. They were close by. Kyle Dunner quickly bent to retrieve the statuette. Everyone knew that the moment he rose, he'd start shooting. What none of them knew, save for Matt, who had surreptitiously slipped his gun out of his jacket pocket, was that Kyle Dunner wasn't going to rise.

HARVEY, MILDRED, George Denk, and Roy Filmore were hurrying to the scene when they heard a single shot ring out. They also heard a pair of gasps. A minute later they discovered who the gasps belonged to. Just ahead of them, also hurrying to the scene of the action, were the two elderly sisters, Eleanor McDermott and Harriet Beecham. As Eleanor anxiously explained to the chief, her granddaughter had finally confessed that while she was in Keith Baron's room the night of John Fossier's murder, he'd slipped out for a few minutes. And it was while he was out that Allison had heard the shots. Keith had pleaded with her not to say anything, swearing his innocence. But after the truth about him being an actor was exposed, Allison became more and more uneasy about not speaking out. Finally she'd come clean.

It turned out that Harriet had caught Keith eavesdropping on one of the extensions at the inn, listening in on

Bri's conversation with Lucy. Being the curious sort, Harriet decided to follow suit on another extension. Which was how she learned that Bri was going to the cemetery. She and Eleanor decided that they had to warn Bri about the dangerous young man. Now, having heard the shot, they were afraid they might be too late.

The others were equally afraid, until they hard Matt's voice call out from the knoll, "Chief, if you're out there, relax. Everything's under control. But we'll need an ambulance. Mr. Dunner's had a little *hunting* accident."

A few minutes later the ambulance carried Kyle away. The chief and his two deputies were just hustling Jillian, Liz and her brother over to one of the police cruisers when Steve Palmer arrived at the scene.

He looked at Liz and shook his head sadly. Then he turned to Bri who was standing beside Matt on the street. "I did try to warn you. If you'd given me the scroll, I might have been able to stop her." He looked back over at Liz who was being guided into the back seat. "I'm sorry."

Bri wasn't sure whether he was apologizing to her or Liz. But it didn't matter. It was over.

AFTER GETTING checked over and bandaged at the hospital, Bri and Matt hightailed it to the police station a short while later to give their statements. When they walked inside, Bri spotted a small dapper man in a navy serge suit chatting with the sergeant at the front desk. She was surprised to see Matt walk right over to the man and throw an arm around his shoulders in a comradely way, asking what took him so long to get there.

Matt waved her over. "Bri, I want you to meet Leonard Roth. My boss. Len, meet Bri, the woman I plan to marry."

Bri gave Matt a double-whammy stare.

Matt gave her one of his impossible boyish grins. "Don't look so surprised, baby. I always told you I was on the up-and-up. As soon as I was able to track Len down, I gave him the word that we might have a lead on the Osiris scroll and he ought to cut his vacation short, come on up here and let me hand it over to him."

Bri had to laugh. "I'd already decided you were on the up-and-up when I was heading over to the cemetery."

"And when did you decide you'd agree to marry me?" he asked, his eyes dancing.

Both Matt's boss and the desk sergeant chuckled. Bri blushed. "Really, Matt, this isn't the time or place," she muttered.

Matt winked at the two men. "At least she didn't tell me I'm being immature again. This is progress, boys."

IT WAS A MUCH SMALLER tour party that was planning its departure from the Sugarrun Inn two days later. The group consisted of Bri, Matt, Eleanor McDermott and Harriet Beecham. Jillian Knight and Kyle Dunner had their own private transportation arranged for them. A special police cruiser was taking them down to Boston and turning them over to the Boston authorities to stand trial for the murder of Adam Quinn. Keith Baron Armstrong was not likely to be returning by van or any other conveyance to Boston and then on to New York City for quite a while. He was being held, along with his sister, in the county prison to stand trial for the murder of John Fossier. So much for the bad guys.

A happier and more attractive looking Anna Khaffir, as the newly appointed representative of the Cairo Antiquities Museum, was flying back to Boston and then on to Cairo accompanied by the museum's insurance representative, Leonard Roth. Very soon the valuable Osiris scroll would be in its proper place. The museum's board of directors had even agreed to put up a special plaque in the museum, honoring the memory of one of their most valued and outstanding curators, Selim Khaffir.

Allison managed, at the last minute, to talk her grandmother into letting her tag along with Anna Khaffir and Matt's boss on the flight to Boston. From there she planned to fly back home to sunny California. She'd had quite enough of fall foliage for one season. Her grandmother had reluctantly agreed it was for the best, although she did try to talk Allison into joining her and Harriet on a winter bus tour they were planning to the Laurentians. As it turned out, the two sisters were avid skiers, having learned the sport a few years back on a trip to Colorado.

Bri was packing in her room when there was a knock on her door.

"It's open," she called out.

Matt came sauntering into the room. "Listen, I've been thinking."

She glanced up at him, but didn't say anything.

"You've done the mystery tour bit, so it doesn't really make sense to repeat yourself. Besides, I doubt you could top this one."

Now Bri was looking at him as if he was deranged.

"So, I have an idea. A new twist. Another unique tour."

Bri returned to her task of packing. "Okay. I'll bite. What kind of a tour?"

He walked over to her and took the folded sweater from her hands. Then he took her hands in his. "A wedding tour. Say in June. Everyone says it's the best month for a wedding. And I don't want you to start worrying about rushing into another marriage. You need some time to get used to the idea and realize it's the right move. And, this time, kid, it's going to be for keeps. So we'll have a nice, long engagement, get to learn how to cope with each other's quirks. And just think." He gave her a crooked smile. "I'll be that much older in nine months."

She opened her mouth to speak, but he pressed his fingers to her lips. "I know what you're going to say. 'And so will I.'"

She grinned at him. "That's how much you know. That wasn't what I was going to say at all."

"Okay, I'll bite. What were you going to say?"

She fixed her eyes on him, a loving smile on her lips. "I was going to say, a June wedding sounds perfect."

He looked at her as if he didn't quite believe her. "You mean it?"

Her smile deepened. "Absolutely."

Epilogue

What's What
by
Mildred Mead

This afternoon at 3:00 p.m. four young couples, all participants in the Boston-based Valentine Tour's unique wedding trip, were joined in holy matrimony at St. John's Church in Thornhill. The tour guide, Bri Graham, herself one of the brides, looked stunning in a pink organdy dress designed by Geoffrey Beene. Her groom, Matthew Sebastian, who met his bride on an equally unique fall foliage tour late last year, cut a handsome figure in a Ralph Lauren navy dinner jacket and white slacks....

The grand reception following the ceremony was held at the Sugarrun Inn, where all four couples plan to honeymoon.

As a special side note, each of the new brides received silver heart lockets from their husbands which they all buried up on a knoll in the old Thornhill cemetery, the four couples vowing to return to dig up their treasures on their twentieth anniversary. To Bri

Graham-Sebastian's delight, the other couples have already placed their bookings. And what a special tour that's going to be!

ROMANCE IS A YEARLONG EVENT!

Celebrate the most romantic day of the year with MY VALENTINE! (February)

CRYSTAL CREEK
When you come for a visit Texas-style, you won't want to leave! (March)

Celebrate the joy, excitement and adjustment that comes with being JUST MARRIED! (April)

Go back in time and discover the West as it was meant to be ... UNTAMED—Maverick Hearts! (July)

LINGERING SHADOWS
New York Times bestselling author Penny Jordan brings you her latest blockbuster. Don't miss it! (August)

BACK BY POPULAR DEMAND!!!
Calloway Corners, involving stories of four sisters coping with family, business and romance! (September)

FRIENDS, FAMILIES, LOVERS
Join us for these heartwarming love stories that evoke memories of family and friends. (October)

Capture the magic and romance of Christmas past with HARLEQUIN HISTORICAL CHRISTMAS STORIES! (November)

WATCH FOR FURTHER DETAILS IN ALL HARLEQUIN BOOKS!

CALEND

HARLEQUIN®
I N T R I G U E®

It looks like a charming old building near the Baltimore waterfront, but inside 43 Light Street lurks danger . . . and romance.

Labeled a "true master of intrigue" by *Rave Reviews*, bestselling author Rebecca York continues her exciting series with #213 HOPSCOTCH, coming to you in February.

Paralegal Noel Emery meets an enigmatic man from her past and gets swept away on a thrilling international adventure— where illusion and reality shift like the images in a deadly kaleidoscope. . . .

"Ms. York ruthlessly boggles the brain and then twists our jangled nerves beyond the breaking point in this electrifying foray into hi-tech skullduggery and sizzling romance!"
— Melinda Helfer, *Romantic Times*

Don't miss Harlequin Intrigue #213 HOPSCOTCH!